W9-BUI-189

NEED TO KNOW

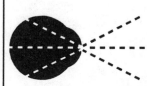

This Large Print Book carries the
Seal of Approval of N.A.V.H.

NEED TO KNOW

FERN MICHAELS

WHEELER PUBLISHING
A part of Gale, a Cengage Company

Farmington Hills, Mich • San Francisco • New York • Waterville, Maine
Meriden, Conn • Mason, Ohio • Chicago

Copyright © 2017 by Fern Michaels.
Sisterhood Series.
Fern Michaels is a registered trademark of KAP 5, Inc.
Wheeler Publishing, a part of Gale, a Cengage Company.

LIBRARY OF CONGRESS CIP DATA ON FILE.
CATALOGUING IN PUBLICATION FOR THIS BOOK
IS AVAILABLE FROM THE LIBRARY OF CONGRESS.

ISBN-13: 978-1-4328-4738-8 (hardcover)
ISBN-10: 1-4328-4738-4 (hardcover)

Published in 2018 by arrangement with Kensington Books, an imprint of Kensington Publishing Corp.

Printed in the United States of America
1 2 3 4 5 6 7 22 21 20 19 18

NEED TO KNOW

PROLOGUE

Eight years earlier

Arthur Forrester squared his shoulders, took a deep breath, and opened the door of sparkling glass in front of him. He did his best to ignore the black-silk wreath that hung in the center of the door. He exhaled and wished that he had not. The overpowering smell of incense gagged him. He hated the somber music that was playing in the background. He hated the place. Hated all funeral homes.

He dreaded going into the viewing room to see the deceased decked out in whatever fashion was current to someone in the entertainment business.

Twice he had met the man laid out in the coffin, also known as the deceased, aka David Duffy. The first time he had met him, they shook hands, sized one another up, and moved on. The second time Forrester had met him, Duffy was with his star client, Garland Lee, and Forrester had taken an active dislike to the man. The truth was, he was jealous and resentful of David Duffy and his close professional and personal relationship with the woman whose phenomenally successful career he managed. He hated the way she deferred to Duffy, hated how she constantly sang his praises, hated that they were personal friends, with all that entailed. But most of all, he hated the fact that Duffy made millions of dollars by representing America's beloved songbird, while all Arthur Forrester got were billable hours, along with the misery he suffered from having to listen to Garland go on and on about how wonderful Duffy was to her and her family.

Arthur Forrester looked around. For some reason, he'd expected to see a gaggle of people crying and wailing. All he saw was the man's widow, dressed in the dark clothing widows wore, sitting with her two sons. Their expressions were set, their eyes dry. All three had rosary beads in their hands. Across the aisle was Garland Lee, who was crying and sniffling into a wad of tissues. Her adult children were next to her. They all looked distressed, but holding up. David Duffy had been the godfather to all of

Garland's children.

He looked around to see who else was in attendance, but all he saw were people who looked like professional mourners — people the funeral parlor hired to sit and look like relatives, so the deceased would have a proper send-off. He thought the whole thing was barbaric. He hated funerals with a passion.

No way was he walking up to that bronze casket to stare down at a man he barely knew and heartily disliked. No way in hell. He sat down next to Garland and tapped her arm. She looked at him in a daze — seeing him, but not seeing him. For some reason, he had expected Garland to throw herself at him for comfort, but she did not do that. What she did was get up and walk up to the bronze box and reach out to touch her business manager's hands, which held a rosary. A strangled sound escaped her lips. He risked a glance at Duffy's wife, who was staring off into space.

Forrester squirmed in his seat. He itched for some reason. He looked around at the sea of flower arrangements. He knew without a doubt they were all from Garland. The scent was overpowering. He had to force himself not to gag. Three days of this, with two viewings each day. Garland would stay the whole time until they kicked her out. That's just how she was. He had been Garland's lawyer for forty years, and he'd often wondered from time to time if she was secretly in love with David Duffy. To this day, he didn't know if she was or not. The fact that Duffy's family members were sitting by themselves, and Garland was sitting on the other side with her children, just seemed to confirm his notion that something was *off*.

Forrester's thoughts raced. Maybe he could step in and take over from David. Garland's upcoming tour would have to be canceled. Knowing Garland as well as he did, he knew she would go into a deep funk and be unable to perform. Never mind that millions of dollars were at stake. She wouldn't care. Who better than he to take over the reins? After all, he was a lawyer, Garland's lawyer. Duffy's 20 percent commission would automatically become his, plus his billable hours. He might have to give up the billable hours in favor of the 20 percent commission. Or maybe he could actually wear two hats and do both. How hard could that be? He could actually see Garland embracing the idea.

Forrester snapped to attention when the mortician, clad in a black suit and smelling of Aqua Velva, approached the new widow and her family. He leaned over and spoke softly. He watched as the family got up and left. Now the black suit was heading toward Garland. He spoke to her, but from where Forrester was sitting, it looked like she was ignoring him. The black suit then motioned to Garland's children. *Come and get your mother.* The children got up and led Garland from the room, her feet dragging every step of the way.

Outside, in the cool evening air, Forrester put his arm around Garland's shoulders. It was time to make nice, time to step into David Duffy's shoes. He could do it. Not only could he do it, he *would* do it.

"Garland, look at me," Forrester said, cupping the singer's face in his two hands. "I'm going to follow you home because I need to get all the files and records you have that David worked on. I know this is not the time and the place, and I know your heart is breaking, but it has to be done. I will take care of it all and leave you and your family to grieve. Trust me, I'm your lawyer. We've been together longer than you've been with David. You know I'll do right by you. Do you understand what I'm saying?"

Garland's head bobbed up and down.

11

Forrester decided it wouldn't hurt him at that moment to sweeten up his words. "I'm truly sorry for your loss, Garland. I know how much you loved and relied on David. He left some very big shoes to fill. I promise to do my best and not upset you in the process."

"All right, Arthur," Garland said wearily.

An hour later, Arthur Forrester carried the last of David Duffy's records and files, or, more accurately, Garland's copies of David's work, out to the trunk of his late-model Mercedes. He had a release in his possession that Garland had signed in front of two witnesses, her housekeeper and her gardener.

Arthur Forrester was now the business manager of one of America's most famous singers, Garland Lee. He had just secured his future with the millions he would pocket over the coming years. And, best of all, he could now tell the sanctimonious bastards at the Ballard law firm to go to hell. Or not. Billable hours would only add to his coffers.

Talk about moving to Easy Street, which would be his new address from this day forward.

Arthur drove away from Garland's home, his spirits as high as they'd ever been in his entire life. As he drove away, he mentally rehearsed the press release he would send out to the entertainment media over the next few days. Decorum dictated that he wait at least until David Duffy was firmly planted six feet under.

Arthur drove to his home on what he now kept thinking of as Easy Street, feeling better than he'd ever felt in his whole life.

CHAPTER 1

Yoko Wong put her hands up to shield her eyes from the bright sun as she watched Kathryn Lucas expertly back up the huge eighteen-wheeler full of spring flowers and seedlings for the Wong Nursery. Out of the corner of her eye, she noticed a luxurious silver Mercedes inching its way into the customer parking lot. The only person she knew who drove a car like that was Garland Lee. Her heart kicked up a beat, knowing that Garland would buy every single flower and seedling the moment Kathryn unloaded the truck. Garland loved flowers.

With one eye on Kathryn and the other one on Garland, Yoko realized it had been *months* since she'd seen her friend. Garland was Beyoncé, Rihanna, Tina Turner, and Madonna all rolled into what the public knew as Garland Lee.

Yoko grinned when she saw her friend step out of her fancy car and wave both arms. Garland looked like a bag lady, dressed in baggy coveralls, black lace-up–to–the– ankle Converse sneakers, and a tattered T-shirt that at one time said MUSIC IS MY LIFE. Most of the letters were worn off, and the shirt was three sizes too big for the songbird. Her long, luxurious, strawberry-blond hair, one of Garland's trademarks, was held in place by a bright red bandanna.

"I'll take it all!" Garland shouted. "How are you, sweetie?" she said, gathering Yoko in a tight bear hug. Up close, Yoko admired the other woman's ageless beauty. Garland's explanation for her looks was that she came from hearty peasant stock. She pooh-poohed those who said she had plastic surgery, telling them that if they could find the surgeon, she would pay them a cool one million dollars. She did, however, admit to dyeing her hair, wearing contact lenses, and having had her teeth capped. She always ended her explanation by saying, "I'm no different than half the women in America." And that was the end of that.

Yoko threw her hands in the air. "Hanging in there, Garland. How about you? I've missed you. Were you on tour? It's been months. I missed our occasional lunches. Uh-oh, something's wrong. I know that look. What? Wait, wait. I have to sign off on this load and pay for it. You sure you want all of it? Because if you do, I have to place my order to replace this delivery."

"I'm sure. Go along, take care of business. I have all day. We can talk when you're finished."

Garland Lee was a very beautiful woman, with a warm smile and sparkling green eyes. Her smile was welcoming and sincere. If Garland welcomed you into her very small inner circle, you had a friend for life. She walked along now, up and down the different aisles where flats and pots of colorful spring flowers filled the nursery. She wondered if what she was seeing would be enough to replace all the damage done from the fire at her estate. She winced when she remembered how the firefighters had trampled her flower beds, how the construction workers had uprooted her beautiful shrubs and flowering trees. It had been necessary, she knew that, but still, she wished it hadn't happened. She loved her mini estate, the beautiful gardens she had designed herself because she so loved flowers. What she missed the most were her treasured lilac bushes. When they were in full bloom, she filled the house with lilacs. She looked around but did not see any. Well, Yoko was a magician when it came to plants and flowers. If anyone could find lilac bushes, it was Yoko Wong. The thought left her feeling better.

Garland's ears picked up the sound of the eighteen-wheeler's powerful engine. She turned around to walk back to the entrance. She smiled at the sound of the air horn and an arm waving out the driver's-side window. Yoko waved back.

Garland laughed. "If I had known this delivery was scheduled for this morning, I could have had you divert the driver to my house. Oh, well, everything happens for a reason. When do you think your people can deliver all of this?" she said, waving her arms about.

"When my afternoon help arrives."

"I didn't see any lilac bushes," Garland said fretfully.

"That's because there aren't any. The lilacs, the red tips, and the magnolias are scheduled for delivery next Wednesday. I guess you want all the lilacs, right?"

"Yes, all of them. I don't care how many you have. But I don't want little bitty shrubs. I want them full grown. At my age, I don't have time to watch them grow like the original batch. Yoko, I cried, do you believe that? All my beautiful plants, the hemlocks in the back, my gorgeous lilacs trampled like roadside scrub. The house . . . I was able to deal with that. It was the garden, my sanctuary, that I hated to lose. But life goes on, so now I'm in a place where I am fortunate enough to be able to replace everything."

Yoko nodded. "Let's go in the office and have a cup of tea so you can bring me up to date on what's been going on in your life."

"Fine, fine. I can use a cup of tea, but I want to be sure your crew will do the entire yard. It has to be graded, fertilized, then planted. I'm not trying to tell you how to run your business, but I just want to be sure we're on the same page. By my best guess, this is a hundred-thousand-dollar job. Possibly more. I can pay you a deposit now. The insurance company settled with me last week."

"Don't worry, Garland. My people know what to do. When they're finished, you'll never know you had a fire. Are you satisfied with the house?"

"I am. It's amazing how one faulty wire could cause all that damage. But that's behind me now. This is a new page in my book of life. How are things with you? Oh, you have those sticky rice cakes that I love so much. Talk to me, Yoko."

"My life is routine. Harry does his thing,

and Lily is happy as a lark and loves her new school. I work here every day. I saved you the biggest, the prettiest Christmas tree, and you never came for it. I think I knew something was wrong at that point. I had heard about your fire. One of the tabloids said you were living in your guesthouse, and another one said you were in Europe. I didn't know what to think."

Garland untied the colorful bandanna on her head, bundled up her hair, and tied the bandanna back in place. "It's complicated, Yoko. I've been in California. That's where my backup sound studio is. I did a lot of crying, but I'm over that now. I think I'm going to retire."

"No! You aren't serious, or are you?" Yoko was so shocked, she was virtually speechless.

"I'm thinking about it. Like I said, it's complicated. Part of it is that crazy lawsuit."

Once again, Yoko was speechless. "That's still going on! Good Lord, that's . . . that's three years!"

"Two years and ten months, to be precise. That low-life, bottom-feeding scumbag is not giving up. I'm gearing up to go to trial because I won't settle with him. By the time it gets to court, it will be well over three years. I've had to spend millions to defend

20

myself. The scumbag does most of his own legal work, and he has his creepy lawyer sign off on it, so his legal bills are nowhere near what mine are. The case is starting to heat up again after months of nothing. Every day, I pray that the bastard will drop off the face of the earth or just disappear into thin air. I keep rooting for a UFO to appear and whisk him away to some deep-space asteroid, preferably in another galaxy, to live out the rest of his life in abject misery. I know that's an impossible dream, but I still pray for it. There are no words to tell you how much I loathe that man."

Yoko poured the tea into pretty little cups and set the rice cakes on a matching plate. She smiled. "I think I have a pretty good idea."

"The thing is, Yoko, if my son hadn't taken over my affairs, I still wouldn't know what he had been doing. Twenty years! For twenty years, I believed him. I thought he was my friend. I trusted him, and he betrayed me. He helped himself to twenty-five million dollars of my money! Not just my money, but the money meant for my charity!" To Yoko's dismay, Garland was screeching now.

"What are your lawyers telling you?"

"They tell me what they think I want to

hear as they run to the bank with all that billable-hours money. Let's not even go there. Things were fine when he was simply my lawyer from way back, when I got my first contract. David Duffy, who became my business manager, had a handle on things and was as honest as the day is long. When he died eight years ago, I was lost, and when Arthur Forrester stepped in and said he could take it all over, I was grateful! Can you believe that? I was actually grateful to the man who proceeded to rob me blind. I must have been out of my mind. But I did ask my son if he'd take over, and he said he didn't think he was capable and really didn't have the time since he was going for his doctorate. I asked my daughter, but Misty was just starting out in her career and was on the road constantly. There was no way the twins could have done it. I had no other choice, or that's how I saw it at the time, other than to go with Arthur."

Yoko's head buzzed. "How did he do it? Rip you off for so much money and you not know it?"

"He did it in small amounts so I wouldn't notice. A little bit off every contract, every record, every dollar in endorsement money. That's how. But worst of all, he took most of it from my charity."

Yoko knew that Garland had created early in her career a charitable foundation that provided scholarships, school supplies, and other opportunities for underprivileged kids. Many times over the years, she had said that she believed in sharing her success with others, and devoted a lot of her precious free time to fund-raising and appearing at events for her foundation. Yoko could tell that most of Garland's outrage sprang from the fact that the money specifically set aside to help others had been misused for individual gain.

"Andy was in a car accident several years ago and had to have extensive rehab," Garland continued, "so he had time on his hands and tried to help me out. He's the one who found out what Forrester was doing."

"I don't really understand, Garland. How could you not have noticed that amount of money going missing? Were you asleep at the switch?"

"No. But I might as well have been. Duffy was so honest, I never thought. . . . It just never occurred to me that Arthur would . . . would cheat me like that. As you know, I'm bipolar. I'm sure, to a certain extent, that plays into it. In my own defense, I had every right to expect that he would act like an honest lawyer. Lawyers are supposed to be like doctors. You're supposed to be able to trust them. The bottom line is, he betrayed me for his own personal gain. When I fired him, he said that I ruined his life and the lives of his family. Then the bastard sued me, and I had no recourse but to sue him back. And here we are."

Yoko sighed as she sipped at her tea. "That is such an outrageous sum of money. I don't deal in those kinds of numbers. What is he suing you for specifically? What does, or did, he do with all his money? Do you know?"

"I don't know this for sure, but one time he told me he plays the stock market and is *not* a very savvy investor. Twice, he claimed, he lost really big. But he's such a liar, I have no idea if that was true or not. Or why he would admit such a thing to me. I almost tend to think it was true because at one point I had to cosign a loan for him to buy some kind of horse ranch in Montana. Stupid as I was, I didn't even question the *why* of it. I just did it because I trusted him.

"I don't want to talk about this anymore, Yoko. It's too depressing, and it's too nice a day to be depressed. I'm going to take a walk around the Tidal Basin because the cherry trees are blooming."

Yoko nodded. "Do you want to take the rest of these rice cakes with you?"

"Such a silly question," Garland said, hugging Yoko.

"Ah . . . Garland, I don't want to seem like I'm inserting myself into your personal business, but I know some . . . um . . . people who could possibly help you. If I could arrange a meeting, would you be interested?"

Garland took a step back and stared at Yoko. "Are we talking about what you do in your other life?"

Yoko laughed out loud. "I can neither confirm nor deny. And you know I have this other life . . . how?"

"Because I'm a good listener, and I've heard things over the years. I know how to add two and two. But, to answer your question, yes, I am up to anything to speed things up. You have my number and know where I live. Just let me know."

Yoko smiled as she watched Garland fish around in her bag for her checkbook. She pulled it out, scribbled on a check, and handed it over with a flourish. "I don't need a receipt. Just these rice cakes. Nice seeing you again, Yoko, and I'm sorry about that Christmas tree. What did you do with it?"

"I put it in the middle of the nursery,

decorated it, and lit it up with two thousand LED lights. I kept it up till the end of January."

Garland laughed out loud all the way to her car.

Yoko waited till Garland's car was out of sight. Then she went back inside to her office and sent off texts to all the sisters. With Kathryn in the area, they'd have a full house. Things just worked out perfectly sometimes.

We need to meet ASAP for possible new mission. My friend is in serious trouble.

It was nine o'clock when the last car, driven by Isabelle, whizzed through the gates at Pinewood.

It was a dark night, and the air was damp. It would rain before long. Isabelle stepped out of the car, looked around at the other cars, and soon realized that she was the last person to arrive. She shrugged. She could not be held accountable for the traffic, even at this hour of the night.

She was greeted inside by comments and laughter. Everyone knew that Isabelle was always punctual to a fault. "Damn traffic" was her response.

"Well, we're just glad that you arrived safe

and sound, dear," Myra said as she led the parade out of the room to the secret staircase that led to the underground tunnels, where Charles and Fergus waited in the war room. She could feel the charged electricity running through the sisters and herself as well. It was always this way when they were about to embark on a new mission.

At the top of the steps, Myra stepped aside and looked over at Lady and her pups. "You know what to do. Guard."

Lady looked up at her mistress and let loose with a soft *woof* before she herded her brood to the kitchen to guard the door that had three special locks on it. None of the locks were more efficient than Lady and her pups.

Down in the war room, Charles was calling the meeting to order, saying, "The hour is late, but no one is complaining. I suggest we give Yoko the floor and hear what she has to say." His suggestion was met with nods of approval.

Yoko leaned forward. She looked at Kathryn and smiled. "This all happened after you made your delivery." To the others, she said, "Kathryn had just delivered a load of spring flowers when Garland Lee pulled into the parking lot. We all know who Garland Lee is, known as 'America's beloved songbird.' She bought the entire delivery, by the way. A while back, she had a fire at her mini estate, and the work crews ruined her property. You know, construction, all that earthmoving equipment. We're friendly, she and I. I don't exactly know how that happened, but we go back almost to the time I opened the nursery. She's my best customer and a wonderful person. She wasn't afraid to ask for advice, and she always followed the advice. I know you all have seen pictures of her estate. It's literally covered in flowers and flowering shrubs and trees.

"We would talk from time to time. She never, not once, used her celebrity with me. She was just a customer. Over time, she talked about her kids, like everyone does. She also talked about her *other* kids, the ones she helps via her charitable foundation. She would talk about how she hated the tours and being away from home. For years now, she has talked about retiring. She's older than she looks."

"Why hasn't she retired?" Nikki asked, a frown building on her beautiful face.

"Ah, you see, that's where the problem is. She told me about most of this earlier today, and then I did some research online. She has this lawyer who has handled her legal affairs for over twenty years. Let me stress the words *legal affairs.* Eight years ago, her agent and business manager, whose name was David Duffy, died. She was so devastated at his passing, she took off a whole year, canceled tours, etc. During that year is when I got to really know her. She came out to the nursery almost every day to walk through the greenhouses, and she attended every class I held for new gardeners. I even got her hooked on my apple tea.

"During that year, her attorney, a man named Arthur Forrester, hounded her relentlessly. He appointed himself her agent, saying she needed to be represented, and the canceled tours and such had to be dealt with. Not wanting to deal with all the threatened lawsuits, she agreed. And, remember, she was still grieving for Mr. Duffy. She always called him Duffy. He was her best friend, her children's godfather. By the way, she has four children. She dotes on them all. She said Forrester would show up with piles and piles of papers and say, 'Sign this, sign that,' and she did. She admits she never asked questions because she trusted him, and he had been her lawyer for over twenty years at that point in time."

Charles interjected a question. "So he took over as her agent, but then what happened?"

"He slowly started to embezzle money, in small sums so to go unnoticed, from all aspects of Garland's earnings. But the majority of it came from the charity that she runs."

"How is that possible?" Alexis demanded.

"I do not know," Yoko said. "If Garland said he did it and got away with it, then believe it. Moving along here . . . about three years ago, she was scheduled to go on a worldwide tour. She said the money was unbelievable, but she didn't want to do it, told Forrester she was going to retire and write her memoirs, but she would do a mini tour, a kind of farewell thing. They argued and fought openly, and she said she saw a side of him she had never seen before. That, according to Garland, was when she finally woke up and smelled the roses."

"What kind of money are you talking about, Yoko?"

"It was fifty-five million dollars for the tour. That's net for her after expenses. Forrester takes his percentage off the gross. If you're asking how much he double-dipped her for, she said it was an astronomical amount. She said her lawyers know to the penny, but she's not sure."

"Well, damn, I need to work for his law

30

firm," Nikki said. Alexis agreed.

"And his firm knew nothing about any of this?" Kathryn said in disbelief.

"I can only tell you what Garland told me. Two years and ten months ago, when she canceled the world tour, Forrester drafted some kind of letter and told her it was to keep the offer of the mini tour on the table. Also, unbeknownst to her, he was out there trying to get a book deal for her memoirs, a deal that she knew nothing about until the lawsuit was filed. It seems he was going on vacation or something at that time. She wouldn't sign it, and it got a little heated. He told her, over and over, that it was not binding and was just to keep things in play. He then told her that if she wouldn't sign it, to have one of her kids sign it through the corporation she owns. She did do that.

"Then, the more she thought about it, the more she didn't even want to do the mini tour. She asked her son, who was in rehab because of a serious car accident, to handle it for her. He had to have both of his knees replaced and had time on his hands. He agreed, and he was the one who discovered all that had gone on. He called in a forensic accounting firm, and they verified it.

"Garland fired Forrester on the spot, once her son told her what was going on. A lot went down, and Forrester ended up suing her. She countersued him. The rest has to come from her. I forgot to mention that Forrester had retired from the firm a few weeks before Garland fired him. She said it got really ugly. He called her, screaming and yelling, saying that she had ruined him and his family. I would assume his plan was to retire, play golf, and live off Garland's money. It got so bad, she had to change her phone number. So what do you all think?"

"What I think is that this guy gives all us decent lawyers a bad name. I met the man once at a dinner somewhere. But while I remember the name, I would be hard-pressed to pick him out of a crowd. What's the name of his firm?" Nikki asked.

Yoko shrugged. "If she told me, I don't remember. She did say Arthur said he hated the people he worked with."

"It's easy enough to Google him and get his profile. Is he a local?"

"No, no. He works in Washington, D.C. Garland used to live there as well. Actually, she was born and raised there and lived in the house she was born in. She still owns the house, but a cousin lives in it, rent-free, and maintains the property."

Yoko looked around at the others. She threw her hands in the air instead of asking if they were in or out. Understanding her sign language, the girls all shouted at the same time, "Count me in!"

Charles and Fergus agreed.

"When can you arrange a meeting with Garland?" Fergus asked.

"I took the liberty of sort of/kind of telling her I knew some people who could help her. She was all for it. I think I can arrange a meeting for the weekend, if that works for all of you."

"That works for me. I have a run and will be back by Wednesday morning," Kathryn said. "I wish you'd all stop pretending that you aren't looking at me. I'm okay. I'm really okay. So Bert is back in the States and is engaged. He wants to get married and raise a family. That's not the path in life I'm on. Yes, he and I talked, and we'll be friends for the rest of our lives. It simply didn't work for us. To show you I am serious, I am going to tell you something. I have a date that I am looking forward to. He understands me, and I understand him. Marriage is not in his DNA any more than it is in mine. At least for now."

"Who is it? Do we know him?" the girls chorused as one.

Kathryn laughed, pure joy in the sound. "Of course you know him. It's Jackson

Sparrow." At the girls' stunned surprise, Kathryn laughed harder and louder.

Ten minutes of hugs and more laughter followed. "As Jack Emery likes to say, 'I did not see that coming,' and I live next door to Sparrow." Maggie giggled.

The group then switched back to the matter at hand and agreed to meet Thursday evening for one of Charles's gourmet dinners, with a special guest named Garland Lee.

"I'm excited, aren't you, Myra? I have every album she's ever made. I know you do, too," Annie said.

"What I always liked about her was how normal she is. She never bought in to all that celebrity nonsense. First and foremost, she always said she was a wife and mother, and singing was just something she did to fill in the blanks. She sings in church, did you know that?" Myra said.

"I do know that, and I couldn't agree with you more. I just hate it when I hear about some man trying to take advantage of a woman. Especially a lawyer. If you can't trust your lawyer, whom can you trust? It's scary, isn't it, Myra?"

"There are a few bad apples in every barrel, Annie. That's why you and I and the

34

girls do what we do. We'll make it right for her."

Maggie, who had been quiet most of the evening, suddenly piped up, saying, "I'd like to do the due diligence on that guy. I know a few really good reporters in Washington whom I can ask for help. I'd like to go to D.C. undercover and infiltrate the firm. That's where I think we should start. If that's okay with all of you, I can have Alexis fix me up so no one will recognize me."

"Alone? Maggie, the boys are on assignment. I'm all for it, but you need a partner."

"I'll go," Nikki volunteered. "The office is slow, no pending cases on my calendar. Alexis can handle the office and anything I would have to deal with."

"All right," Annie said. "But not till after our meeting with Garland."

"I wish you girls weren't driving back to town. It's so late, and you are more than welcome to stay. Please send a text when you arrive home safe and sound," Myra said, her face creased in worry.

"Not to worry, *Mom,* we'll be a caravan all the way into the city," Maggie drawled.

Lady and her brood followed the girls out to the courtyard parking area and gave the girls a rousing send-off. They waited until the huge iron gates closed before trotting back to the kitchen.

Pinewood, their kingdom, their domain, was now safe for the night.

CHAPTER 2

It was still full light, thanks to daylight saving time, when the caravan of cars sailed through the open gates at Pinewood. The evening was almost balmy, with a slight breeze wafting through the ancient oak trees that surrounded the farmhouse. Even out here in the large courtyard, the girls could smell delicious aromas coming from the open kitchen door, where Myra and Annie stood waiting for the girls and their special guest to cross the cobblestones and make their way up to the porch. Lady and her pups, tails wagging, furiously barked a continuous greeting.

"*Exactly* who lives here, Yoko?" Garland Lee whispered.

Yoko smiled. "A very special lady named Myra Rutledge. The lady standing next to her is my adoptive mother. She adopted all of us," she said, waving her arms about. "Her name is Anna de Silva."

"*Countess* Anna de Silva?" Garland asked, obviously in awe. "Damn, I should have gussied up. I look like a bag lady."

"The one and only. You look fine. We only dress up for weddings and funerals. Trust me, okay?"

"If I didn't trust you, Yoko, I wouldn't be here."

It was pure bedlam as it always was when the women got together at Pinewood. It didn't matter if they had just seen each other five minutes earlier, they still hugged and giggled and played with Lady and her pups, all the while commenting on the delicious aromas coming from the stove, where Charles presided, along with his right-hand man, Fergus Duffy.

Introductions were made and hands were shaken, followed by flattering comments on Garland's music. She blushed and thanked everyone and even hugged the dogs, one by one. "I love animals. They love unconditionally, and they never betray you," she said, downplaying her personal accomplishments, which endeared her to the others immediately. Yoko was right; Garland was just an ordinary person with a special talent.

"Amen to that," the girls chorused.

Garland looked around expectantly. Charles nodded and said, "We have an hour till dinner. I suggest we go belowdecks and take care of business." He fixed a steely gaze on Garland, then said, "Yoko has vouched for you, and her word is good enough for all of us. Having said that, we are going to take you down below to an area that only a handful of people know about. It's where we conduct our . . . business. So, if you follow me, we can get things under way."

Garland held up both hands, palms outward facing the girls. "This may surprise you, but I do know who you are. You're the Vigilantes. Back in the day, I supported you and cheered you on, never dreaming the day would ever come that I would need your help." She pointed to Annie. "I didn't know about the countess, though. Someone is missing, though. The plastic surgeon, right?"

"She passed away," Myra said softly. "Annie took her place."

Garland nodded. "You have no worries where I'm concerned. I'm just grateful for your help. I'm ready to get this show on the road — oops, that's a show business expression — if you all are ready."

There were no gasps, no sign of surprise from Garland, when Charles pressed a rosette on the built-in bookshelves to reveal a steep stone staircase that led to the old dungeon, which had been renovated by Isabelle to make room for what they all called the war room, and where the sisters always conducted business.

The first one into the room, Charles set about pressing light switches and turning on the various computers and the giant TV that hung from the ceiling. Lady Justice appeared to a muted drumroll. Garland fired off a snappy salute, to the sisters' absolute delight.

Fifteen minutes whizzed by as everyone got comfortable. Chitchat was about the beautiful spring weather and the cherry blossom festival, which they had all missed for one reason or another. They were waiting for Charles to call the meeting to order, which he did by stepping down from his perch on the dais and standing behind Myra's chair. He was rewarded with instant silence.

"Ms. Lee . . ."

"Please call me Garland. I feel like I'm among friends, and I'd like you all to consider me one, too."

Charles nodded. "Garland it is then. And, of course, you know all of us, so first names are the order of the day. Now, Yoko has filled us in. I'd like to go over what she's told us to date, and if anything is missing, please feel free to enlighten us, so we can do our best to help you." Garland nodded as Charles repeated virtually verbatim everything Yoko had shared with the group. "Am I missing anything?"

"Yes and no. We are coming up to three years from the date Arthur sued me. I've had enough. I've had to spend several million dollars in legal fees. I want that back. My position is I did nothing wrong. Arthur lied to me, and everything in the suit is a lie. I suppose most defendants say that, but in my case, it is the God's honest truth. Arthur is the liar. I now know more about the legal system than I ever wanted to know. The fact that Arthur is a lawyer himself puts me at a disadvantage. We had a mandatory meeting, there's a legal name for it, and it was a disaster. I think the magistrate who oversaw it was on Arthur's side. Maybe paid off by him. My lawyers thought so, too. Neither side gave in. We still do not have a court date, and settlement talks are a pure joke. Right now, we're waiting for a judge to rule on a summary judgment that my lawyers requested. He's had the case for four months."

"Sometimes judges do take forever," Nikki said. Alexis nodded agreement.

"What would you like us to do for you, Garland?" Myra asked.

Without missing a beat, Garland leaned forward and spoke quickly and concisely. "I would like you to get all my money back, the monies he stole from me and my charity, my legal fees, and for him not to be able to take another cent from me. I'd like to see that sack of pus living in a tent and pissing in the bushes. I'm sorry for sounding so crude, but that's what I would like to see happen. Arthur put me through hell these past few years, but mostly I want him to pay for betraying me. Please understand something. It's not the money. It's the fact that the man who I thought was my friend and protector put himself before me when it was his fiduciary duty to put me first. If I get all those monies back, I will donate them to the charity. Not just the one I founded, but others as well. I read what you are doing with the veterans, Cou . . . Annie. I'd be happy to donate to those fine men and women who did their service for our nation. And I'd like to donate to animal shelters across the country. Now, is that possible? Whatever you need me to do, you can count on me to do it. Is it possible?" she asked anxiously.

"Oh, yeah," Kathryn drawled.

"All things are possible," Annie said, and smiled.

"We just have to make a plan. Maggie has volunteered to go to Washington, along with Nikki, to scope things out. Some things just need to be done in person. Then we'll get back to fine-tuning what has to be done to make you whole again," Myra assured Garland.

"For now, we want you to talk to us. Maggie will record it all and transcribe it for us later, so we each have a copy. Tell us everything you know about Arthur Forrester, from the day you met him until this moment. Even if you think it's silly or not important, tell us, anyway. We need the big picture," Annie said, her eyes sparkling with excitement.

"Even the part about my praying for him to drop dead, then asking God to forgive me for my evil thoughts?" Garland grinned. She liked these ladies. Really liked them.

The sisters laughed. "We don't kill people. What we do is we make them wish they were dead," Isabelle said with a smile in her voice.

"Ladies, if you can do that, then it works for me. Have at it," Garland said.

"Now that you ladies have taken control, Fergus and I will go topside to see about dinner." Charles looked down at his watch. "You have thirty-four minutes, so talk fast,

Garland. I've found over the years that one has trouble being productive after a heavy meal. If you don't finish up in your allotted time, we will have to reconvene another day."

Garland did as instructed and was only interrupted once by Maggie, who had Googled Arthur Forrester's old firm for a picture of the lawyer. "Here he is, girls, take a look at what Garland calls a 'sack of pus.' Arthur Saul Forrester! He looks like one of the Seven Dwarfs. Grumpy, to be precise."

The girls all leaned forward to stare at the picture on Maggie's laptop.

"What's with the rosy cheeks?" Alexis asked.

"He has rosacea," Garland said. "You need a more recent picture. He looked awful when I saw him last year at a deposition. It's not like I saw him a lot. Maybe once a year or so. We mostly sent texts, e-mails, and, of course, had lots of phone conversations. I heard through the grapevine that when a partner retires from that firm, the firm has a big dinner and the departing partner is given a gift of some kind. But nothing like that, I was told, was done for Arthur when he retired. He just walked away and didn't look back.

"True or false, I don't know, it's just what

I heard. I also heard that the firm was going to sue him, but I never heard if that happened."

"Okay, okay, here's one. Taken in a group shot at the firm's annual barbecue the year he retired. He looks kinda like Dopey in this one. Kind of like a hound dog. He doesn't appear to be very tall."

"He's only five-one. He also wears lifts in his shoes. I think he suffers from short-man syndrome. Look at all the other partners in that picture. They're all six feet or so."

"I guess that could play into his psyche," Myra said.

"What about his family? What do you know about them, Garland?"

"Not much. He has four kids, two boys and two girls. His wife is a blend of something, Asian and American, I think. I think she's a nurse or a nurse practitioner. He never really talked about his wife. His children are beautiful. The wife, not so much. She's small, tiny actually. I remember thinking a good wind would blow her over. I guess she gives off the appearance of being fragile. I only ever met her once, so my memories of her are hazy.

"She didn't like me, and I didn't like her. He never talked about her to me. The kids, yes. Because . . . I was invited to his kids' birthday parties and graduations, the weddings, the births of the grandkids, the grandkids' birthdays and graduations. For gifts, obviously. I never went to any of them, but I always sent generous gifts.

"Arthur once told me how much some wedding he had attended cost, and it boggled my mind that someone would pay a quarter of a million for a wedding. I think it was his niece's wedding, though I'm not all that sure. Now that I think back, I guess he was bragging. Why he thought he had to brag to me is wild.

"He paid for the graduation parties for two of his grandsons. And each of them cost almost as much as that wedding. Just for the hell of it, I had my son match up the bills to the dates of those graduation parties, to see how much he was billing me for, and sure enough, it did look like *I* was the one who paid for his grandkids' parties," she said, holding back a guffaw. "I guess I want that money back, too."

"Of course you do, dear, and we're going to see that you get it," Myra said cheerfully.

"Anything else we should know?" Yoko asked.

"He likes to play the stock market, but he admitted he isn't very good at it. He took some big hits when the economy tanked there for a while. He did talk a lot about how successful his two brothers were compared to him, who was just a plain old lawyer. I sensed some jealousy in that regard. One of his brothers is a world-renowned thoracic surgeon and travels all over the world. The other brother married some French billionaire's daughter and swims in money. Jealousy just oozed out of Arthur's pores. That's just my opinion, now."

"So what you seem to be saying is Arthur has no money. No serious money from his profession. Am I right on that?"

Garland nodded.

"That means he counted on you to keep him afloat and in the style he wanted to live." Garland nodded again. "If he has no money, how are we going to get yours back, dear?" Myra asked.

"He has malpractice insurance. Since this all happened while he was a member of the firm, he was covered under that umbrella. I don't know the dollar amount. By the way, if I didn't make it clear before, when we countersued Arthur, we also sued the firm. For the five years he was both my lawyer and, unknown to his firm, my agent, he was a partner in the law firm. They owe me, too."

"It would appear so," Annie said. "I so

love going after people and taking their money, then putting it to good use. You, my dear, are in good hands."

"And just in time," Kathryn said as she heard the dinner bell Charles was ringing at the top of the brick steps. If any additional proof was needed that dinner was indeed ready, Lady barked shrilly.

"You're going to help me, then?"

"Of course we are. We will make you whole again. All you have to do is trust us. Can you do that?" Annie asked.

"Of course I can." Garland turned to Yoko and hugged her. "Thank you for bringing me here. How can I ever repay you . . . all of you?"

"By keeping our secret," Myra said. "And if you ever give another concert, getting us front-row seats."

"Deal." Garland laughed.

Dinner was a lively affair, with Garland fitting right in. As the sisters said later, it was like she was one of them. She ate like Maggie and Kathryn, and said she no longer worried about her weight and was so glad she didn't have to stuff herself into a nasty corset to project a tiny waist. She didn't bat an eye when she held out her plate for seconds.

The conversation quickly turned to Kathryn, as she knew it would. "Come on, Kat, tell us about your date last night with Jackson Sparrow," Nikki teased.

Garland's eyes went wide. "You had a date with the former director of the FBI? The Jackson Sparrow who told the president to take a hike and now works for Annie with the veterans? That Jackson Sparrow?"

"The one and only. Okay, you want it, here it is. We went to a Thai place, and the food was out of this world. We then went to a movie and had popcorn and Jujubes and one of those large sodas, which we shared. Two straws. He's funny, he's witty, he's charming. Murphy, my dog, adored him. That's a plus right there. He kissed me good night, and my toes curled up, and my eyeballs about exploded."

Charles cleared his throat as Fergus scrambled to his feet. "Ah . . . ladies, I think Fergus and I will retire to the kitchen while you . . . um . . . discuss whatever is to come next."

"Ooh, just one kiss?" Yoko asked.

"Well, no, there was another one, but neither one of us could catch our breath, so we left it at one and a half." Kathryn giggled at the expressions on the sisters' faces. "No, I did not invite him in," she said between giggles. "That's for another time."

"So how do you think he'll be in bed?" Maggie asked boldly.

Kathryn laughed out loud. "I'm thinking *spectacular!*"

"Make sure you take notes for your memoirs down the road," Garland said.

"When are you going to see Jackson again, dear?" Myra asked.

"The next time I'm in town. Just enough time for me to buy some . . . you know, some frilly, gossamer nothings."

Inside the kitchen, Fergus leaned toward Charles and hissed, "Does that mean what I think it means?"

"You're asking me?" Charles dithered as he waved a dishcloth around and around.

The general consensus before the girls called it a night was that they had never seen Kathryn so happy.

Maggie settled herself in the buttery-soft client chair across from Nikki's desk. "You called, I'm here," she quipped. "The truth is, if you hadn't called, I would have called you. I couldn't sleep last night. All I did was think about Garland Lee and that *sack of pus* ex-lawyer of hers. I have an idea. Want to hear it?" Maggie said, leaning forward, her eyes sparkling.

"I'm all ears, girl, hit me!" Nikki said,

reacting to what she was seeing on the reporter's face.

"*Okayyyyy.* Last night, we talked about Alexis fixing us up so no one would recognize us when we go to the firm, right? I think we need to give that up and go with who we are. Bear with me now, because we can only do this with Annie's approval. I think she will give her seal of approval, but with Annie, you never know.

"You will be Annie's . . . I don't know what term to use . . . chief of staff, her front person, her right hand, whatever. You tell whomever we get to speak to at Forrester's old firm that Countess de Silva is looking for a law firm to handle her real-estate holdings and that she is considering that firm and one other. We need to be up front with that to make them want her business so bad they can taste it. If we have to give a reason as to why she's doing this, we just say her holdings are so vast she no longer wants to keep everything under one umbrella. You rattle off the amount of one hundred million dollars, and they'll sit up and take notice."

Nikki leaned over the desk until both women were almost nose to nose. "And . . ."

"That's when you speak up and say that the other firm the countess is considering has a clean slate, whereas sack of pus's firm has this huge lawsuit pending, along with a few others over these past years. I checked them out last night. The firm has had four serious high-dollar lawsuits filed against them. The malpractice insurance was forced to pay out on all four. Two of their attorneys were disbarred for unethical practices, two as a direct result of one of the lawsuits. Don't you lawyers describe this as *due diligence*?"

Nikki nodded. "Okay, I see where you're going with this. It's doable. I think we can make it work. What role are you going to play?"

"Myself. Intrepid reporter and former editor in chief who works for the countess, of course, who owns the *Post*. I report on anything and everything the countess does. If you're okay with this, I'll clear it with Annie. And then we call ahead for an appointment and drive to Washington. I'm okay either way. What do you think, Nikki?"

"I've been researching Ballard, Ballard and Quinlan. They are a top-notch, white-shoe law firm, if you believe their hype, with over sixty lawyers, twenty of whom are partners. Their website leaves a lot to be desired, and it hasn't been updated in a while. Forrester's picture is still on there, and there was no indication he had retired. You'd think they'd update it at least once a year, but the last time it says it was updated was three years ago, before the suit against Garland Lee was filed.

"I personally know several lawyers who work for a good old Irish firm in D.C., O'Malley, O'Shaunnesy and McCallister. We can float that firm out there as our due diligence. As far as I know, they, the firm, have never been sued, but I'll check that out." Nikki got up and walked around her desk. The two women hugged. "Want to go out for coffee?"

"Love to, but I can't. The boys are up in Delaware and will be gone for ten days or so, so I'm holding down the fort, so to speak. I'll call Annie, and you call the Ballard firm for an appointment. Walk me to the elevator. What's your feeling on this, Nikki?"

Nikki winked at Maggie as she pressed the button for the down elevator. "I'm thinking Mr. Sack of Pus Forrester is going to wish he were dead before we're through with him."

Maggie laughed. The women had one more hug before Maggie stepped into the elevator. Damn, she felt good. Not just good, but *really* good. In her mind, there was no better adrenaline rush than going after a bad guy and making him wish he'd never been born.

By the end of the day, Maggie had Annie's permission to do whatever was needed to move the mission along. Nikki reported back that the meeting with three senior partners of Ballard, Ballard & Quinlan was scheduled for 11:00 A.M. Maggie's clenched fist shot in the air the moment she disconnected from the call with Nikki. She just *loved, loved, loved* it when a plan came together, especially when she was the one who had originated the plan in the first place.

CHAPTER 3

Myra stirred the fluffy scrambled eggs on her plate as she stared across the kitchen to the window, where she could see bright, golden sunshine streaming into the room. "A penny for your thoughts, old girl," Charles said jovially.

"I'm not sure my thoughts are worth even a penny right now, Charles. By the way, these eggs are delicious."

"I can see that," Charles quipped, motioning to the uneaten pile of protein sitting on her plate. "So, would you care to share what is making you so pensive this morning?"

"I was thinking about Garland Lee. I really like her, Charles. She's what I call *real people.* She never got caught up in that celebrity lifestyle, and she never lost her values. I just hope we can make her whole again. I've been thinking about asking Annie to go with me to her house to pick up all her legal files. We really need to go through them, and she did say she would be happy to turn them over to us. She said she has them all packed up in boxes. I thought that among all of us — you, Fergus, Annie, and me — we could get a leg up before Monday, when Nikki and Maggie head to Washington. What do you think, dear?"

"I think it's a marvelous idea. So I guess what you're telling me is I should count on doing a lot of reading through the weekend. Like a campout, so to speak."

"Exactly," Myra replied, beaming at Charles.

"Consider it done, old girl. I don't suppose you would be interested in cleaning up now, would you?"

"I would not. I have things to do, dear, and cleanup is not among them, and you do it so well. Everything sparkles when you do it."

Charles laughed. "You do know how to flatter me. Aside from picking up Ms. Lee's files, what else is on your agenda?"

"For starters, I think one of us needs to call Mr. Snowden to reserve his services. Do you want to do that, or should I?"

"I can multitask, so I'll call him. Anything else?"

"Actually, yes. Charles, do you remember

back when we did our first mission how we plotted and planned and had our mission laid out almost like a military drill?" Charles nodded. "I'm thinking we all need to pair up and head to Washington to check out Mr. Sack of Pus Forrester. I really hate that term, even though it's apt where he is concerned. I think I'm going to refer to him from now on as Mr. SOP. What do you think?" Myra asked fretfully.

Charles laughed out loud as he scraped Myra's eggs onto a plate for Lady and her pups, who devoured them in less than a minute. "It works for me, my dear."

"You know the boys' schedules better than I do these days. Is there any point to asking Abner if he can hack into Mr. SOP's bank accounts to ascertain his financial worth, or should we just leave it to Mr. Snowden and his people? And the firm's, of course. Although I'm beginning to think that might have to be done by someone like Abner's friend Philonious. Any thoughts on that, Charles?"

"Not off the cuff, but I will certainly look into it all. Sunday evening is our next scheduled meeting. I'm sure we'll have more information than we need at that point. So, until then, make a note of anything you think will be relevant in our quest for justice."

Myra merely nodded as she tapped out a text to Annie. She waved airily as she left the kitchen to shower and dress for the day, with Lady and the pups on her heels.

Left to his own devices and his kitchen duty, Charles did a little two-step as he swished the dish towel overhead. At last, some action, something to bite down on. He could hardly wait to get down to his lair to start the ball rolling.

Garland Lee heard the car the minute it turned onto her gravel driveway. *Company?* She wasn't expecting anyone, so she frowned. No one ever came this far out, unless they called in advance. Those same people who called also knew that Garland was not partial to company and liked her privacy, so callers were few and far between.

Garland bounced upright and shook the dirt off the knees of her coveralls. She stripped off her gardening gloves to shield her eyes from the bright sun. A low-slung sports car. "Hmmmmm." Three light taps of the horn told her she had nothing to fear because she saw an arm waving out the driver's-side window. Countess de Silva and Myra. "Hmmmmm," all over again. She waved back as she walked forward to meet the two women.

"I hope this isn't an imposition, Garland, but you did say you would turn over all the legal files to us. Annie and I decided to get a head start on picking them up, so we can go through them over the weekend."

"No problem. Everything is boxed up and ready for you. I added the last few items that had not been packed already, when I got home last night. I can have Jose put them in the trunk of your car, if you open it up. How about some tea? Or coffee? Or a glass of lemonade?"

"Tea would be nice," Annie said. "Your grounds are beautiful. Do you do all the planting yourself?"

"No, but I do a lot of it. Jose lets me putter, then when I'm not looking, he moves everything to where it should go. It's pretty much maintenance, since Yoko's people did all the designing and heavy lifting. I just love digging in the earth. I like catching all the earthworms for Jose's sons. We have a pond, way in the back, and they like to fish there. Come along. It's a beautiful day, isn't it?" Garland gurgled as she led the way up to the house. "It's okay, you can say something." She continued to gurgle with laughter.

59

"It's . . . ah . . . beautiful."

"You know, it really is, after you get used to it. Architects throw up their hands, then take a step back and try to come up with something suitable to say. I designed the house myself for my wants and needs, because no sane architect would ever sign his or her name to such a structure. The builder had fits over it, but when it was done, he told me if I ever wanted to sell it, to consider him. My kids love it. Arthur said it was an abomination, but I could see that he was just jealous. *Even back then.* He lives in a condo."

"Is the whole back end glass?"

"From top to bottom, yes. That's where I work. The bottom is my small recording studio, and the second floor is where I paint. No, I'm not really an artist, but I love splashing color on canvas. I also work on my memoirs there. The third floor has a one-bedroom suite, along with a monster bathroom. I sleep there sometimes so I can look out at the stars at night. Mostly on nights when I'm stressed out.

"The front, as you can see, is half-Tudor and half-Federal. I just like the look. Inside, the rooms are all different. Come along, and I'll show you." Garland stopped and waved to a little man pushing a wheelbarrow.

"Jose, can you put the boxes in the kitchen into the lady's trunk for me? Don't carry them, they're heavy, so put them in the wheelbarrow. I don't want you hurting your back. Annie, Myra, this is my friend Jose. He is in charge of the gardens and has been with me for almost forty years. Jose, these lovely ladies are helping me with some . . . some problems I'm having."

The little old man was shy, and he held out his hands to show they were dirty, so he couldn't shake their hands. He nodded and smiled and scurried off to do Garland's bidding.

"Jose should retire, but he refuses. When his knees protest too much, he has his grandchildren help him. They all live here in a house I built for them. To me, there is no greater love than loyalty, and Jose has proven it over and over from the day we first met. He has two sons, one is an orthopedic surgeon and one is an architect — and, yes, he helped with the house." Garland laughed.

Garland led Myra and Annie along a flagstone path, which took them to a tiny alcove that led to the kitchen. The door was ornate, a Hansel and Gretel affair that was not unpleasing to the eye. They entered a mudroom, where Garland kicked off her work boots and walked barefoot down a short hall into a kitchen that left both Annie and Myra gasping. It was all brick, except for one wall of glass, right down to the brick floor. Moss and other mossy plants grew out of the brick walls. Bright red ladybugs climbed the walls. "I made the ladybugs," Garland said proudly as she pointed out the massive fireplace, which was big enough to hold a party within. "My publicity people wanted me to host a luau for some important music people about ten years ago, and we roasted a whole pig."

The furniture was old, hard maple that gleamed from years of polish and wax. Colorful place mats adorned the table, whose centerpiece was a cactus plant with seven arms. "That cactus is fifty years old. My husband gave it to me for my birthday one year. We were too poor back then to buy gifts, so he found it somewhere and put it in a little cardboard box, and here it is. One of my most valued treasures. Arthur called it an eyesore." Garland sniffed to show what she thought of her former lawyer's opinion.

Annie and Myra looked around, loving the homey feel of Garland's kitchen. "Who hooked all these colorful rugs?" Myra asked.

"Me. It's what I do . . . did when I would get back from a tour. It helped me unwind.

Most of them are pretty old, so we have to wash them by hand and let them dry in the sun. I wouldn't part with them for anything in the world. This is where I spend a lot of time. Please sit down while I make tea. Hot, not ice, tea, right?"

The far glass wall of the kitchen drew Myra and Annie like a magnet. They looked around at the bushel-size ferns hanging from the old rafters, then down at the window seat, which ran the entire length of the window wall. Colorful pots of flowers, every hue of the rainbow, were luscious and healthy-looking. However, the drawings lying on the face of the window seat caused them to gasp out loud.

"I thought you said you liked to smear paint on canvas. This looks more like something a real artist would draw," Annie said in awe.

Garland walked over to the window. She was blushing. "It's a hobby. I like doing caricatures. These are all people who are important in my life. Or, were important. It's how I see them. My husband, my kids, Duffy, and even Arthur. A few old friends who are gone now. Arthur said it was an infantile hobby. I don't think he liked my rendition of him, with the dollar signs for eyes." Myra and Annie laughed.

"I can't wait to set eyes on that man," Annie said. Myra agreed.

"How do you water those gorgeous ferns? Don't tell me you climb on a ladder," Myra said.

"Nothing that dangerous. Jose rigged up a mister with a timer. It mists everything twice a day. The light is filtered from the windows. He said it cost fourteen cents for each mister. Every so often, he takes the ferns down to fertilize them. I take care of the plants on the window seat. Jose is very conscientious."

Myra and Annie walked around, viewing the eye-catching end of the kitchen, before they walked back to the table and sat down. Looking around, they continued to let their gazes sweep the one-of-a-kind kitchen, which held all of Garland's treasures. "Did this kitchen get damaged in the fire?"

"Only one corner. Mostly the Tudor side and some of the back. A lot of the glass had to be replaced. You'd never know there was a fire, at least that's how I see it. I just love it here. It's where I raised my children. My husband died here. He's buried in a special place Jose created for him. When my time comes, I'll lie next to him. As you can see, I'm quite happy here. The only black mark on the tapestry of my life is Arthur Forrester. If I lose this lawsuit, and it is entirely possible, I could lose this house. Just between you and me, if that were to happen, I would burn it to the ground before I let him have it. He knows how much it means to me, and that's what he'll go after if he wins. The law is all a matter of interpretation. And he knows judges, plays golf with them. Need I say more?"

"That's not going to happen, Garland. That's a promise," Annie assured her. Myra seconded Annie's promise. Garland beamed her pleasure as she poured boiling water into a red ceramic teapot. "It's Yoko's special blend of apple tea, which she keeps me supplied with. In turn, I paint ladybugs for her so she can nestle them in and among her plants."

Sipping their tea, relaxed and feeling comfortable with each other, Myra said, "When you were out at the farm, you were tense and stressed. We're on your home turf now, so talk to us about Mr. SOP. By the way, that stands for Sack of Pus. Just talk, even if you think it's not important. We'll sift through it and make it all work."

Garland nodded. "He's a bully. Back in the beginning, when I didn't know any better, I thought of it as him just being aggressive. I was so naive. I guess I thought that's the way lawyers were supposed to be. He's very controlling. David Duffy, my one and only business manager, tried his best to warn me about Arthur, but he would never come outright and say anything bad about him. You would have liked David. He was one of those rare people who walk the walk and talk the talk. Honest as the day is long. He'd give you the shirt off his back, and if you needed a dollar and he only had fifty cents, he'd find a way to get you the other fifty. I mourned his passing like no other. He was like the brother I never had, the beloved uncle, the treasured grandfather, all rolled into one. I just loved and adored him."

"What did, or didn't, he say about SOP?" Annie asked.

"Not to turn my back on him. He said there was something about him that did not compute. Arthur was always about the money. You couldn't have a conversation — unless it had to do with money. You could be talking about a day at the beach, and he'd find something to say about money.

"Arthur, excuse me, SOP, did not come from money. Although I think his family was comfortable. His mother passed first, then his father retired to Hilton Head in South Carolina, I think, or somewhere else warm, and he and his siblings had to help pay for his care. He resented that. He talked about that quite a bit, about how he had to write out a check every month. And then, when his father passed away, he was the first one there to sell off everything so he could get some of that money back. His siblings didn't care one way or the other was how I understood it."

Annie grimaced. "The man sounds like a real prince."

"Usually, it's women who like to keep up with the Joneses, as the saying goes. Arthur was like that. He joined a ritzy country club that even he admitted he couldn't afford. He said it was all about doing deals on the golf course and drinking at the clubhouse while eating some rare Kobe beef. The man lived to play golf, and it's my understanding he's an excellent golfer.

"When he retired, right before I fired him, he sold his house and moved. He said he didn't need all that room anymore. I think he only moved a few miles away. I wasn't that interested, so I didn't pay that much attention at that point in time. He also gave up his membership at the ritzy country club, so he could get his two-hundred-thousand-dollar membership fee back. It sounded to me at the time like he needed money and was downsizing.

"One day, I sat down and tried to figure out what the man's living expenses were, since he was so obsessed with money. I recalled he told me once that his property taxes on his house were forty-eight thousand dollars a year. I do remember being shocked at the amount, especially when he said his house was only twenty-five hundred square feet, with no backyard to speak of. And he had a septic tank. And a well. He lived in Riverville, Maryland, in a very upscale, wealthy area, a couple hours' commute to his office.

"I know he shared his secretary with another attorney, but the firm pays the salaries of support staff. Of course, all those expenses reduce his share of the partnership profits. Add to that the cost of utilities for the house, car insurance, house insurance, commuter fees. Then there are the credit card bills, day-to-day living expenses, clothing, and all those vacations he took. It all added up to a princely sum. My final assessment was that he couldn't possibly live the way he did — unless he had the money he was making from me. If I needed any further proof, it came when I fired him, and he said that I was destroying him and his family. That's the moment his true, ugly colors came out."

"Did something happen, some financial disaster, anything like that?" Myra asked.

Garland shrugged. "I don't know. Like I said at that point in time, I had already become disenchanted with him. What I do know was he was livid when I said I was not doing the tour. I guess he was counting on the up-front monies. And then he tried pressuring me when I made the mistake of telling him I was writing my memoirs. Another commission lost. If I had agreed to a publishing contract, he would have gotten a chunk of money right off the top. He turned really, really ugly then."

"Would it be wrong to assume that when he retired, he planned on living off you? Was he planning on taking any favorite or old clients with him, do you know?"

Garland poured more tea for everyone. Her brow furrowed in thought. "My lawyers think, but cannot prove, that he was asked to leave the firm. They think he just said he was retiring, to save face. They think the name partners found out about me and called him on it. Now, if that played into his possibly not being able to take clients, I don't know. I would assume he got some kind of financial payout, since he had to buy in to become an equity partner, but, again,

I don't really know how that works. Maybe everything is like in limbo, pending the outcome of this lawsuit."

"Was he a litigator?" Myra asked.

"No, he did corporate law. He said he hated it because it was boring, but 'it was a living' was how he put it. I don't know anything about his clients. From time to time, he would say they were all dry as cardboard. I remember once asking him if he ever said anything nice about anyone, but he ignored the question."

"Did he talk about his home life, his wife or children?"

"Yes and no. Not so much when the boys were young. Rarely about the girls. He wasn't one of those Little League dads, if that's what you mean. He put in long days with his commute. He hardly saw them. They did not have live-in help, I do know that. I guess Mrs. SOP did all the house-work, but I don't know that for a fact. He did talk a lot when it was time to pony up for the grandkids' birthday and graduation parties. They were quite lavish, but he was trying to prove something to his siblings, I think. Keeping up appearances with the in-crowd.

"Oh, this probably means nothing, but you said anything I could think of. Mrs.

SOP was a health nut. Arthur said he took sixteen vitamin supplements every day."

"Anything else you can remember?" Annie asked.

"He leases his cars. Is that important? Always the latest-model Mercedes. Turns it in every year for a new one. I guess it was about keeping up appearances, too. He once told me, years ago, that he made his kids work to pay for half of their vehicles and insurance. I thought that was good thinking on his part. He also made them apply for student aid when they attended college. They got some, but not very much, so he had to foot the bill for that. All four of them went to Ivy League schools."

"Did he gamble?" Myra asked.

"I don't know. He never ever said he was going to Las Vegas. He and his wife did take a lot of vacations, which were ten days at a time. He would always notify me when he was going on a vacation, in case I needed him. I never did. I really can't think of anything else other than what I already told you."

"I guess, then, you wouldn't have an opinion on how he is managing these past three years with no money coming in, eh?" Annie said.

"I'm sure he has a pension fund, and

there's his Social Security. I would assume his wife would have the same, so he can't be desperate for money. But if his legal bills are even half of what mine have been, then he might have a problem, but I have no way of knowing that for sure."

"Why didn't you fire him a long time ago? It sounds like you never much cared for him," Myra said. "My biggest problem with all of this is how he got away with it at the firm. Working for you and handling his legal clients so he could pile up billable hours. Everyone knows that with lawyers, it's all about billable hours."

Garland made an ugly sound in her throat. "It's really quite simple. After Duffy died, he took all the files. All he had to do was make phone calls and plug in numbers on contracts. He wasn't out there beating the bushes for new business. He didn't bring one thing to the table for me. He literally just stepped into Duffy's shoes — shoes that he was never quite able to fill. The only thing he would have accomplished would have been a book contract or turning me into a brand. But, again, all he did was call a publisher to ask if they were interested in my memoirs, then he called several other publishers to see if he could get a bidding war going. Then I shut him down. I nixed the brand business the moment he brought it up. It was all very easy for him to get away with at the firm."

Garland got up and threw her hands in the air. "I don't know how I let it all happen. I was used to him. He had always been there in the background to help me, at least that's what I thought at the time. When Duffy died, he took over. He just stepped in and took over. I was a basket case, and I allowed it to happen. I own that. I trusted him. It wasn't that I disliked him. It was more like I simply wasn't comfortable around him the way I was with Duffy. But in point of fact, I had not really had a lot of up close contact with him when he was just the lawyer we went to when something came up that required a legal eagle.

"Maybe, secretly, down deep, I knew he didn't really like me. He did like the money he made off me, however. I guess I knew that, deep inside, and it bothered me, but I wouldn't own up to it.

"If I had a fairy godmother who could grant me one wish, it would be that I had retired when Duffy died and fired Arthur at the same time. You have no idea how many times I have wished that over these past years. You cannot *un*ring the bell, as they say, so here I am."

"And here we are, right alongside you," Annie said happily. "Thanks for the tea, it was good. I'm going to have to ask Yoko to get me some. I think Fergus would like it."

The women talked for another hour about anything and nothing, with Annie jotting down in the little spiral notebook she always carried in her purse any recollection that would come out in regard to Arthur Forrester.

Myra got up, and the three women embraced. "Trust us. Can you do that?"

"Absolutely," Garland said as she bent down to pick up a fat yellow cat who appeared out of nowhere. "Meet Henry!"

Myra and Annie oohed and aahed over Henry, who purred his contentment.

Garland walked her guests out to the car. She admired the racy set of wheels, then laughed out loud as Annie slid into the low-slung sports car and gunned the engine.

"She's fearless," Myra said, sliding into the bucket seat. "She's also an absolute menace on the road. Evel Knievel in a skirt!"

"Drive carefully, and thanks for everything."

"We'll call with progress reports. I love your house and the gardens, Garland. Be happy, you hear?" Myra called out the open window as Annie pressed the gas pedal.

"Always," Garland said, choking back a deep laugh. She looked down at Henry, and said, "I think my new friends are really going to pull my feet out of the fire, and all our worries will be over." Henry snuggled deeper into Garland's arms and purred his song of contentment.

CHAPTER 4

Myra's kitchen was in a state of bedlam as the sisters ran across the courtyard to the kitchen through the torrential rain. Lady and her pups barked and howled as the soaking-wet women grumbled and complained while Myra handed out large, fluffy yellow towels, and Charles and Fergus tried to wipe up the floor so the dogs wouldn't slip and slide, thinking it was all a big game.

"April showers, my foot," Alexis groused. "It's like a blinking tsunami out there."

"And it's cold as well," Nikki said, her teeth chattering uncontrollably.

"I don't see any spring flowers," Yoko grumbled.

"Run upstairs and get changed, girls. You all keep clothes here. Scat now before you catch a cold. I'm going to turn up the heat."

"Your outside thermometer says it is only sixty degrees," Maggie called over her shoulder. "Some spring this is! Whatever happened to global warming? Or is that climate change?"

Isabelle shouted to be heard over the dogs barking and the girls screeching that Kathryn was on the road and would not be attending the meeting.

"I think some hot chocolate would be good, dear," Myra said, reaching for the can of hot chocolate mix in the overhead cabinet. She blinked when she noticed Charles already pouring milk into a saucepan. "You're always one step ahead of me, aren't you, dear?"

Charles laughed. "Only at times, and mostly it's because you allow it."

Myra sniffed. "There is that," she agreed, then laughed out loud.

"So we have a full house, with the exception of Kathryn," Fergus said as he pulled out cups and saucers from the cabinet. "Where are the marshmallows? You can't have hot chocolate without marshmallows." Charles pointed to a cabinet to Fergus's left. "They're colored!"

"But they all taste the same." Myra giggled. "I think they just color them for the children. Like sprinkles. When children see all the colors, they smile."

Lady and her pups suddenly reared up and ran from the kitchen as whoops and hollers of pure joy invaded the room.

"The girls are sliding down the banister!" Annie laughed out loud. "I remember your telling me that the first time you all met, it was a stormy night like this, and Kathryn was the one who slid down first, and the others followed. You said that was the moment you all bonded and became the Sisterhood. I'm sorry I wasn't here to experience that," Annie said wistfully. "But I do remember how our daughters used to do the same thing when they were little. We'd put pillows down to catch them. Such happy memories, and yet those very same memories make me sad."

Myra wrapped her arm around Annie's shoulders. "Don't be sad. That was then, and this is now." She leaned closer, and whispered, "Later, you and I can try it as long as we put a lot of pillows at the bottom. Our bones aren't what they used to be." Annie nodded, and Myra was grateful that Annie was able to shelve her memories for the moment.

The girls swooped into the kitchen like a gaggle of wild geese, laughing, talking, and rubbing their rear ends. "We aren't ten years old anymore," Nikki observed, giggling. "But it was still fun!"

Fergus poured hot chocolate into cups as

the girls sprinkled the tiny colored marshmallows into their cups.

Ten minutes later, the empty cups were
soaking in the sink, and the team was on
the way to the war room, where Lady Justice
presided. As was their custom before taking
their seats, the sisters saluted the lady wearing a blindfold.

"Let's get to it, girls!" Charles said as he
handed out colored folders. "As you know,
after our last meeting, Avery Snowden said
he and his team were free to help us on our
new mission, so I dispatched him to Washington immediately. He's there with a team
of six operatives. As yet, he has not checked
in, but he did say he would be in touch
sometime today so that Nikki and Maggie
won't be heading in blind tomorrow when
they take the early shuttle to meet with the
partners at Mr. Forrester's old law firm.
What you have in front of you in the folders
is what Fergus and I were able to come up
with, plus some other material that Maggie
found for us in the *Post*'s archives. By no
means does it tell the whole story of Mr.
Forrester and the firm, but it is a jumping-
off place."

Isabelle's hand shot in the air. "Yoko and
I were talking on the way here, and she can
take a few days off, and so can I. We'd both

like to head to Washington, along with Nikki and Maggie. We thought since Garland said SOP's wife was such a health nut, it's possible she patronizes a gym. Maybe we could meet her there if we can figure out where she goes or even *if* she goes. We think it's worth a try, but if you all think it's a waste of time, we'll just forget it."

"I think it's a good idea," Nikki said. The others agreed.

"I can't really do anything this week. I'm starting a trial tomorrow, unless the opposing side decides to settle, which I don't think will happen," Alexis said. "Even my nights won't be free, so I'm not going to be much help. I'm sorry if that's going to leave us short, what with Kathryn on the road."

The others assured Alexis that it wouldn't be a problem, but they all agreed they would miss her expertise.

"What? Did you forget us?" Annie barked. "What, are we chopped liver?"

"Absolutely not, my dear. More like rare Kobe beef," Charles said cheerfully. "We're just waiting for your input."

"In that case, then, Annie and I will go to Washington, too, and take on the bank Mr. SOP uses," Myra said forcefully.

"And do what?" Nikki asked. "They won't give you the time of day, and rightly so. Doing something like that will throw up all manner of red flags. I think you need to rethink that idea."

Charles groaned inwardly. He knew from long experience that all anyone had to do was tell Myra and Annie they couldn't do something, and between the two of them, they would move mountains to prove them wrong. He itched just thinking of their response.

"To try and find out whatever we can about Mr. SOP's financial situation. It is entirely possible Avery may have gotten his account numbers, which, of course, would make things easier. But if not, Annie and I can be very resourceful when we have to be. We're going!" Myra said adamantly. Annie's closed fist shot high in the air.

And that was the end of that.

Charles felt light-headed at his beloved's words. He risked a glance at Fergus, who nodded. *Escape* was the message.

Charles cleared his throat. "Fergus and I will leave you all to peruse the folders in front of you while we go topside and prepare dinner. Hot roast-beef sandwiches and vegetable soup. Seeing what a miserable day it was going to be early on, we thought that would work better today than a light supper of cold cuts. Cherry cobbler for dessert."

When there were no favorable comments, both men quickly beat a hasty retreat.

The sisters got right to it.

"I guess this is as good a time as any to tell you all that Abner is not going to be able to help us, at least not in the next few days. Something big is going on at the CIA, and he's in lockdown mode and can't leave the premises. As it is, I haven't seen him for two days, and he said he was looking at another three to four days," Isabelle said.

"Then I guess we'll just have to muddle through on our own. It won't be the first time that's happened to us," Myra said airily.

Nikki nodded as she looked across the table at Myra and Annie. "I see where you two are going with this, what with Abner out of the picture for the time being. Seriously, how in the world do you think you're going to get access to Mr. SOP's accounts? Without ending up in jail?"

Myra flinched at Nikki's words. Not so Annie, who glared across the table. "We're not idiots, Nikki. I'll open up a sizable bank account, and that will put us on friendly footing. I'll insist on doing business with a bank officer, so that means a private office to conduct business. Myra will come up with a plan to trick him or her, as the case might be, to leave the room, at which point I will type in Mr. SOP's Social Security number, which Garland was kind enough to provide, and voila! We're in business. Unless, of course, Mr. Snowden comes up with the number of Mr. SOP's bank account, which will make it even faster on my part. With a flash drive, I think I can get all we need in six minutes."

"Uh-huh" was all Nikki could think to say.

"Have you given any thought to security cameras?" Yoko asked.

Myra went pale. Once again, Annie jumped in.

"Of course we have. They don't have cameras in the private offices. Everyone knows that. How else can all those rich bankers carry on their dalliances behind closed doors? But if it will make you feel any better, we will obviously check, won't we, Myra?" Myra's head wobbled from side to side, but her color was returning as she fingered her lifeline, the heirloom pearls around her neck.

"Uh-huh," Nikki said again.

"Moving right along here. Nikki and I have our game plan worked out. Annie, we need a letter from you on that gorgeous fancy-dancy stationery of yours, appointing us as your financial representatives. I don't suppose you travel around with that special stationery, or do you?" Maggie asked.

"I have some upstairs in the room that Myra graciously allows me to use when I stay over. I can do that when we go up for supper. What's your plan, dear?"

Maggie laughed. "Pretty much like yours, Annie. We're going to wing it. But we will pit the firm against the Irish firm Nikki and I updated you about after our last meeting. Think of it as high-tech blackmail."

"I love it when you talk like that, dear," Annie said. The sisters burst out laughing.

As one, they knew when they were on a roll.

"Guess we're up next," Isabelle said.

"What's your plan?" Alexis asked. "I have to admit, I am so jealous, I'm turning green that I'm not going to be able to participate."

"In Maggie's research, she came up with Mrs. SOP's name. Nala. Once we find out where she goes to stay in shape, we'll figure out a way to get to her. Yoko will approach her about something or other. Like the rest of you, we'll be winging it. Sometimes the best-laid plans go awry for one reason or another. There's a lot to be said for serendipity and operating on the fly. I do guarantee we will come up with something, though."

The sisters leaned in close across the table and high-fived each other, meaning they were all on board for whatever was on the horizon.

"C'mon, girls, tell me what you think of my profile of Mr. SOP," Maggie said, her grin stretching across her face. "I worked really hard to make him come out . . . likable, but as you can see, it wasn't in the cards. Opinions, please."

"For starters, if my vote counts, the guy's a little shit," Alexis said.

"I was going to call him a turd," Isabelle said.

"A little Napoléon," Nikki said. "Short-man syndrome," she clarified.

"A bully," Yoko said. "He needs to be brought down to Lilliputian status."

The girls roared with laughter.

"He's not even fit to listen to Garland's music. It says here he is into classical music and even plays the piano. Chopin is his favorite composer. Nothing wrong with that, but to denigrate Garland behind the scenes, while he steals her money, is not all right," Nikki said.

All eyes turned to Myra and Annie for their assessment of Arthur Forrester.

"The man is everything you all say he is, and more. He's conniving. He's also a liar,"

Myra said.

It was Annie's turn. "He's a wannabe. I'm just not sure what it is he wants to be. Does he want to excel beyond his brothers? Even he must know that's not possible. Perhaps that's what makes him do what he's been doing. In his mind, he has a pinnacle to reach, but no way to get there now that his goose isn't laying her golden eggs any longer."

"And that about sums up Mr. Arthur Forrester, also known as Mr. Sack of Pus," Nikki said, tongue in cheek.

Up on the dais, the fax machine beeped its warning signal that a fax was coming through, just as Fergus appeared in the doorway to announce that dinner was ready.

"I guess the fax will have to wait," Myra said, getting up from the table and leading the way up to the kitchen.

They all knew that when Charles cooked, nothing and no one interfered, not even Avery Snowden.

Dinner was a lively affair, as usual, with the topics of conversation consisting of the weather, Kathryn's new relationship with Jackson Sparrow, and a lengthy report on Annie and Myra's new venture with the veterans. All were careful to obey Charles's rule not to discuss business at the dinner table.

Dinner over, the girls fell to their jobs, and, as per usual, cleanup was completed in thirteen minutes. Seven minutes after that, they were assembled in the war room, waiting for Charles and Fergus to share Avery Snowden's documents, which he had e-mailed in sections, all neatly labeled.

As the sheets crawled out of the printer, Fergus slapped them into a high-speed copy machine so that each sister would have a copy. "There has to be a speedier printer somewhere. This one is slow enough to make me want to pull my hair out," Fergus grumbled.

"It's the latest one on the market, mate. We just have to live with it. We're looking at well over a hundred pages. The last section is coming through now. Just grab them, and we can get on with it," Charles said, his voice sounding patient.

Snowden's report in hand, the sisters read Arthur Forrester's profile. It didn't take long, since they already knew most of what was included in the report.

Charles picked up the report and leafed through it, stopping at a section he wanted to read aloud. "Guess he wasn't the brightest student in his graduating law class. He graduated in the bottom half of his class. His first job was at a small firm, but he couldn't make any money, so he left and started up a firm with a friend. That venture went belly-up after two years. All told, we are talking about two and a half years of his life. From there, he went to work for an insurance company. But that didn't last long, either, a year and a half. If his wife weren't working, they never could have survived, and they had a baby on the way.

"His two brothers, who are older — Mr. SOP is the youngest — were already established, and he was floundering. He was unemployed for ten months until he finally landed the job with Ballard, Ballard and Quinlan. With a taste of how cruel the world can be, he hunkered down and stayed with the firm for thirty-five years. There was nothing outstanding about his thirty-five-year tenure. He put in his time, billed his hours, made partner, and went home at night.

"Garland was one of his early clients. The usual stuff, real-estate closings, a car accident, a dog bite where someone sued her, the ordinary things people need a lawyer for. Things did not change until her career took off like a rocket, four or five years later. Her business manager and close friend, David Duffy — and, no, he is no relation to Fergus — would send Garland's contracts to SOP for him to look over.

"I could be wrong, but I don't think so. I think once SOP saw the astronomical amount of money Garland was bringing in, something snapped in him. Here was this little down-home gal, with no college degree, making all this money that he could only dream about and lust after. Not to mention her celebrity. When Garland's business manager died, SOP didn't miss a beat. Here were the ingredients to make all his dreams come true. He stepped right in and took over. Garland was so overcome with grief, as she told us, that she let it happen. And do not forget to factor in her bipolar condition and the lithium she takes, the dosage of which they were trying to regulate at the time. That's pretty much Forrester's life, up until she fired him.

"What Mr. SOP has done during the past two years and nine months is something we are not privy to. Avery is working on that as we speak," Charles said.

"What about the wife?" Maggie asked. "She doesn't do Facebook, which I think is odd. I couldn't find anything about her kids doing it, either. Hard to believe they aren't into social media."

"Maggie's right. Avery says they are not into any type of social media, and that goes for the whole family. Second-to-last page at the bottom. As for Mrs. SOP, there isn't much here. She worked at a hospital most of her life. She was pleasant, but made no lasting friendships. She did lunch from time to time with some of her peers, but was not one to confide anything about her personal life. She volunteered like the rest of the staff when she had to. She retired when SOP retired. She was raised as a Buddhist, but changed her faith to Protestant for her husband. Her so-called conversion seems to be pro forma at best.

"She's not into fashion and is a plain dresser. Shops for bargains. Only buys organic food. Buys lots of vitamins from GNC. Avery's operator said she came out of the store with a heavy shopping bag that looked to be full.

"One thing did jump out at me from the report," Charles said. "Two years and ten months ago, around the time SOP sued Garland, Nala started doing some private-duty nursing for wealthy people. The report says she's an excellent nurse and got top dollar, or one hundred dollars an hour. She often worked double shifts, if she was needed. Ask yourself why she would do that at that point in time. Legal fees would be my guess. This is just a guess on my part, but I tend to think she might have resented having to go back to work."

"Any clue in this report as to what kind of relationship the two of them have?" Nikki asked.

"Avery has only been there three days. Both husband and wife have been covered twenty-four/seven, but they are rarely together. They take turns going to the market. No trips to the dry cleaner. One trip to a drugstore. No movies, no rentals. No car trips. SOP did go to his lawyer's office the first afternoon, stayed for ninety minutes, then went home. Stopped for gas and bought a lottery ticket."

"What about the kids?" Isabelle asked.

"Actually nothing. They all live within an hour's drive. There were no visits this week. Avery has an operative on each kid, but thinks it's a waste of time and money, but he is sticking with it. He doesn't expect anything to come of the surveillance. He did post a note saying he was surprised the kids didn't visit SOP and his wife, since the wives don't work. Guess that beyond springing for big fancy birthday and graduation parties, they are not into their grandkids, which is surprising."

"So where does that leave us?" Myra asked.

"Where we were before we read this report," Annie snapped. "I have to say I was expecting . . . something . . . more. Wishful thinking that there would be a smoking gun of some kind."

"That just confirms that we wing it tomorrow when we get to Washington and hit the bank," Myra said.

A long discussion followed as the sisters mapped out some plans for the following day, leaving open their return, should they need to stay on an extra day. The one thing they agreed on was to meet up at five o'clock to discuss the day's events.

Back in the kitchen, Charles turned on the outside lights to check on the rain. "It's not as heavy as it was earlier," he said. "And the temperature is rising."

"Make sure you all call to check in, once you arrive home safe and sound," Myra cautioned. "Annie and Fergus are spending the night, so we'll meet you in the morning, unless we're delayed. We'll text you if any problems crop up. Drive carefully, girls."

"Nikki, how are you getting home?" Fergus asked.

"I came in the golf cart across the field. I'll just cut around and take the ring road.

The field will be too soggy. Not to worry, Jack put a headlight on the cart, and it has a roof, so I'll be fine. Maggie is spending the night. We'll get up early enough to stop by her house, so she can pack a quick bag. Night, all."

"Oh, to be that young again," Annie said wistfully as she watched the last car go through the open gate. Lady barked a belated good-bye before Myra turned off the outside light.

"But only if we could know then what we know now. Otherwise, what's the point of the whole thing? You ready for our *adventure*?"

"What adventure would that be, dear?" Charles asked.

Fergus took one look at Annie's gleeful face, and said, "No, no, no!"

"Yes, yes, yes. Let's go, Myra."

"Come along, mate, we need to stand at the bottom of the steps to catch these lovely ladies, who are determined to break their bones," Fergus said.

"We dare you to take a turn," Myra heckled her husband.

"I would have to be out of my mind to try something like that at my age," Charles sniffed.

"We are going to put pillows down in case

we land on our bums," Annie said. She turned to Myra, and said, "I told you they can talk the walk, but can't walk the walk or however that saying goes. What it means is these handsome, dashing men are both *wusses.* However are we going to be able to look up to you two after this, if you're afraid of a slide down a banister?" Annie taunted.

"They're baiting us. Do not fall for it, Charles," Fergus said in a shaky voice. He knew he was going to slide down the damn banister if he wanted to stay in Annie's good graces. From the look of things, Charles was thinking the same thing.

"Let's do it!" Annie said as she rushed to the living room to gather up all the pillows and spread them out at the bottom of the stairs. "Who wants to go first?" she yelped in excitement.

"I will," Myra said, running up the steps, Annie right behind her. Charles squeezed his eyes shut while Fergus turned around, afraid to look at what he was certain would be a mass of broken bones.

"Here I come!" Myra bellowed as she sailed down the banister to land in the nest of pillows. She got up and staggered over to where Charles was standing. "That was worth the pain in my bum, dear. Your turn!"

Annie whooped and hollered as she slid

down the banister and landed on her feet. "It's like flying. It's magical."

Charles clenched his teeth, closed his eyes, and slid down the banister at a speed he was totally unable to control. He landed in a heap and rolled over, laughing uncontrollably.

Fergus followed, Annie cheering him on. He landed exactly where Charles had landed, but he wasn't laughing; he was grimacing. "My bum will be sore for a week." Annie laughed even harder.

"I think we should make a decision right now never to do this again," Myra said as she hobbled into the kitchen, her hand massaging her backside. "Two fingers of cognac, Charles, and no ice."

"Coming right up, dear," Charles said as he imitated his wife's movements.

"I'm so proud of you, Fergus. I will reward you later," Annie purred.

Fergus Duffy was no fool, because he knew exactly what that reward would be. He laughed and hugged Annie so hard she squealed.

And yet another day at Pinewood came to a happy end.

CHAPTER 5

Maggie Spritzer adjusted the handle on her small travel bag. She kept looking over her shoulder to see the rest of the team, but to no avail. "I guess they'll catch up."

"It would appear that way," Nikki said, looking around to see if she could spot the others. "We have time, so let's do the coffee thing once we get to town. I need my caffeine fix before we beard the lions of Ballard, Ballard and Quinlan. At least we have a nice day to be in Washington. I love the city."

Maggie read an incoming text from Myra, followed by one from Isabelle. "They're running late. I'm up for coffee and some donuts, if we can get some. Let's hope there's a café or coffee shop in the building. You feeling any anxiety, Nikki?"

Nikki laughed. "Not one little bit. Just for the record, I really don't think we're going to get much in the way of information. Lawyers do not talk, they listen. I might have to use a few tricks, and depending on how sharp they are, they might work. But then again, they might not. Just for the heck of it, I'm thinking positive. Annie's letter of introduction should have them salivating over the possibility of landing her account."

"I can't get over what a nice day it is. Especially after that awful storm at home yesterday. I wonder if it's coming this way."

"Nope!" Maggie said as she tapped at her smartphone. "Clear skies and sunny for the next two days. Spring has definitely come to Washington!"

"Here we go," Nikki said as she got into her car. Maggie slid into the passenger seat. Nikki typed the address of the Ballard law firm into the GPS. Within minutes, they were cruising along on their way further into the city.

"There is a coffee shop inside," Maggie said once they had parked. She stared down at the app she had just clicked on. "If we want, we can even get a full breakfast. We have an hour to kill, and I am hungry."

Nikki laughed. "When aren't you hungry, my dear?"

"When I'm sleeping, and even then, I dream about food," Maggie said as she pushed through the revolving door. She looked around at the ornate lobby. "Nice digs. Good address. All to impress clients, right?"

"Pretty much," Nikki agreed.

"According to Google, some wealthy Hungarian guy owns the building."

"And we need to know this . . . why?" Nikki asked.

"Well, information is power. The more you know, the more power you have. That's a given. I'll bet you five bucks Annie knows the guy or knows someone who knows him, and if she put the word out, the Hungarian could evict Ballard, Ballard and Quinlan. He's probably one of those Hungarian oligarchs, like the ones in Russia with money to burn."

Nikki giggled as she slid into a leather booth whose seats were patched with gray duct tape. She picked up a paper menu, which had seen better days, and said, "And . . . your point is?"

Maggie grinned as she looked up at the hovering waitress, and said, "I'll take one of everything. The Big Breakfast. Make the bacon snap-in-two crisp, and I like the butter soft for my toast, three slices, and your syrup is warm, right?"

Nikki ordered an English muffin and coffee. She raised her eyebrows at Maggie.

"Well, if we don't get anywhere with the

firm and Mr. SOP, Annie could ask the Hungarian to boot them out. You know, like blackmail."

Nikki couldn't help it; she laughed out loud. "Okay, Wizard Spritzer, send Annie a text and ask her if she knows the guy. Then send Avery Snowden a text and ask him when Ballard's lease is up." Getting caught up in Maggie's excitement, Nikki continued, "Or maybe Annie could buy the building from the Hungarian. That way, she could boot the firm out, unless the lease covers a buyout, but there are even ways around that."

Maggie stared across the table at Nikki. "Seriously?"

"Hey, you threw the ball. All I did was catch it." Both women giggled as their waitress poured their coffees. "Think about this. During our meeting, how cool would it be for us to know — secretly, of course — that it is a possibility as we play cat and mouse with the partners. Pretty darn cool, I'm thinking."

Maggie giggled again, but nodded in agreement. At the moment, the only thing she could concentrate on was her one-of-everything-on-the-menu breakfast.

Forty minutes later, Nikki paid the bill. Then it was a trip to the ladies' room before the two of them headed for the elevator that would take them to the fourteenth floor, which housed the main office of Ballard, Ballard & Quinlan.

"Four minutes to spare," Maggie muttered as they opened the heavy mahogany doors leading to the reception area of the prestigious law firm. They both looked around in awe at the expanse of shiny green marble that covered the floors and walls. The reception desk was covered in expensive tooled leather, which was an off shade of green, with gold stripes running through it. The lighting was subdued. The cozy seating arrangements and the fresh-looking magazines were beckoning. Brilliant-colored flowering plants dazzled under the lighting and looked lush and festive.

"It won't make a difference," Nikki murmured. "I dig this place. They'll keep us waiting for at least fifteen minutes to show us how important they are. I give them seven minutes, and we're out of here."

Nikki handed her business card to the tony receptionist, and informed her, "As you can see, we're on time. We will wait seven minutes. If your people can't see us in that time frame, it's their loss. Ticktock," she added, smiling.

"Um . . . yes, yes. I'll ring for someone to

escort you to the conference room. Please take a seat."

"That won't be necessary. Seven minutes go by very quickly."

Nikki turned around to admire the artwork hanging on the wall. She fixed her gaze on Jackson Pollock's *Autumn Rhythm.* Definitely not one of her favorites because it reminded her of some crazy wallpaper she'd seen in a Southern antebellum mansion.

"Two minutes and counting," Maggie said.

Nikki whirled around. She smiled, a cat-ate-the-canary smile, which caused Maggie to laugh out loud. The tony receptionist frowned at the levity. "Seventy seconds and counting."

Huge double doors behind the receptionist were thrust open, and a pert young person said, "Ms. Quinn, Ms. Spritzer, please follow me." Which they did, with only thirty seconds to go on the countdown.

To Maggie's chagrin, the room was empty.

"As I said before, it's all a game," Nikki whispered to Maggie. "Don't read anything into the fact that this room is empty."

To the pert young person, she said, "I have thirty more seconds before we leave. You can either stay to usher us out or we can find our own way."

101

Flustered, the paralegal turned pale. "I . . . I thought . . . they said they . . . they said they would be here."

"Obviously, they did not mean what they said. So, when we exit this room, we go back down the corridor and make a right, then the very next left. And that will take us to the reception area, right?"

"Um . . . yes, but I think I hear them coming now. Please take a seat, whichever one you want. Ah, yes, here they are," the pert young thing said as she held the door open for three elderly gentlemen. After they had entered the conference room, she quickly closed the door and ran to tell the rest of the staff about the bitchy women who were meeting with the senior partners and making said partners dance to whatever tune they were playing. The other staff members thought wistfully how much they would enjoy being flies on the wall.

Introductions were made; handshakes ensued; offers of coffee and pastries were declined. Nikki opened her Chanel briefcase, which cost more than three months of the tony receptionist's salary. She withdrew Annie's letter and handed it over to Henry Ballard, the managing director and founder of the firm. He read it quickly and passed it to his brother, Alvin, who then passed it to

Robert Quinlan.

"I would be remiss if I didn't say I'm flattered that Countess de Silva would consider our firm for her needs. I think I speak for Alvin and Robert as well." Both men nodded. "Would you mind telling us how our firm came to the countess's attention?"

"Oh, she's friends with your landlord, Yuri Yonovich," Nikki said airily. "Oh, dear, I hope I'm not spilling secrets here. I just assumed you knew that she's considering buying this building."

Maggie almost choked; then she pretended to cough to cover up her surprise at Nikki's statement and the looks of stunned surprise on the partners' faces. The cough caused the glasses perched on the end of her nose to fall to the table, then to the floor. Her heart beating trip-hammer fast, she bent down to pick up her glasses and, at the same time, reached up under the table to stick the listening device Fergus had handed over to her as they were leaving for the airport. "If you get the chance, stick it wherever you can," he had advised.

When she sat up again, she noticed that Quinlan was the first to recover, and he said in a rich baritone, which probably at one time served him well in the courtroom, "We did hear something to that effect a while back, but when nothing came of it, we just assumed nothing was going to happen. By that, I mean we heard Yuri was trying to sell the building, but no names were ever mentioned as to who the buyer might be." Henry's and Alvin's heads bobbed up and down in agreement. *Such a blatant lie,* Nikki thought. But Quinlan was nimble on his feet, and she had to give him credit for his quick thinking. Never let your opponent think they knew something you did not.

"You lease five floors, is that correct?"

"Yes, it is. Is that important?" Henry asked sharply.

Nikki leaned back in the buttery-soft leather chair and, with a cool eye, looked at the three men. All had white hair. All wore contact lenses. All appeared to be in their mid to late seventies. All wore thousand-dollar suits. All wore spit-shined wingtips. All sported manicures and wore Rolex watches. They fit right into this lavish conference room, with the one-of-a-kind teak conference table, with seating for eighteen. The artwork alone was worth a fortune. The eighteen chairs by themselves had to have cost a fortune. The green plants were so lush, they looked like they'd just come out of some rain forest.

"I don't know, Mr. Ballard. I was just

repeating something the countess said to me. We need to be clear on something. Should the countess choose your firm, she only wants it to handle her real-estate holdings. If I'm not mistaken, the number the countess spoke of was around, give or take, four hundred million. Please don't confuse that with her shipping holdings. That's for another firm. I would be remiss if I didn't also tell you that the firm of O'Malley, O'Shaunnesy and McCallister is also being considered to handle her real-estate business. In fact, Ms. Spritzer and I will be in discussions with the senior partners of that firm later this afternoon."

Maggie watched the partners closely and stifled her grin. None of them liked what Nikki had just said, but she would have bet a year's salary that all three would put on their game faces. And so they did.

Alvin cleared his throat. His voice was raspy. Cigarette and/or cigar smoker. Maggie looked at his fingers, nicotine stained. Confirmation.

"Excellent firm. Can't say a bad word about them. Topnotch. Henry, Robert, and I play golf with Seamus and Sean every Saturday morning. And as much as I hate to admit it, they're actually better *golfers* than we are. Are they better lawyers? Well, that's a different question, isn't it? Still, I think I can speak for the three of us and say we're flattered to be considered along with them. Having said that, tell us how we can help you.

"Do you want to ask us questions? Does the countess want us to open our books to her financial people? We'll certainly co-operate in any way we can."

"That's for another day and meeting. The countess only has one area of concern, and she thought this face-to-face could put her mind to rest."

"What would that area of concern be, Ms. Quinn?" Robert Quinlan asked. His tone sounded so neutral, Nikki flinched inwardly. Her first thought was that he already knew what was coming.

"The five lawsuits brought against your firm in the past. The countess has read up on all of them, and I believe that she understands the *how* and the *why* of all five. It's the lawsuit pending with one of your ex-attorneys against Garland Lee that has her concerned. I should tell you, the artist is a personal favorite of the countess. She has every single album she's ever made. As an attorney who advises the countess, I have to ask you, gentlemen, since your firm is involved, where is this suit going? It's coming up on three years now, and there doesn't seem to be any record of settlement talks, and your firm is right in the middle. The burning question Countess de Silva has is this. Did Mr. Forrester leave your firm of his own accord, or was he asked to leave? We also understand he was of retirement age when he left. The countess is very big on transparency and full disclosure. Just so you know."

Maggie and Nikki both loved the look of surprise on the faces of the three name partners. To say all three were frustrated would be to put it mildly. Henry Ballard stood up first, shook down his designer jacket's sleeves, and motioned for the others to join him. "I think a small break is called for here so Alvin, Robert, and I can discuss this matter. I hope you don't mind. In the meantime, please avail yourselves of the coffee. It's very good. We have it flown in from Brazil once a month."

Nikki just nodded as she tapped out a text to Maggie:

Do not talk, text. I'm sure this room is bugged. I am not referring to your bug, either. Obviously, we need to make an appointment with the Irish firm, like in *immediately,* since these guys play golf on Saturdays with the big honchos in that firm. Try to make it right after lunch. Apologize for not giving them more time.

Maggie nodded as her fingers flew over the mini keyboard. "Coffee, Maggie?"

"Sure, why not? I don't think I ever had coffee fresh from a coffee farm in Brazil, have you?"

"Not that I can recall. These paintings are beautiful, aren't they? The countess would love them. I wonder if they'd mind if I took pictures on my phone to show her. I think I'll take them, then ask them. If they object, I'll erase them," Nikki said.

"I'm sure they won't object. They seem like nice people, don't you agree?"

The text message she sent read: Three stuffed shirts full of themselves if I'm not mistaken, but I kind of like them.

Nikki's return text read: They're salivating over the possibility of getting Annie's business. But they aren't going to tell us anything substantial, even though they'd love to spout off. That's just my opinion. They'll come back and say they can't discuss ongoing litigation. At the very best, they might drop a few hints, but I seriously doubt they'll go that far.

"Mr. Ballard is right, this is excellent coffee, don't you agree, Maggie?"

"Absolutely I do. Now I'll be spoiled, expecting every cup I drink from here on in to taste like this."

The door to the elaborate conference room opened to allow the three partners to reenter. They were all big men, and the room suddenly seemed full. Nikki looked at them expectantly as they took the seats they had been sitting in earlier.

Henry Ballard, obviously senior of the threesome and their spokesperson, held up his hand to show he was going to take the floor. "Alvin, Robert, and I spoke, and I'm sure you know, being an attorney yourself, that we cannot comment on ongoing litigation. We can, however, answer some general questions. First of all, you are wrong to assume that no settlement talks have taken place. Actually, we've had two such discussions, but nothing was resolved. Ms. Lee's attorneys filed for summary judgment, but so far the judge has not ruled on the matter. I don't know if you are aware of that or not."

The lawyer cleared his throat, then continued speaking. "The watercooler talk in town is that there are those who hope the judge rules in favor of Ms. Lee and tosses our case to the four winds. I've also heard rumors that people have been encouraging Mr. Forrester to drop the case. There are some who — and, again, this is rumor outside the office — have said that Arthur is a greedy opportunist. That's just idle midmorning talk at break time and over three-martini lunches." Nikki just nodded, surprised to have been given as much as she had.

"Yes, we are involved in the lawsuit through no fault of our own. We have malpractice insurance, as I'm sure you know. The insurance lawyers are representing us in the matter, with input from the most-senior firm members.

"The other question you asked concerned Arthur's retirement. When Arthur left the firm, he was of retirement age to do so. He did not have to retire. I will tell you that, to my knowledge, no one at the firm encouraged him to stay or even tried to talk him out of retirement."

Well, Nikki thought, *that's one way of saying Mr. SOP was asked to leave, without coming out and saying those words.*

"And knowing what you already know, I imagine your next question would be what happened to the lawyer Mr. Forrester enticed to file his complaint after he left the firm. She was discharged. I do not know where she is or if she's even practicing law any longer. There are those who believe Arthur tricked her. True or false, it doesn't matter. It was unethical, and we had no other choice but to discharge her. Her name was Adela Ash. We have the firm's reputation to think about. Shenanigans like that are simply unacceptable. As you probably also know, it is Zack Ash, Adela's husband, who, along with his partner, is representing Mr. Forrester in the original suit. I believe their firm is located in D.C., near where Arthur lives. Somewhere along the way, I also heard a rumor that Zack and Adela had separated and were about to divorce. It may have happened already, seeing as how it's been three years, but I cannot confirm that. As I said, it's just a rumor, and as a lawyer, I shouldn't even mention it. I think that about sums up what we, the three of us, are comfortable saying. If it turns out to be a game changer in regard to the countess, I'm sorry. I meant what I said about the O'Malley firm. I'd like the countess to choose this firm, but I understand the circumstances. Is there anything else?"

Nikki stood up and offered her hand across the table. "No. I appreciate how forthright you've all been without violating your ethical obligations. I will convey everything we've said here today to Countess de Silva and show no bias whatsoever. Nor will Maggie, who, by the way, is the former editor in chief of the *Post*. The countess relies heavily on Maggie, so she and I will be sure to tell her how forthright you've been. By the way, you were right, that was the best cup of coffee I've ever had. Thank you for sharing it with us both. Oh, one last thing. I hope you don't mind, but I took some pictures of your beautiful artwork to show the countess. She loves art. Of course, I can erase them if you object."

Alvin beamed. "Not at all. We're very proud of our artwork *and* our coffee. Would you like a packet to go?"

"I would love that," Nikki gushed.

"I would love that, too," Maggie said.

Alvin scurried out of the room and returned with two five-pound foil-wrapped bags of coffee. The aroma even through the bags filtered all about the room.

"Oh, my," Nikki gushed again. "When you said packet, I thought you meant for one cup. We insist on paying for this, don't we, Maggie?"

"No, no, *no*! We don't want anyone to construe this as a *bribe.* It's a gift from one coffee connoisseur to another."

Nikki nodded solemnly. "You're right, of course. Well, thank you so much. Each time I have a cup, I'll think of you."

"Now you're getting it." Alvin laughed. Everyone joined in, but to Nikki's ears, the laughter sounded forced.

Another round of handshakes followed; then the two women were in the elevator, which now smelled heavenly of coffee, on their way down to the lobby. Neither spoke until they were outside in the balmy spring air.

"Well, I thought that went well, what do you think, Maggie?"

"I actually kind of liked the old buzzards. I think Mr. SOP sucked them into this. I read up on those other five cases, and they're standard, nothing earth-shattering. Every firm has a few. You?" Maggie asked.

"As for Adela Ash, I didn't find anything in my various searches. I'll try again, but from where I'm standing, it sounds like a dead issue," Maggie said.

"I'm with you. They did try to help and still fulfill their ethical obligations. I am referring to the watercooler comment. You did pick up on that, right?"

"Uh-huh. Look, Nikki, there's a UPS Store. Let's go in and ship this coffee home. I don't fancy walking around the rest of the day carrying a five-pound bag of aromatic coffee or carrying it on the plane. TSA would probably confiscate it, anyway," Maggie said.

"Good idea, works for me," Nikki said

agreeably. "Jack is going to go over the moon when he tastes it. So, are we on for the Irish firm or not?"

"Two-thirty. Gives us time for some lunch."

Nikki stopped in the middle of the street. "You just had breakfast!"

"Yes, but by one o'clock, I'll be hungry again. Just a quick bite, maybe soup and a sandwich. Nothing big. Hold on, don't go in the store yet. A text is coming in from Annie."

Nikki leaned up against the plate-glass window of the UPS Store and watched the foot traffic as Maggie read, then tapped out a response. "Well?"

"They're at the bank now. A cab just dropped them off. Annie said it's a Bank of America. It's not that far from here. Do you want to head up there after we send off our coffee? Moral support, or in case they end up in a sticky situation."

"Good idea. Let's do that."

The ride to the bank was short, traffic being light even though it was the lunch hour, with busy office workers stampeding to the streets to enjoy the beautiful spring day even if it was just for an hour or so.

Nikki and Maggie entered the bank. Both

women looked around to see if Annie and Myra were visible. They were not. "What should we do?" Maggie hissed.

"Let's go over to the counter and pretend we're filling out deposit slips. Then we can get in one of the long teller lines that are about out the door. This is the lunch crowd doing their banking before they head back to the office," Nikki said quietly.

"I'm thinking Annie, even Myra, would insist on talking to one of the head honchos. If I'm right, that means they're behind closed doors. See that row of shiny doors with the blinds drawn on the plate-glass windows. That's probably where the high muckety-mucks conduct business," Maggie said as she scribbled something on a deposit ticket. She turned around to see where the longest line was and nudged Nikki in that direction. "Where the heck are they? One or the other of them should have gotten in touch with us by now. How long does it take to open an account, even if you are Countess Anna de Silva?"

If someone had been able to answer Maggie's question, he or she would have told her that both Annie and Myra were sitting in the president's office, filling out papers that would allow both to open sizable brokerage accounts.

Annie looked at the stack of forms in front of her and grimaced. "Mr. Holiday, before we continue with our business here, would you be so kind as to show my sister your vault. We're going to require four safe-deposit boxes. One stand-up and three of your biggest boxes. I'd go with you, but when we came here, I stepped off the curb the wrong way and my ankle is starting to throb. While you do that, I'll finish all this paperwork so we can be on our way. You don't have a problem with that, do you?"

"Absolutely not, Countess. Do you want one of my people to help you?"

"No. I'm fine. Just close the door when you leave. I don't like people staring at me and nudging their friends to notice me."

"I totally understand. If you're sure you're okay, then I'll be happy to show Ms. Cabot our available vaults," Holiday said, using the name Myra had given him when they were introduced.

Annie thought she would explode right out of her skin as she waited to hear the door close. She already had the tiny flash drive in her hand. Seven minutes was all she needed. Or was it ten? She wasn't sure. She catapulted out of her chair, stood up, and swung the computer around until it was facing her. She inserted the flash drive and

116

then typed in Arthur Forrester's Social Security number and waited as she hardly dared to breathe. A blizzard of numbers, symbols, and what looked like spreadsheets appeared on the small screen. Annie clicked the keys and started to pray. "C'mon, c'mon," she muttered under her breath as she watched the minute hand on the treasured Mickey Mouse watch that adorned her wrist, the watch she was never without because she so loved the great big numerals. She was so light-headed from what she was doing that she almost blacked out. "Faster, faster," she muttered. She squeezed her eyes shut, then opened them. She was getting everything, Mr. SOP's checking account, his IRAs, and his brokerage accounts. She tried to focus; then she tapped in letters that would give her Mr. SOP's entire banking reports from the day he opened his first account. The knowledge of what she was downloading, along with a vision of herself in an orange jumpsuit, waiting in some federal prison for visitors, was almost more than she could bear.

Annie looked down at the minute hand on her Mickey Mouse watch. Seven minutes, seven and a half minutes. Maybe it was a mistake to ask for the entire banking history. The computer pinged. Download

117

finished. As quickly as she could, she removed the flash drive and tapped again so that the original screen appeared. She swung the monitor around so fast, she thought it was going to sail right off the desk. Eight minutes total. *Damn, I'm good.* The vision of her in an orange jumpsuit, waiting for visitors, disappeared. She closed her eyes and dropped her head to her knees, taking deep breaths; *four-seven-eight,* they called it. Four deep breaths, hold for the count of seven, and then exhale to the count of eight. She had to do two series of four deep breaths before her heart rate returned to normal.

Annie quickly reached for the pen and finished filling out the papers in front of her. She finished just as Kyle Holiday ushered Myra back into the room. Both were smiling.

"Ah, I see you finished. And we were successful with the vaults. Your sister has the keys to all four of them," Holiday said as though he were offering up the Holy Grail.

"That's wonderful, Mr. Holiday. I just called my financial manager and he will be calling you in the next hour or so after he returns from lunch. From here on in, you will be dealing with him. His name is Connor. It was a pleasure doing business with you, Mr. Holiday. I hope all my financial dealings with your bank will be just as pleasant."

"I think I can guarantee it, Countess. Let me walk you out."

That was the last thing Annie and Myra wanted, but they obediently followed the bank president out to the lobby of the bank, where the teller lines had dwindled to a mere trickle.

"Quick! Quick! Your ten o'clock. There are Myra and Annie, with, I assume, a bank officer," Maggie sputtered.

Myra spotted Nikki and Maggie out of the corner of her eye. Stunned, she stumbled, but the banker quickly reached for her arm.

If nothing else, Annie was quick on the draw. She saw Nikki and Maggie at the same time Myra did, but she didn't stumble. "That's so like you, little sister. Just because I hurt my ankle doesn't mean you have to, too." She giggled as she pushed her way through the revolving door, with Myra behind her and Nikki and Maggie behind Myra. Both women waved to the banker, who waved back.

"I don't know about the rest of you, but I'm going to look for the nearest bar and order a double or triple shot of something. I got it all. Honest to God, I got it all!" Annie cackled as she set off down the street, her "twisted ankle" totally forgotten, and the others running to catch up with her.

"All his banking records?" Nikki asked in awe.

"Every last one." Annie cackled again.

"Then all right! Let's find a place for food and drink to celebrate! It's lunchtime," Maggie said. "Of course, to my way of thinking, it is always lunchtime somewhere in the world. Don't you all agree?"

CHAPTER 6

Avery Snowden walked nonchalantly around the block, pretending to talk on his cell phone. He was still practicing the tradecraft he had perfected back in the old days with MI5, when he and Charles Martin worked for the queen of England. Old habits served him well in his new endeavors. The truth was, he was in tune with his surroundings. He could hear a dog barking down the street; he noticed a fat pigeon on the lookout for a stray crumb here or there. He noticed the pedestrians on their way to do whatever they did during the noon hour here, during one of the busiest hours of the day. He was aware of the light breeze, the warm sun, and, of course, the high-rise condominium building where Arthur Forrester and his wife, Nala, lived. It was a high-security building, but that didn't worry him. There was no lock known to man that he couldn't open.

Snowden turned the corner, jammed his phone into his pocket, then crossed the street and headed back the way he had come. He had the uncanny knack of being able to see everything without turning his head. What he was looking for, in particular, was any sign of Nala Forrester returning to the condo.

Charles had dispatched him and his team last Thursday. The condo and the Forresters had been under surveillance twenty-four/seven since the moment the team had arrived. Unfortunately, there was very little to show for their efforts. The Forresters didn't go out much, and when they did, they stayed planted at their destination until it was time to head home. As far as he could tell, they had no friends and no social life. Arthur Forrester played golf three days a week, Monday, Wednesday, and Friday. At least that's what one of the staff at the Golf Shack told him. He'd also said that sometimes, weather permitting, Forrester would play a round on Sunday. He went on to say Forrester had no golf buddies. He showed up and waited to see if he could join a foursome, which happened most times. He confirmed that the scuttlebutt was that Forrester was an excellent golfer.

The wife, Nala, went to a place called

Lady's Fitness every morning, stayed for three hours, then hit the Organic Market, where she bought fresh fruits and vegetables. When she had finished shopping, she walked back to the condo, carrying her workout bag on her shoulder and a string bag with the produce. She rarely left the condominium after that.

Arthur Forrester usually returned at around three o'clock and, like his wife, never left the building afterward. Except for one day, last Friday, when he had returned from his golf game. On that day, he had gone into the condo, changed clothes, then emerged and drove six blocks to his attorney's office, where he stayed for ninety minutes.

Avery had explained to Charles in his late-night call yesterday that he didn't have a *feel* for the guy yet. He'd gone on to tell Charles that he needed a few more days to make any real kind of assessment.

When asked about Mrs. Forrester, his response had been she was a nonstarter. He took that one step further and said he wasn't 100 percent sure Nala Forrester even knew about the lawsuit. He explained it was just a gut feeling, and he couldn't explain it any better than that.

Snowden stopped under a colorful awning

and pretended to light a cigarette he didn't want. He didn't smoke and only used cigarettes as a prop, when needed. Pretending to be interested at what was on display, he looked in the store window at a variety of hiking boots on pedestals. He winced at the discreet price tags, which barely showed. He was in midpuff on the cigarette when his cell phone vibrated in his pocket. He dropped the cigarette, crushed it out with his shoe, then picked it up and put it in one of the pockets of his cargo pants. "Snowden," he said by way of greeting.

The voice on the other end of the phone sounded breathless and hushed at the same time. "The Forresters are leaving in the same car. I can't follow them, as I'm wedged in here. I updated Kelly, and she's two cars behind them. I took the liberty of alerting Duke to get in front. We have it covered. What do you want me to do?" Sasha Quantrell asked.

"I'm headed your way. Stay put till I get there, which should be in about eight minutes. This might be my only chance to get into their condo. I want you with me."

Snowden set off at a jog and appeared at Sasha's car in seven minutes. "Let's go. We'll go in through the garage and take the service elevator up to the ninth floor, where the Forresters live. I checked the ownership records at town hall last night, and this building seems to be made up of seniors, which, to me, means it's pretty much a mind-your-own-business kind of establishment, no little kids permitted. A high-end establishment, mainly for senior citizens. There are, however, about a dozen middle-aged investment-banker types who live here, but they work during the day. Just act like you belong or are visiting friends or family."

Sasha laughed. She'd done this type of thing so many times, she'd lost count. Still, she nodded. After all, Avery Snowden was her boss and signed her paychecks. If he wanted to share totally unnecessary reminders about how to do her job, who was she to object?

"So if anyone asks questions, who are we today? FBI, Homeland Security, ATF, or DEA?"

"We'll just wing it. Okay, showtime," Snowden said as the elevator doors opened. Snowden took a moment to look at the arrows that indicated which way to go. "Apartment 909 is to the left. We knock as per usual, just in case," Snowden said, his lock-picking kit in his hand. "Eyes everywhere, Sasha." She nodded as Snowden pressed the doorbell and was rewarded with a pleasant chime. He waited a few seconds, then pressed the button again. When nothing happened after that, he selected the tool he wanted and was about to insert it in the lock when the door suddenly opened to reveal a woman wearing a bandanna on her head and an apron. She had a feather duster in her hand.

The woman looked puzzled, like she'd never opened the door to guests before. "Can I help you?"

Snowden reached into his pocket and withdrew a folded leather wallet. He flipped it open to reveal an FBI shield, compliments of Jackson Sparrow. "I'm Special Agent Jonathan Ryan, and this is Special Agent Martha Blake." Martha Blake, aka Sasha Quantrell, held up her own badge. "We'd like to talk to you. May we come in?" Snowden's tone clearly said he would not take no for an answer.

The maid or housekeeper, her hand over her heart, stepped aside, her eyes full of fear. "Mr. and Mrs. Forrester are not at home. I have a green card," she blurted fearfully.

"I know that. We're not here for you, but we do want to talk to you. When will the Forresters be home?"

"They say . . . not till late. They tell me to lock up when I leave. I have a key."

"Do you know where they went?" Snowden asked.

"They did not tell me, but I heard Mr. Forrester say to his wife they had to go to where he used to work in the city. I did not hear anything else."

Snowden nodded to himself. *That makes sense,* he thought, *since Nikki and Maggie did pay a visit to the firm earlier today.*

"We have a warrant," Snowden said, waving a paper under the woman's nose. She jerked back, but didn't bother to read what was on the paper. "What that means is my partner, Special Agent Blake, is going to search the premises while you and I talk. I mean you no harm, so please do not be afraid. You have done absolutely nothing wrong. I'm going to ask you some questions, and if you know the answers, I want you to tell me the truth. If you lie to me, I will have to ask the proper authorities to take another look at that green card you have. Do you understand what I just said?"

"I do. Do you want to go to the living room or the kitchen to talk? I can make coffee for you or give you cold fruit juice."

"The kitchen will be fine. Tell me everything you know about the Forresters. How long have you worked for them?"

"I used to work for them before they

127

moved. Maybe for ten years, once or twice a week. They sold the house and moved here, but they said they didn't need me any longer. I found other work. Then eight months ago, Mrs. Forrester called and asked if I would come to work one day a week. She said she would pay my travel expenses. I said yes. The work is easy. There are no children or pets, not like before."

"Mr. and Mrs. Forrester are retired?"

"Yes. But on the days he does not play golf, Mr. Forrester works in his office here. Many, many papers, but he will not let me clean his office. It is . . . how you say . . . a *pigsty*. Yes, pigsty. They . . . they are different now from before, when I worked for them. Not mean, but not nice. They do not talk. They fight and argue over money all the time. Last week, I heard Mrs. Forrester say that she no give him her money. Her money is for her children and the children she helps with her charity. They closed the door so I would not hear, but I could still hear. Did they do something wrong?"

"We can't talk about that. And your name is?"

"Elena Mendez. Am I in trouble because they pay me cash?"

"It's a problem, but I'll take care of it if you cooperate," Snowden said smoothly.

"I will do what you say," Elena said fervently. "I do not want trouble for me and my family."

"I know that, and we're here to help you. Now, this is what I want you to do. I want you to call either Mr. or Mrs. Forrester and tell them there is an emergency in your family, and you won't be returning to work. Tell them you will leave the key on the counter. You said you have a key of your own, right?" Elena nodded. "Then thank them for being so good to you." Elena grimaced. Snowden grinned. "Okay, you can leave that part out. From that point on, I don't want you to have any further contact with them. If they call, do not answer the phone. Is that understood?"

"Yes. Yes. I understand. I understand that through no fault of my own, I am losing a job I depend on. It is not fair. I did nothing wrong." Tears welled in Elena's eyes.

Snowden felt lower than a snake's belly at Elena's words. "We at the Bureau are not that heartless, Elena. We understand, and we are going to make it right for you. If you do everything we say and do not speak of this to anyone, and you will have to sign off on that, then we're prepared to help you."

"How will you help me?" Fat tears rolled down Elena's cheeks.

Snowden pulled off his rucksack and rummaged around until he found what he wanted, a thick envelope full of cash. "There is five thousand dollars in this envelope, a tidy sum to hold you over until you can find additional work. Will that work for you?"

The tears were gone, and the woman's smile was brighter than the sun outdoors. "Yes, that will work for me. What do you want me to sign?"

A good question, Snowden thought. He fished around inside the rucksack again and came up with a paper that he didn't have time to read, something to do with his last car maintenance. "Just sign on the bottom, and we're good to go." He watched as Elena signed her name carefully and handed the paper over. Snowden folded it in two and slipped it back into his rucksack. "Make the call now."

"I will call Mrs. Forrester. Her number is here by the house phone. Mr. Forrester might not answer the phone." As it turned out, Mrs. Forrester didn't answer her phone, either, so Elena left a clear, concise message, ending by saying, "I will leave the key on the kitchen counter under the phone. Thank you for giving me the opportunity to work for you." She made a funny little face at Snowden, who just smiled. "Is there anything else?" she asked after hanging up.

"Not unless you think there is something I should know?"

Elena shook her head. "They are different people, it seems to me, from when I worked for them before. Mr. Forrester is a cold, heartless man. He only cares about himself, and all he talks about is money. But I only see him a bit one day a week, so I am sorry I can't be more helpful."

"Do his children and grandchildren ever come here? Or do they go to visit them?"

Elena shook her head. "I don't know. They have never been here when I'm here. I don't know if they visit the children. Once I heard Mrs. Forrester talking to one of her daughters about a Sunday dinner. Oh, every six weeks or so, they drive to Hilton Head, South Carolina, and stay for ten days. They call to tell me they don't need me during that time. They own a house there. Mrs. Forrester doesn't much like going there, but Mr. Forrester likes the golf course. Should I leave now?"

"Yes. Remember everything I said, Elena."

"I will not forget."

"Give me your cell phone number and your home address in case I need to get in touch with you. Here is my card. If the Forresters harass you or do anything, I want you to call me right away. Is that clear?"

"Yes, it is clear. They do not know where I live. They never cared enough to ask me, and I never volunteered the information. I will not answer the phone. Thank you for the money. It will be a big help to me and my family. I will not tell anyone about my fairy godfather," she said, a smile tugging at the corner of her mouth.

Sasha appeared in the doorway. "I checked everything." Snowden nodded as he escorted Elena to the door. They said goodbye; then he closed and locked the door.

"I planted four listening devices," Sasha continued. "I copied everything on Mr. Forrester's computer. I took pictures of the paperwork on his desk. Do you want a bug on this kitchen phone?" Snowden nodded as he eyed the key on the counter. "Did you happen to notice any candles around here?"

"There's one in the guest bathroom. Ah, you want to make a wax impression of the key in case you need to get back in here, eh? I'll get the candle."

While Snowden melted the wax on the candle, Sasha looked around the kitchen, poking in the cabinets and fridge. She blinked, then blinked again, as she counted twenty-two bottles of vitamin supplements on the counter. *Crazy health nuts,* she thought. She checked the mini laundry room, but nothing caught her eye. "I'm not getting this, Avery. Are these people supposed to be rich? If they are, they certainly didn't furnish this place to impress people. I have furniture that's better than some of this stuff. The word *spartan* doesn't cover it."

Snowden shrugged. "Not our problem. Did you wipe down everything that you touched?" Sasha nodded. "I'm going to take this candle with us and hope they won't miss it, since it's never been lit. A blackened wick might cause suspicion." Sasha nodded.

"Time to leave. Do you want to go to your hotel? I can have Steve stake out here."

"I could use a shower and a nap, so I'll head for the hotel. If you need me for tonight, give me a call. Here are the flash drives. I almost forgot to give them to you."

Both operatives walked out of the Forrester condo without encountering anyone. They parted company outside, with Sasha driving away and Snowden heading down the street to where he'd parked his car earlier. He sat for a while, his brain racing before he called Charles to bring him up to date. "I'm going to head over to a FedEx office and overnight the flash drives, then have a key made. I'm staying on with my people. I'll check in later this evening when the Forresters return. The minute I found out the Forresters were headed for the city, to his old firm, I called one of my operatives to stake out the lobby of the building to see when he leaves. I'm told he and his wife took the train in. He'll follow them back here. If Maggie was successful planting the bug at the firm, my night is going to be busy listening to what went down there and what's going on in the condo. I'll be in touch later this evening."

Snowden signed off and put the car in gear. *Nice town,* he thought as he drove up one street and down the other. *Nice place to retire if you're an old fuddy-duddy.* It was not for him, though. When it was time for him to walk off into the sunset, he wanted bright lights and noise, to prove he was still alive.

Annie, Myra, Nikki, and Maggie settled down at an outside café to talk. Myra was looking at an incoming text from Charles that said Isabelle and Yoko never made it to Washington. Something went awry at a job site that required Isabelle to be there, and Yoko didn't want to make the trip alone. She shared it with the others, who just shrugged. They ordered coffee from a waiter as an excuse for taking up a table. Maggie grimaced; she was so counting on food. And it was *almost* the supper hour.

"Should we go home, or stick around and spend the night?" Nikki asked.

"Your business is finished, so other than taking a trip to Riverville, I don't see any need to stay," Annie said. "Unless we can think of a way to get more personal background on the Forresters."

"I thought Avery Snowden had that covered," Maggie said, eyeing the menu the waiter had left with their coffee. "Has anyone heard from him?"

"I'm calling him right now." Annie held up her hand for the girls to be quiet as she listened intently to what was being said. "First things first. We're going to take the six o'clock shuttle home. You are not going to believe what Mr. Snowden told me. Listen up, girls." She quickly and concisely repeated everything Snowden had accomplished, ending with, "As we speak, the Forresters are right now traveling to the Ballard law firm's offices. Seems their day lady overheard a phone call in which the husband and wife were talking to each other. I guess it was a command performance, although I don't see Arthur Forrester dancing to anyone's tune but his own. That tells me it was a threatening phone call. And it hap-

135

pened after Nikki and Maggie left their offices. What do you think, Nikki?"

Nikki offered up a low chuckle. "I think the firm wants your business so bad, they can taste it. They know that if your business goes to the O'Malley firm, it will be because of Forrester. They'll threaten him with lawsuits till the end of time and bleed him dry. Whatever they threatened him with, it was enough to make him hightail it into the city. With his wife, no less. Must be some kind of package deal. The thing is, this is all make-believe. Although I have to say, I did like the partners at O'Malley. I liked that they didn't try to impress us. If this was for real, I'd recommend them over the Ballard firm."

"When things settle back down, I'll personally send both firms letters thanking them for their interest and tell them this isn't quite the right time to separate my holdings, but will keep them in mind," Annie said.

"Sounds like a plan," Maggie said as she ran her finger up and down the plastic menu.

"You know what the best part is. Avery will get it all in real time, since I planted that listening device under the conference table. When Fergus handed it to me at the last minute, I have to admit I was a tad worried how I'd get to do it and get away with it. I vote that we head for the airport and go home when we finish our coffee," Maggie said.

The women reached out and high-fived each other, wicked smiles on their faces. They had really pulled off their little caper, with no one the wiser.

"Mr. Arthur Forrester, aka Mr. SOP, you are toast!" Myra said, shooting two thumbs up in victory.

Nikki looked around at the sisters. "What can I say? When you're good, you are *soooo* good!"

Another round of high fives was followed by hilarious laughter, which had the other patrons smiling, wishing that they were part of whatever happy-making events were taking place at table four.

As the sisters were high-fiving each other, Arthur Forrester and his wife were stepping out of the cab they had taken from Union Station onto the sidewalk in front of the building in which Ballard, Ballard & Quinlan was located. Arthur looked at his wife, but didn't say anything. He then looked at the building where he'd worked for thirty-odd years. His stomach muscles tightened.

This was the first time in close to three years that he'd come anywhere near to the building where he had plied his trade for all those years. Since retiring, he had avoided this area as though it were the locus of the latest plague. He thought of the work he had done at Ballard, Ballard & Quinlan as having slaved his life away.

"What are we doing here, Arthur? I don't understand why I had to come here with you. What are you waiting for? Open the damn door and let's get this, whatever this is, over and done with. I don't mind telling you that I am really fed up with this mess you've gotten us into. I mean *really* fed up, Arthur."

"You asked me the same question on the train ride in four times, and four times I told you I do not know the answer. It was the malpractice lawyer who called this meeting. I have to be here. And, to answer the second question, yes, I am stalling. I do not want to go into that building any more than you do. I hate this place with a passion. When I walked away from here, I never thought I would ever come near it again, and yet here I am."

Forrester drew in a deep breath and opened the heavy plate-glass door to allow his wife to go in ahead of him. She side-stepped him neatly. With his wife walking behind him, he marched across the cavernous lobby to the bank of elevators. He pressed the button and could not help but remember how slow the elevators always were.

He turned to his wife. "Listen to me, Nala. I don't want you to say anything, and for God's sake, do not volunteer anything, even if it is to comment on the weather. Do you understand me?"

His tone was a low snarl. Nala reared back, her eyes narrowing. "You're the idiot in this family, Arthur. Don't you tell me what to do. The days when you could tell me to jump and I would ask 'how high' are long gone. Do-you-understand-*ME*?"

They were alone in the elevator, riding up to the fourteenth floor, before Arthur Forrester spoke. "Seriously? You expect me to respond? Just do as I say, so we can get out of this place."

His breathing in check, Forrester walked over to the courtesy desk. This was going to be awkward. His stomach muscles started to tense up. "Hello, Carol. I have a meeting scheduled with Henry. Could you tell him I'm here?"

The receptionist turned pink. "Ah . . . Arthur . . . ah, nice to see you again. Hello,

Mrs. Forrester." Nala nodded a greeting. "Mr. Ballard said to bring you right back when you got here. I . . . ah . . . I know you know the way, but I . . . have to . . ."

"It's not a problem, Carol. We'll follow you."

The room was full. The Ballard brothers and Robert Quinlan all sat in a row. Juan Lorenzo, the malpractice attorney, sat across from them. There was no coffee on the credenza, no bowls of fruit or pastries. Not even bottles of water. Nothing for the pariah. That was fine with him. He sat down next to Juan Lorenzo, with Nala on his other side. He clamped his lips shut and waited for what was to come. He knew that the partners would say nothing, giving the floor to Lorenzo. He leaned back, but he didn't take his eyes off the three men sitting across from him — the three lawyers that he, along with all the other drones who worked at the law firm, had helped make rich over the years. The three men he hated more than anything in the whole world. If they thought he was going to speak first, they could wait till hell froze over.

Forrester was stunned when he heard his wife say in a voice that could have chilled Jell-O, "Why are we here? More to the point, why am *I* here? If you do not, at this

140

very moment, give me an answer that is acceptable, I am walking out of here. And if you think you will ever get me to come back, you all need to have your heads examined."

Forrester wanted nothing more than to strangle his wife right then and there. He did his best to hold his emotions in check as he schooled his face to impassiveness. He looked like it was carved in granite.

"Yes, I'm sure you do want to know, and, of course, you have every right to know, so I am going to tell you." Juan Lorenzo smiled. "*Right now.* This morning, two young women came into this very room and talked to Henry, Alvin, and Robert. They were, for want of a better term, fact-finding for their employer, who is considering this firm, along with another firm, to handle a portion of her very extensive real-estate holdings. I believe," he said, looking down at his notes for confirmation, "somewhere in the neighborhood of four hundred million dollars is what the firm would be managing, should it be chosen. The client's name is Countess Anna de Silva. She was represented here today by one of her attorneys, Nicole Quinn, who owns a twelve-member, all-female law firm in Georgetown. The other woman was the former editor in chief of the *Post,* which the countess also owns. Quinn has impressive credentials and was named Lawyer of the Year three years running. Maggie Spritzer has several Pulitzer Prizes to her credit. Having said that, I'm sure you can see that everyone is taking the possibility of securing the countess's account seriously."

Forrester wanted to outright slap his wife silly when she said, "I don't see what that has to do with me or my husband, especially since my husband no longer works for this firm. If there's a point to this, get to it, please."

"Ah, yes, the point. The point is, the countess is aware of your husband's lawsuit against Garland Lee, as well as this firm's part in it all. While Ms. Quinn didn't come out and directly say the countess would not consider the firm until the lawsuit is settled one way or the other, reading between the lines, the partners believe that is her intent. Which then will mean the countess will more than likely take her business to O'Malley, O'Shaunnesy and McCallister because Ms. Quinn mentioned them as the alternate firm. Which, by the way, is a sterling firm, as your husband can tell you."

Lorenzo stretched his neck so he could see past Arthur Forrester to his wife, to whom he was responding. "As you know, we're in limbo here with the judge, who has not ruled on the summary judgment motion filed by Ms. Lee. We can settle this now and avoid a trial. It is, after all, a trial your husband can't possibly win. All three of the lawyers in this room and I can cite you a thousand cases where celebrity wins out. The firm is prepared to drop their case against your husband and would like to see your husband drop his suit against Garland Lee. Everyone picks up his marbles and just walks away."

"You forgot to say empty-handed," Arthur Forrester said coldly. "I have no intention of walking away or settling. I earned those monies held in escrow. I put the deal together. I earned my percentage. What part of *that* don't you understand?"

"The part where you are a greedy idiot. You hoodwinked Garland Lee. You know it, and we know it. All you did was plug in numbers and make copies. And that movie deal you tried to engineer without telling Ms. Lee! The deal where you appointed yourself her agent, her manager, and anything else you could tack on to make you money. In the end, you would have made more off the movie deal than Garland Lee would have. But, once she had her eyes

143

opened to what you were doing, she chopped you off at the knees and refused, just the way she refused to do the book deal and the branding deal. A jury will see right through all of your sanctimonious nonsense and see what a greedy son of a bitch you really are. You violated every ethical stricture in the book when you conspired against your own client for your own personal gain.

"You're finished, don't you see? Why are you being so blind? Going through a trial, putting your family through that spectacle, only to lose — because you are a greedy bastard — can't be your endgame. You'll spend all of your pension, your retirement, only to come out the loser by going through a trial. In addition to that, if the firm loses the de Silva account because of you, you will be sued up one side and down the other. You will be defending yourself in courtrooms till the day you die. Don't be stupid, Arthur, you cannot win. Either drop the suit or settle," Lorenzo said, his voice a virtual snarl.

"So you say. I want my day in court. I will not be denied that which I earned," Forrester said, bitterness ringing in his voice at the threats raining down on him.

Lorenzo appealed to Nala. "Is this how you want it to go forward? Is this what you want for your family? For your retirement?"

Nala Forrester looked shell-shocked. She recovered nicely and sucked in a deep breath, her eyes lasers of hate directed straight at her husband of forty-some years. "This is how I see it, gentlemen. You can't fix stupid. I do not plan on standing in the wings to watch what you described happening. This might surprise you, but I happen to agree with everything you've said here. Now, if you'll excuse me, I'm leaving." Nala Forrester turned to her husband, and said, "I'm going to stay in town tonight. I'll return home when, and if, I feel like it. Good-bye, gentlemen."

Arthur Forrester stared at his wife, disbelief at her betrayal plainly showing on his face. Gone was any attempt to keep a poker face. If he had a gun, he would have shot her stone-cold dead.

All the men rose to their feet, except Arthur Forrester. The sound of the door's closing was so loud, it sounded like thunder in the quiet conference room.

Juan Lorenzo shot Arthur Forrester a pitying look. "Look, Arthur, I know this came as a shock to you today. Why don't you go home, think it over, and call us in the morning. Please don't make a decision that you'll regret for the rest of your life. And while you're at it, you might want to try to make peace with your wife."

Arthur Forrester stood up, shook his shoulders, and looked around at the four men. "Do me a favor. Go to hell. But before you leave for that burning inferno, kiss my ass, boys!"

No one blinked. No one said a word. No one even breathed until the door opened and Arthur Forrester walked through it.

Henry Ballard looked at his two partners. "Draw up the complaints. Charge the bastard with anything you can think of. I want everything ready the moment I say to go."

Juan Lorenzo sighed, as did the others. "We tried."

"Yes, we did," the three partners said in unison. "Yes, we did."

CHAPTER 7

Forty-eight hours after the girls had returned from Washington, Charles called a dinner meeting to further strategize about Garland Lee's mission. The girls were cleaning up with their usual zest and thoroughness. "We shaved off a second," Yoko giggled as she hung up the dishcloth to dry. The others high-fived her, laughing as they always did over their impeccable timing where cleanup was concerned. Yoko was last in line to exit the kitchen for the trip down the moss-covered steps that led to the war room.

As was their custom, they all turned silent as they saluted Lady Justice in all her majesty. They took their seats and started to chatter nonstop, bringing everyone up to date on what each one knew and didn't know.

Nikki spoke first. "I'm taking ten days off. I'm between cases, and there is absolutely nothing urgent that the others can't handle. I'm available for whatever I can do."

"I'm with Nikki," Alexis said. "I won my case yesterday, and the rule at the firm is ten days off to celebrate. I'm also available."

"I got a text from Kathryn, who said she's rolling into town tomorrow for ten days. Ten days must be our magic number. She has to have her rig overhauled. She said she might even be here two full weeks. As for me, I'm good. My college boys finished up and are available twenty-four/seven," Yoko said happily.

"I don't exactly have ten full days, but I can guarantee seven," Isabelle said. "My project is ahead of schedule. I do have to be available, however."

"I'm good for whatever I can do, as long as Annie cuts me some slack," Maggie said.

"You have all the time you need, my dear," Annie said generously.

"I think I speak for Annie, as well as myself, by saying we're here to do whatever is needed, and we don't have any time constraints," Myra said.

Charles and Fergus walked down the three steps to the main part of the war room to stand behind Annie's and Myra's chairs. "We're here for Avery Snowden's report. He should be checking in momentarily. I do believe he has some information that will aid us in our next moves. He'll be on speakerphone and answer any and all questions you might have. Please hold your questions till *after* he has given his report. While his report will be verbal for now, he's overnighting a full written report. He also said we might want to arrange a face-to-face with Ms. Lee after we hear the report, since he said he picked up some information she either forgot to mention or doesn't want to talk about."

Myra and Annie looked at one another.

"Garland seemed very forthcoming when we visited her. We kept asking if there was anything else, and she said no. She's not the kind of person who would knowingly withhold information. I think we'll find out it is just an oversight, whatever it turns out to be," Myra said. Annie nodded in agreement.

No sooner had the words rolled off Myra's tongue than the phone in the middle of the table shrilled to life. Nikki reached out to click it to the ON position, and then hit the SPEAKER button. The sisters leaned forward, not wanting to miss a single word of Avery's verbal report.

"Evening, all. Let's get right to it. Some of what I have to tell you is good and some not so much. All of the listening devices we planted are prime and working well. I've spent the past two days listening to conversations among all parties. For starters, let's go with the device Maggie planted at the firm. I was able to listen to the entire meeting the partners and their malpractice lawyer had with Mr. and Mrs. Forrester. That meeting did not go at all well. In fact, the partners did not say a single word the whole time the Forresters were in the room. They left it all up to Juan Lorenzo, the malpractice attorney. And that's the way it should be.

"Mrs. Forrester reared up and spoke her piece and left the meeting, saying she was *not* going home. One of my operatives followed her, and she took a cab, by the way. She and her husband had taken the train into Union Station. The cab took Mrs. Forrester uptown, where she entered a doorman-monitored building. My operative logged the address, but was unable to garner any information on who lives there or whom she is visiting. More on that later.

"Lorenzo presented Mr. Forrester all the information the partners had shared with him about Countess de Silva's account possibly coming their way. He spoke about Nikki and Maggie and how Nikki was named Lawyer of the Year several years in a row. He spoke about her firm to show that this was serious business and, of course, Maggie's role as the former editor in chief of the *Post*. Forrester made no comment. In point of fact, he was pretty much silent, till the very end.

"I think it's safe to say the meeting was intense. Forrester said he had earned the millions being held in escrow. Lorenzo said all he did was plug in numbers and change the dates, yada yada yada. Forrester countered, and they argued back and forth, until Lorenzo zapped him with some movie deal he tried to get going about Garland Lee's life, which she knew nothing about. It sounded like Mrs. Forrester didn't know about it, either.

"The deal would have him, had it worked out, getting the lion's share of the profits, had a movie been made. He had himself down as manager and any other titles he could give himself. Plus his twenty percent, plus his hourly legal fee, and the guy was going to make out like a bandit. Had the deal come off, the guy would be living on Easy Street for life. So, when Lee nixed the deal, he went nuclear on her. I'm not sure of the timing, exactly, but I think that's when things started to go south.

"Then there was the book deal, the memoirs he tried to peddle, that Lee shut him down on, too. I don't remember exactly where I heard this, but it was a ten-million-dollar deal, with him getting his twenty percent, or two million dollars, plus his hourly rate, plus his percentage of the royalties, if there were any. Any foreign rights percentages were on top of all that. Lorenzo made it sound as if Forrester had already spent the money when Lee shut him down.

"The man is beyond bitter. The more Lorenzo tried to talk him into dropping the case or trying to settle, the more it made Forrester dig in his heels. To me, and this is just my opinion now, it's all about vengeance and getting back at Garland Lee for ruining the good life he had planned for himself. His parting shot to Lorenzo and the partners was to go to hell and to kiss his ass on the way. Then he stormed out of the room and took the train back to Riverville. The operative who followed him said he burned up his phone. I assume he was trying to reach his wife, but was apparently unsuccessful, because he just kept doing it, one call after the other. I'm sure the wife turned off her phone, because she sounded way beyond angry when she left.

"After Forrester left the office, the partners talked, and they're going ahead with their threat to sue him for anything they can. They told him in no uncertain terms that he would spend the rest of his life defending the suits. That's it on that part. We can move on now to what transpired in Riverville as all that was going down.

"Sasha, one of my best operatives, and I managed to get into the Forresters' condo. We planted four listening devices, copied everything off his hard drive, and took photos of everything we saw in his office. We ran into a bit of a diversion because the maid was there, but we made that right with the proper gratuity and a thinly veiled threat. We also copied her key, so we have access to the condo whenever we want to go in there, providing no one is home. We had her call Mrs. Forrester to say she was leaving and wouldn't be back, but no one answered. She left a voice mail for her. And she promised to call if there was any kind of blowback. Since she was positive that the Forresters did not even know where she lives, blowback is unlikely. I think she'll keep her word, and, of course, the gratuity helped with that a bit.

"We've been on the job almost six days now. I still really don't have a feeling for the guy. It's like he's a robot. Usually, by this stage of a mission, I've figured things out.

They're an odd couple. They do not appear to be close to their children. I don't know if that's true or not, but that's how it appears. The maid said she heard the wife refuse to give her husband money, or to let him use her money, because it was for her children and the children helped by her charity. She said the Forresters argued behind closed doors, but she could still hear them. She's the one who tipped us off that a phone call came in for Arthur to come into the firm for a meeting. *Stat.* They dropped everything and left. The missus didn't want to go, but she did end up going. They took the train into D.C., then took a cab to the office building.

"The condo has been silent the past two days. Arthur did not go out to play golf today. He did go to the market and brought food home. He has not spoken to anyone on the phone, so if he has been in touch with anyone, it is via e-mail or texting. He does not talk to himself, sing while he shaves, or anything like that. I do not know what he's been doing, so all we have at the moment is dead air coming out of the condo.

"My operative told me that the first night of our surveillance, Mrs. Forrester and a female friend went to dinner at a little café around the corner. An Italian place. They drank two bottles of wine and had spaghetti and meatballs for dinner. They had to hold on to each other for the trip home. Mrs. Forrester cried in her wine. They were there three hours. They do not go anywhere during the day. The second night, they went to a different place, a bistro, where they only drank one bottle of beer each and just had appetizers. They were steady on their feet walking home.

"One other thing. It's my opinion that Forrester is doing the nitty-gritty on a lot of his legal work, and his attorney here is signing off on it. To keep the bill down, I would assume. You did tell me, Charles, that Annie got a copy of his financials. I'd like to know how much he's actually paid out in legal fees. I know the malpractice guy, Lorenzo, is paid by the insurance company.

"That is pretty much my report, and you can ask me questions now. I'll do my best to answer them."

The sisters looked around at each other, their eyebrows raised. They shrugged their shoulders at the same time.

"So he's not willing to settle, and he refuses to drop his suit against Garland. That's a given, right?" Annie said.

"That's what I got out of it, yes," Snowden

responded.

"So what happens now? When do they set a date for the trial?" Yoko asked.

"I have no clue," Snowden responded.

"Probably whenever the judge rules on the summary judgment," Alexis and Nikki said in unison.

"When you say the condo is dead air, does that mean no TV, no stereo, no phone calls where he left messages for his wife?" Isabelle asked. "Seems to me if the TV or the radio was playing, maybe he made calls and your device didn't pick up on it."

"Good point. Yes, he does keep the TV on — all night, as a matter of fact. He has it set to the Fox cable network. It's very muted. I could hear fine. My bad here. He did make one phone call the night he got back after his meeting in Washington. He called his wife, but he had to leave a message, which he did, and it was not very nice. Not very nice at all. He chastised her, and also said if she didn't return home ASAP, he was going to file a missing persons report on her. That, I believe, was an idle threat, which I'm quite sure she recognized. Because, for all intents and purposes, it looks like she's hunkered down at the current location for the foreseeable future.

"Before you ask, the woman she's visiting

appears to be the same size and build as Nala Forrester, so I assume she's lending Mrs. Forrester clothes. My people are trying to find out the name of the person who either owns or is leasing the apartment. We have to comb through all the tenants, and even then, we don't know which floor she lives on. The doorman is exceptionally tight-lipped, and bribes don't work.

"My next question to you all is, do you want us to check out the kids? I know your rule on that, but I still have to ask."

"Our rule has always been, and always will be, that children, no matter their age, or grandchildren, along with animals, are off-limits. Even if they know something, we leave them alone," Annie said forcefully. The others nodded in agreement.

"Anything else, ladies?"

"What about the e-mails back and forth with his attorney up there in Riverville and the ones to Lorenzo?" Nikki asked.

"I'm wading through them now. I'll report first thing in the morning. What I've seen so far is that they are not nice. Forrester is very demanding. He wants what he wants when he wants it, and not a minute later. From the way they read, I would surmise that his attorney up here is just a puppet, and the guy resents it. I saw a few in which he dared to offer advice, and Forrester shot him down. There was one very personal one where he blamed Forrester for breaking up his marriage, to which Forrester replied that his wife was a big girl and could make her own decisions. He obviously has no remorse whatsoever that the woman was terminated for helping him file suit against Garland Lee. Knowing what little I know of him, he probably views it as acceptable collateral damage, though I suppose that he would consider any damage to others perfectly acceptable. He is not a nice guy. If there's nothing else, I need to get back to work."

The girls agreed that they had no more questions. Charles terminated the call and waited for the comments to come.

"What do you think, Charles?" Myra asked.

"Fergus and I are going to need a few more days to go through all the bank records. We need to take our time and make sure we get it right the first time. The minute Avery sends me his written report, we'll make up copies for everyone. I'd say three days. By then, Kathryn will be back, and we'll have a full house."

"Tomorrow, first thing, Myra and I will pay Garland Lee a visit and ask about the movie deal that she forgot to mention. We'll get more particulars on the book deal, too. I think it will help us a great deal if we can come up with numbers, to determine how much money he thinks he lost because Garland fired him."

"So what you're saying is once we get everything all nice and neat, we have two choices. We either wait for that judge to rule on the summary judgment to set the trial date, or we snatch Mr. SOP and end it *our* way, right? But, I think before we make that decision, we should ask Garland's opinion. I know she said she doesn't have the stamina for a full-blown trial, even knowing she'll win. She doesn't want to go public and have that circus all over the media, and I can't say that I blame her," Nikki said.

"What I don't understand is why Mr. SOP would want to put himself out there for the world to see. Doesn't he care about what that will do to his family and his reputation? Not to mention what it will do to the firm. Where is that man's head?" Alexis barked angrily. "What kind of person is this we're dealing with?"

"A greedy son of a bitch with absolutely no conscience," Annie said. "Add that to the fact that he is just not a nice person, and I think we need to teach him a lesson. So I'm all for the snatch. From here on in, we'll make all his decisions for him."

"Damn straight," Nikki said.

The sisters banged their fists on the conference table, shouting, "Hear, hear!"

Fergus shivered. Charles trembled. He knew what those words meant. If he needed any additional proof, all he had to do was look at the gleeful expressions on the women's faces.

Not a single one of the sisters felt the least bit sorry for what was going to befall Arthur Forrester.

Myra eased up on the gas pedal as she approached the entrance to Garland Lee's property. "Annie, do you see what I'm seeing?" she asked in awe.

"I do, I do. How did she do all this? Granted, she has a gardener, but still. . . . We were just here a few days ago, and now the place is an oasis covered in flowers. Acres and acres of flowers, as far as the eye can see. Every color of the rainbow! I don't think I've ever seen anything as beautiful as what we're looking at. There must be like . . . I don't know, fifty thousand plants with flowers on all of them. Shangri-la, a tropical paradise, I don't know what to call it. Imagine waking up each morning and looking out the window to see all this," Annie said, waving her arms about.

"Garland did say her gardener was a magician when it came to plantings. I assume Yoko's people did a lot of the work. Before we leave, we have to take pictures. The girls will love seeing this magical place, and it is *magical,*" Myra said.

"Look! Garland is walking down to meet us. Look at that grin on her face!" Annie laughed.

"How do you like it?" Garland asked.

"It's magnificent," Annie said.

"Come along. I was so happy you called. I made us some lunch. I like talking over lunch. I don't know why that is."

"We do, too. You shouldn't have bothered, but I have to admit I am hungry," Myra said.

"Shrimp scampi, salad, and some garlic twists. Iced tea. It was no trouble. I don't get much company, and, believe it or not, I do like to cook. So you have me all atwitter. What brings you out here in the middle of the day?"

"A number of things. We wanted to bring you up to date, ask your opinion on a decision we need to make, and ask you some additional questions."

"Sounds serious, but I'm your girl. Lunch is ready, so if you want to wash up a bit, the powder room is off the hall. While you're doing that, I'll get things ready."

Seated at the table, Annie said, "If this tastes half as good as it smells, we're going to want seconds."

Garland beamed her pleasure at the compliment. "Talk to me," she said.

Annie and Myra brought her up to date, with Annie going first, then stopping to eat as Myra picked up. Finally, when their plates were empty for the second time, Myra wound down by saying, "We have to make a decision, but we don't want to do that until you tell us what you want. But before we get to that, we have to ask you a question. When we were out here the first time, why didn't you tell us about the movie deal that never materialized?"

All the color seemed to drain from Garland's face. She wore the look of a startled deer caught in the headlights. "Because until just this minute, I haven't allowed myself to think about that. When I found out what Arthur had done, I had a meltdown. A real meltdown. I had to see a therapist for a while. The movie people tried to sue me, and I didn't even know what they were talking about. I had to hire a boatload of entertainment lawyers to make it all go away. It was all Arthur's doing. It was a very,

very bad time for me. Even now, when I think about it, my heart starts to race, and I break out into a cold sweat. I didn't deliberately withhold the information. I just never allow myself to think about it, so I *won't* have to talk about it.

"The book deal was bad, but the movie deal was much worse. I don't know what to tell you. I have everything boxed up in the closet in my room. All the therapist's reports, the lawyers' reports, affidavits from Arthur. That was the beginning and the end of him with me. I fired him right after the book deal went sour. He dived into that project immediately after the lawyers shut him down on the movie deal. The canceled tour was in between the two. I was out of it for a while. Otherwise, I would have fired him on the spot. I guess that's no excuse to your way of thinking, but had you been me, you might feel different.

"The last thing in the world I would ever want is for a movie to be made of my life. I am no different than anyone else where their private life is concerned. I have my skeletons I don't want to share with the world. Let's just say I was not always the person I am today. I want to keep it that way. The money . . . the money that could have been made was so astronomical, I couldn't believe it. It seems like I would have been a big box-office draw. I found out later that Arthur was planning to buy a brewery with his share of the money. Actually, he had invested heavily in it, even before, but planned on buying out his partners with his share of the movie rights. At least that's what my lawyers told me when everything was said and done." Garland pushed her plate to the side and gulped from the glass of iced tea. "I think I just lost my appetite."

"Then what happened?" Myra asked.

"From there, he tried to arrange a tour to recoup the monies he lost on the movie deal. I said no. Then he went for the book contract. I said no again. That was the end. I'm sorry I didn't tell you. I just . . .'"

"It's okay. We know now, and it certainly answers a lot of our questions. We're not blaming you. We just need to know *everything,* Garland," Myra said soothingly.

"We certainly know now what and whom we're dealing with. As Myra said, you just cleared that up for us. I'm sorry if we upset you. That wasn't our intention."

"Oh, I know that. It's me. It's just that I hate to remember and realize how stupid I was back then. Thinking about it now is like reliving it all over again. So what is the decision you want me to be part of?"

Annie peered at Garland, glad to see the color returning to her face. She appeared calm now, her hands weren't shaking, and her eyes were clearly focused. At that moment, Annie knew that she was capable of strangling Arthur Forrester for what he'd done to this kind, wonderful lady sitting across from her.

Myra took a deep breath. "Here it is in a nutshell, Garland. We told you what went down at the meeting at the firm yesterday. Mr. Forrester said in no uncertain terms that he was not going to settle or drop the case. That means that unless you get a summary judgment, there will be a full-blown trial, probably six or eight months down the road. Possibly, a trial date could even be set for early next year, maybe sooner. We just don't know at this point. It depends on how crowded court calendars are.

"Here are your choices, and you do not have to make a decision right this minute. Take as much time as you need. Talk to your family about the trial only, nothing where we're concerned before you make a decision. Do you understand what I just said?"

"I understand completely. What is my second choice?"

Annie laughed out loud. "I think you will like the second choice."

165

Garland smiled. She adored these two women sitting at her kitchen table. Her eyes sparkled. "Lay it on me, ladies," she quipped.

"We do a snatch. We'll make all his decisions going forward, and it will be over for you, once and for all," Annie said.

"That's a no-brainer. Count me in for the snatch. Are you sure you can actually do that? Arthur is a wily little bugger, just so you know."

"Does the pope pray? Of course we can do it, and we're going to love every minute of the time we spend doing it," Myra said.

"Do you need me to do anything? I'm up for . . . whatever."

"I think we have it covered. We'll update you in a few days. We're still working on things. In the meantime, all you have to do is enjoy all those wonderful gardens you have out there. You should let them feature your grounds in some garden magazines."

Garland shook her head. "No. If I did that, it wouldn't be mine alone anymore. This is my sanctuary, one I share with only family and one or two good friends. I hope you understand that."

"We do," Annie said agreeably. "We should be getting back. You said you had a box to give us."

166

"Yes. I'll go and get it."

When the kitchen door closed behind Garland, Annie looked at Myra, and said, "I'm okay with how this all went down. I believe everything she said, and I understand her completely. You?"

"Absolutely. Oh, Annie, I cannot wait till we have Mr. SOP in our clutches."

"We aren't making any money on this mission, you know that, right?" Annie said wryly.

"Annie, some things are just more important than others. I think we can make do. Our coffers are full. Pro bono is a wonderful thing sometimes. Shhh, I hear Garland on the stairs."

"Here you go, ladies," Garland said as she reentered the room, carrying a large box. "I have to be honest with you — I am so glad to turn this over to you, so glad to get it out of my house. I don't know why I never burned it. I wish I had, but if I had done that, I wouldn't be able to turn it over to you. When you're finished with it, you have my permission to burn the whole darn thing. That's when I'll know it's finally over, and I can have peace in my life again. Come along, I'll walk you out to your car."

The good-byes were warm and sweet, with hugs and promises to stay in touch. They were five miles away when Myra said, "I forgot to take pictures."

"In the scheme of things, I don't really think it matters much, Myra. Just concentrate on your driving. It would be more than okay with me if you sped up a little. This is a sixty-five-mile-per-hour stretch of road, and you're only doing forty."

"Suck it up, Annie. At least I'll get us home in one piece. Those hair-raising rides you force on me leave me traumatized for weeks on end."

"Once a complainer, always a complainer. That really was a superior lunch, wasn't it? Watch that truck!"

"Shut up, Annie!"

Annie clamped her lips shut and looked out the window. She later told Fergus that if she'd wanted to, she could have reached out and plucked the leaves from the bushes because that's how slow Myra was driving.

Fergus knew better than to comment on his beloved's daredevil driving feats. All he said was "Uh-huh."

CHAPTER 8

The exact moment Arthur Forrester heard the *ping* of the front door opening, thanks to his intricate alarm system, he moved like he'd been shot out of a cannon. He was in his wife's face a second later, demanding to know where she had been and why she had not responded to all the calls and texts he'd sent her way. His face was blustery with rage.

Neither the spittle flying out of her husband's mouth nor the rage she saw on his face affected Nala Forrester at all. She didn't back up, but stood her ground. "Get out of my way, Arthur" was all she said, and she tried to shove him in response. When her husband didn't move, Nala walked around him and headed for her bedroom. It had been years since they had shared the same bed. Actually, she remembered the precise day and time she'd relocated all her things into the spare room.

It had all happened on the very day he had filed suit against Garland Lee. The papers had been filed at 4:45 P.M. on a Monday. And he spent the next ten minutes explaining to her in minute detail what he'd just done. At five minutes past five, she'd marched into the bedroom and started to empty out her closet and dresser drawers. Her husband hadn't tried to stop her. He'd just made angry animal sounds as he stormed his way to his office, which was off the family room. The room where he spent twenty hours out of every twenty-four hours a day. Except for the days he played golf. Most nights, he slept on the couch. Not that she cared one way or the other.

Inside the small bedroom, Nala pulled out two dull-looking, soft-sided suitcases and proceeded to fill them. Her motions were precise, quick, and fluid as she gathered up her belongings. How sad that all she was taking with her were clothes and one picture of her along with their four children, taken when they were younger, more than thirty years ago. She no longer kept count of how many years she had been married to her low-life husband, because she no longer cared. And all she had to show for it were her two suitcases filled with clothes that had seen better days. She made a mental note to get a new wardrobe soon.

Nala knew that her husband was standing in the doorway, his face beet red, but she refused to look in his direction. She refused to give him the satisfaction. She continued to move with quiet efficiency. It was her way, and the main reason she'd been such a good nurse practitioner, or at least that's what the doctors she worked with had told her.

"Where do you think you're going? What's gotten into you? You embarrassed me at the firm. That is totally unacceptable, Nala. You need to show me respect — I'm your husband," Forrester snarled. Nala ignored him as she wrapped her rubber-soled white shoes in paper towels from the small bathroom, which was neat as a pin.

"Where have you been? What the hell is wrong with you?" He advanced a step into the room. Nala whirled around, her arms thrust forward, ramrod straight, palms facing her husband. "Take one more step, and I will gouge out your eyes. Step back, Arthur."

Forrester surprised himself by stepping back to his position in the doorway. "We need to talk."

"No. We. Do. Not."

The sound of the zipper's closing the

suitcase was louder than any thunder crack. The second zipper's closing even louder.

Nala yanked the cases off the bed, jerked open the handle that released the wheels, and headed for the doorway. "Get out of my way, Arthur."

Once again, Arthur Forrester surprised himself by stepping outside the room to let his wife pass him. He followed her to the foyer, where she set the bags against the wall. She looked around, trying to figure out if she was missing anything, before she headed back to her bedroom to get the backpack that she used in lieu of a purse. *Ah, yes, the things in the bathroom.* She gathered everything up, put it all in a ziplock bag from one of the drawers, and stuffed it into her backpack, which was already jammed full almost to overflowing.

Forrester tried one more time. "Why are you doing this, Nala?"

Nala Forrester decided it was time to talk. "I'm doing this because I cannot stand the person you've become. You've been a miserable father to our children, a less-than-satisfying husband to me. You aren't even a good lawyer, in my opinion. Since you took over from an agent who was as ethical as the day is long, and totally committed to doing what was best for his client, you

172

preyed on Garland Lee. *You* robbed that woman blind. And now it's time to pay the piper, as they say. I'm sick and tired of your get-rich-quick schemes, which have eaten up all our money. I'm sick and tired of your trying to pretend you are as rich as your brothers. I'm sick and tired of your pretending to be someone you are not. It's taken me a while, but I finally came to the only conclusion possible. You are stupid, Arthur. Beyond stupid, actually.

"To answer your other questions, I am moving into the city with a friend. I'm going to go back to work at her street clinic. It's a clinic I'm going to invest in. And, before you can ask what I'm going to make on the deal, here's my answer. Maybe two or three thousand dollars a year. I'm not doing it for the money. I'm doing it to help people who can't help themselves. My reward will be to see them smile, knowing I helped make their lives at least a little better. My life will be better, too — blessed, if you will — because I won't be standing by someone who is stealing, lying, or cheating other people like you have. I'll be able to sleep at night and look at myself in the mirror when I get up in the morning.

"I'm going to get a new phone, so forget my old number and do not call me and do not try to find me. If you do, I will swear out a complaint against you. We're done. Since you are so stupid, let me spell that out for you. You and I are done as in *done.* You spell it, *d-o-n-e!*"

Arthur Forrester brought up his clenched fist. Nala once again held her ground. "You *might* land one punch, but I *will* gouge out your eyes!"

The sound of the door's closing behind his wife was quiet, like she was.

Three blocks away, Avery Snowden listened, his jaw dropping at the intense happenings in the Forrester household. The girls were going to love this when he reported in.

Arthur Forrester stomped his way through the condo to his office. He wanted to put his fist through something, anything, preferably Garland Lee's beautiful face. When he finished with her, then his wife's face. Rage flowed through him as he scratched and picked at his rosy cheeks. When he saw blood on his fingers, he cursed. He made his way to the small bathroom off his office, where he soaked cotton balls in peroxide. He yelped in pain at the burn. He quickly lathered on a prescription cream, which was supposed to alleviate the itch, but was, in his opinion, worthless. He risked a glance in the mirror and cringed. He looked like he'd been in a catfight and had come out the loser. Worse, he looked like his wife had scratched the bejesus out of him. What all that meant was he was now housebound until his face healed up. Unless he wanted to wear the theatrical makeup his dermatologist had given him. No way was he going out so people could see all the long scabs on both his cheeks. "Son of a bitch!" he seethed to his reflection in the mirror.

Back in his lair, his nest, he settled into his chair and stared off into space. How in the hell had it come to this? He knew how, but he just refused to admit it.

Like he was going to cave in now? Be made a laughingstock. That simply was not in his DNA. He had no other choice but to go through with the trial, assuming he survived the motion for a summary judgment.

Yeah, sure, it was going to cost him a bundle. If he lost, and he didn't think he would, but if he did, he could always appeal, and that process would take years. And money. He still had enough in the bank to pay for that. But then he had to think about the firm. He believed them implicitly when they said they would file every suit they could under the sun to tie him up in the courts for the rest of his life. Maybe. Then again, maybe not. He knew things about all the partners, things no one else knew. Things they wouldn't want getting out. He was glad now he hadn't played those cards. Always keep something in reserve when it looked like a situation might reach the point of no return. The word *blackmail* simply was not a word in his vocabulary. A good decision on his part. Just like all his other decisions were good, so why give up the ghost now?

Maybe what he should do now was concentrate on finding a buyer for the craft brewery he was so heavily invested in. If not an outright buyer, then possibly some investors. Maybe what he should do was go out to the kitchen, make himself an early lunch, brew a fresh pot of coffee, and actually sit down in the breakfast nook and eat while he watched all the political bullshit going on with the Republican and Democratic presidential nominees who couldn't get their crap together. Not one of the candidates was worth a good spit. In the end, he thought, why should he waste his vote on such losers. He simply wouldn't vote this year.

Forrester looked down at the sandwich he'd made himself, rare roast beef, sliced turkey, Virginia ham, Swiss cheese, mayo, lettuce, on soft white bread with a pickle on the side. It had been years and years since he'd had a sandwich like this. He himself had bought all the food on his last trip to the store. If Nala had made the sandwich, it would have been on ten-grain bread and had tofu, avocado, and sprouts, with some kind of spread that tasted like motor oil. Her version was guaranteed to clear out one's arteries, while his was guaranteed to clog them. Like he gave a good rat's ass about his arteries right now.

He bit into the six-inch-high sandwich and rolled his eyes in delight. As he chewed and watched the TV, he knew he needed to come up with a plan. A plan that would get him out from under and send the firm's partners scurrying for cover.

Charles hit the SPEAKER button so Fergus could hear Avery Snowden's incoming message. They looked at one another in shock and surprise at the news the operative was sharing. Snowden wound down and ended the call by saying that his people were still shadowing the wife and would continue the stakeout on the condo and keep their eyes peeled in case Forrester decided to go out for some fresh air. He went on to say the wife had driven her car into the city. "I'm finding it strange that Forrester hasn't been in touch with his local lawyer, the one whose wife filed the original suit. For some reason, I thought that would be the first thing he would do when he got home after the meeting at the firm. Unless he's thinking the guy is going to push him under the bus, too. Then he will have no other recourse except to find another lawyer dumb enough to take him on, or he'll just represent himself.

"If you go with the former, and the guy dumps him, he can stall for months and months until his new lawyer gets up to speed. This guy is just blowing my mind, and I don't mind admitting it, either."

Charles and Fergus agreed with Snowden and ended the call.

"The girls are going to love this. I think they'll want to move up the time and the date to do the snatch. No sense giving Mr. Forrester any more time to plan and scheme. Did you pick up on the fact that Mr. Forrester didn't seem all that upset about the firm's partners suing him for all he's worth? That bothers me, Ferg."

"I did notice that, mate. Do ya think maybe he has something on them? Maybe some skeletons in their closets. That's where

178

my mind is taking me right now."

"If that's true, he's not talking about it. We only have sound to go by. If he's texting or e-mailing, we aren't privy to that. I say we notify the girls, check to see where Kathryn is, and call a meeting for tomorrow. For now, let's finish up on these financials and see what we have. I'm going to go topside and whip us up some lunch. While I'm doing that, call Maggie and have her check to see what she can come up with on that craft brewery. I don't think we have a name for it, do we?" Fergus shrugged.

"What's for lunch?" Fergus asked.

"Well, your beloved, also known as Countess Anna de Silva, requested weenies with baked beans and coleslaw. I made some tapioca pudding earlier, and made it just the way you like it, Ferg, with raisins — yes, the yellow ones — and crushed pineapple. Lunch will be in one hour. Does that work for you?"

"It does."

Both men laughed at the thought of one of the world's richest people, the Countess Anna de Silva, scarfing down her favorite food on earth, hot dogs with the works.

CHAPTER 9

Maggie Spritzer stared out the *Post*'s window at the rain slapping against the building like a million jackhammers. She wondered if all the ducks in and around the Tidal Basin were safe. Such a wild thought. Then again, maybe not so wild. Still, it was better than to keep dwelling on Arthur Forrester and the meeting that was supposed to have taken place in forty-eight hours, but Charles had canceled because of flooding on the roads leading to Pinewood.

The only topic of conversation on television was this latest freak spring storm that rivaled a tsunami. Stranded motorists sitting on the roofs of their cars, houses flooded to the second floors, and all the creek beds overflowing to create a monster lake were the only things to be seen on the local television channels. Residents were advised to stay in their homes and not take to the roads. Virginia was the state in the area being hit the hardest. D.C. and the metropolitan area were flooded, to be sure, but that was nothing compared to Virginia. She'd spent the night here at the *Post.* She'd checked in earlier with Jackson Sparrow, who was living next door to her house in Georgetown, in the house that Jack Emery used to own before he and Nikki moved out to the country. Months ago, they had traded house keys and agreed to watch out for one another. He'd checked on Hero, her cat, cleaned his litter box, and put down fresh food and water and said her basement was dry. So she was good to stay here another day, if need be.

Another glitch, according to Nikki, was that Avery Snowden was pulling out of Washington and heading to Delaware because he was needed by the boys. His rationale for switching up was that surveilling Forrester was about as meaningful and rewarding as watching paint dry. He agreed to leave one operative behind to, as he put it, "babysit the package." *The package,* of course, was operative speak for Arthur Forrester.

He added that the wife was clearly not involved in her husband's high jinks, so there was no reason for a full crew when the boys needed their services. Surprisingly,

Charles had not only *not argued* with Snowden about his decision, but had actually given him permission to go ahead.

Maggie, who for a long time had not been a full-fledged member of the Vigilantes, and so had participated in many fewer assignments, wasn't sure how she felt about that and complained to Nikki that she kind of felt like they were being treated as second-class citizens. To which Nikki had replied, "Think about it, we can do the snatch as well as he could have. All we need to do is set up a plan, set it in motion, and it's a done deal." Maggie agreed, her mood brightening immediately.

Maggie turned around to head to her desk when she had an epiphany. At least she thought it was. She immediately called Annie for permission; then she called Garland Lee to see if she was okay with what they planned to do. After a few questions, the singer gave her verbal okay to go ahead.

It took Maggie a full hour to set up a conference call with all the girls and manage to get Kathryn to stop long enough at a rest stop to be patched through so she could participate. She was sitting in the *Post*'s conference room now, waiting for Kathryn to call so she could ring the others, who were all standing by. She'd worried about

Myra, and Annie, who were stuck out at the farm, and Nikki, who lived nearby and was unable to get into her law firm, but in the end, the telephones were still in operation.

While she waited, she spent her time calling a friend and colleague, Carlie Mason, who worked for one of the major newspapers in Washington. After the social amenities were over, Maggie cut to the chase. "I'll share the byline if you can guarantee that Garland Lee's picture goes above the fold and the story underneath, but it has to be the front page. I'll do the write-up, since I have it sitting in front of me. No one needs to know you didn't share in the writing. This is important to me, Carlie, really important, or I wouldn't involve you. It's a win-win for you, Carlie. What do you say?"

The voice on the other end of the phone bellowed in delight. "I'm in! Give me twenty minutes, my boss just went down to the cafeteria. I'll get back to you within the hour."

"Great. I'll be on a multiple conference call, so leave a message. I'll have the picture and the text to you by late afternoon, in plenty of time for tomorrow's early edition. Thanks, Carlie," Maggie gushed.

"Hey, girl, it's the other way around. A

byline on page one, and I don't have to do a thing. It doesn't get any better than that, ya know. Aside from all of that, I love and adore Garland Lee. Who doesn't?" Both women laughed; then the connection was broken.

The phone in the center of the long conference table shrilled to life. It took eight minutes for everyone to say they were on board and could hear what everyone else was saying. Kathryn said she had excellent reception and was barely ninety miles away and on her way home.

"Since this call is of your making, dear, I suggest you tell us what it's all about," Myra said.

"Right, right! Well, I was staring out the window, and suddenly I had this epiphany. Or the epiphany's cousin. Whatever . . . I want to do an article for tomorrow's early edition saying that Garland Lee is planning a world tour. I called her, and she gave me permission to write whatever I want. She really trusts us. It will be half article, half interview. In the interview, she will be coy, neither confirming nor denying the world tour. She'll say she's coordinating it herself because her last agent/business manager had seemed more interested in his own financial well-being than in hers. In other words, and this is not in the story, he treated her like his own private piggy bank, ripped her off — none of which she can say without opening herself up to a charge of slander. No names need to be mentioned.

"I can have the story ready for the early edition tomorrow morning. I called a colleague in D.C. and promised her to share the byline if she could get front-page coverage tomorrow also. Every news channel and all the wire services will be repeating it on the hour. Garland Lee is a household name, like a combination of Frank Sinatra and Barbra Streisand. We both think it's a go, but Carlie has to get approval. She should have it in about an hour. The object, of course, is for Mr. SOP to hear the news and read the paper so he turns himself inside out and hopefully does something stupid. That's as far as I got in my thinking."

"And what will this do for us?" Alexis asked.

"It will throw Mr. Sack of Pus for a loop. Garland said he devours the morning papers. Reads them all. At least he used to, when he did his commute into the city when he was working. If that was his habit, then chances are that he still does. Retired people always read the paper, either the actual paper or online. And older people are known for watching the early-morning news with their coffee."

"So it throws him for a loop. What is the end result?" Kathryn asked. "Am I missing something?"

"I'm not getting it, either," Yoko said.

"So Mr. Sack of Pus gets upset, so what? What does his getting upset do for us?" Nikki asked.

Maggie had a moment of self-doubt. She raked her hands through her hair and stared at the wall. "I guess what I was thinking was he'd get so furious, he'd do something really stupid. Like try to get in touch with Garland, or maybe try to sue her all over again. I know he'll try to do *something*. With Mr. Snowden's leaving us high and dry to help the guys on their mission, we have to do our own snatch. That is not going to be easy. The guy is alert to what's going on. For crying out loud, he has turned into a virtual recluse. A Garland Lee worldwide tour is easily worth a billion dollars. That's gross, of course. If SOP were arranging the tour, he'd be taking his twenty percent right off the top. Then he'd bill hourly for the time he spent, and anything else he could get away with. I'm told by those in the know that if this tour was Garland's 'Farewell

Tour,' it could bring in more than a billion. Remember now, the article will say she is coordinating it herself, so she's saving that twenty percent and the legal fees she would have to be paying out if SOP was running things.

"It was my thinking that he lost out on all those millions from the tour she turned down and fired him over, which resulted in the current lawsuit to recover the money in escrow, and now to lose out again. . . . Well, I figure that when he hears about this new tour, he would go off the deep end."

"That's all well and good, dear, and I think you're right, but, again, to what end? He can't very well sue her again. She's a free agent these days. She can do whatever she wants. Do I have that right, Nikki?"

"You do. Again, Maggie, what stupid thing do you think he'd do once he reads about it?"

Maggie, her hair standing on end, threw her hands in the air until she realized the others couldn't see her. "So I guess what you're saying is I went off the rails here, and my idea out-and-out sucks. Do I have that right?"

"Pretty much, dear," Myra said. "Unless your idea is to make him go insane with jealousy, but that still won't help us, either.

Having said that, I do like the idea of taunting him."

"He'll just rot from the inside out, but we won't see it," Alexis said. "We need to *see* it. Garland needs to *see* it. The firm where he used to work needs to *see* it."

"I don't see its having the effect I think you're hoping for, Maggie, which was that he will be so devastated, he'll just drop the case against Garland Lee," Kathryn said. "Nikki, Alexis, are we right in assuming he can't sue Garland on this proposed tour? The original case has not been settled yet. Won't this be more like an extension of the first one, where he claims she cheated him, and that's why he sued her in the first place?"

"I'm reasonably sure that is correct, but I would have to research it further," Nikki said. "There can always be extenuating circumstances. Like I said, Alexis and I will research the matter."

Maggie heard the doubt in Nikki's voice and pounced on it. "Anyone can sue anyone for anything, right? Doesn't mean they'll win in a court of law. He can bring the case to court himself. Or find a way to get the firm behind him on this. With millions and millions at stake, perhaps Ballard, Ballard, and Quinlan, the name partners, not the firm itself, might take a second look at things and side with him. Money rules here, and if you think otherwise, then you are wrong. It's all about the money."

The room was silent for several minutes before Annie spoke. "I can almost see that happening for some ungodly reason."

An argument ensued, with everyone talking on top of everyone else. The tone was shrill and bombastic. The moment it turned ugly, Annie whistled sharply for order and told everyone to calm down or she was ending the call. "Now, one at a time, speak."

When no one said a word, Annie turned the floor over to Maggie. "What do you want us to do, dear? What do you *see* us doing is more like it?"

"Well, girls, I hate to admit this, but I do not have an answer. That's why I asked for this conference call. I'm just a reporter. You guys are the foot soldiers here. You're still the ones who make it come out right in the end. It seemed like such a good idea when it popped into my head a while ago that I just ran with it. I've always relied on my gut, my instincts, and I did the same thing this time.

"Maybe in the back of my mind, I was thinking we should snatch him ASAP, *before* he could come up with something dastardly to do. We have a decent window of time here. If we grab him now, no one is going to be looking for him. Certainly not his wife — at least for the foreseeable future. It's doubtful his kids will sound an alarm. There's no one left who would care if he took off for the hills. His lawyer, if interested enough, would probably be relieved not having him to deal with," Maggie said.

"There has to be a reason why SOP is holding out. It sounds so open-and-shut to us, and we all heard what went down in the firm's conference room. They want to settle. That pretty much says to me, and I'm no lawyer, that they know they can't win if it comes to a trial. And the only way it does not come to a trial is if Garland does not get a summary judgment in her favor. And if she does, they lose without a trial. Hence the offer to settle.

"It can't just be simple greed on SOP's part. Somewhere in that ugly head of his, he has to have some brains. So why is he holding so firm and not taking the settlement route?" Yoko asked, her tone frustrated.

"Do you mean like perhaps he has a rabbit-in-the-hat kind of thing? If he does, what could it possibly be? Nikki and Alexis have pored over all the legal filings, as did we, and there is nothing there that any of us could see," Annie reminded them.

"Yes, a rabbit-in-the-hat kind of thing. He has something, or thinks he does, that he's waiting to spring at just the right moment," Kathryn said.

"Let's explore that a little further and call it what it is in plain English, *blackmail*. Whom would he blackmail? Certainly not Garland. That leaves the firm. At least to my way of thinking. Did they do something he was privy to and kept quiet about? But if that's the case, whatever it is, he was a party to it. Unless he found out through other means and simply kept quiet because he was a member of the firm, and that's where his share of the partnership profits came from."

"I just had a thought. The listening device is still under the table in the conference room. That means everything that goes on in that room is still being heard by Snowden or his people. I totally forgot about that. Should we try to get it back? We don't have the right to listen to what goes on in that room between clients and the lawyers who represent them," Maggie said.

The others hooted with laughter. "Considering all the laws we break, do you think this is anywhere near the top of the list? We aren't going to do anything with the infor-

191

mation, unless it turns out to involve Mr. SOP. Don't give that another thought, Maggie. You did say the device couldn't be traced back to us, right?" Isabelle said.

"Right. Okay, then. It stays until someone finds it," Maggie said with a lilt in her voice. "Where does all this leave us now?"

"Hold on, everyone! Charles is right here next to Myra and me, and he just said he's getting a text from Avery. Okay, okay, seems Mr. Forrester is finally making some noise in that condo. He's making a phone call. As they say, we're going live here. Avery's operative is listening in on his end of the conversation. Bear in mind she can only hear Mr. Forrester's end of the conversation," Annie said.

Everyone started talking at once, until Annie whistled sharply. "If you all keep talking, I can't concentrate on what Charles is telling me."

The phone lines went silent. The conference room went as silent as a tomb. Maggie twitched in her chair as she nibbled at the cuticle on her thumb. She made a mental note to stop chewing her nails. She'd made the same mental note hundreds of times before, all to no avail. She was a nail nibbler, bottom line.

■ ■ ■ ■

Not so the home office where Arthur Forrester sat behind his desk, his phone to his ear. Sound could be heard, although it was muted from a television tuned to Fox News. Sasha, Avery Snowden's operative, had her cell phone pressed so hard against her ear that she was getting a headache. She listened, her eyes wide, her jaw dropping as she listened to Arthur Forrester's venom directed at the party he'd called.

"I want you to listen to me, Henry. And, yes, I agree it did take some nerve on my part to call you just now, especially after the way we parted company the last time we were all together. I want you to cease and desist on planning to file any lawsuits against me. The reason I say this is that if you don't, I will go to the bar association and file a complaint about your conduct in *Tram* v *Oden.*

"Depending on my frame of mind at the time, I might even throw in Matthew Spicer's name, Tram's star witness, the one you guys dug up out of nowhere. I have the complete file. I copied it and took it with me when I left. Knowing the way you and the senior partners operate, I thought I

193

might need some leverage someday. I guess that someday is here."

Sasha listened intently to the small silence that ensued. She almost jumped out of her skin when she heard Forrester say, "Calling me a scumbag isn't going to change a damn thing. I learned everything I did from the best, you and the other name partners.

"Now this is what I want. So listen up, and listen good, because I am not going to repeat a word of what I'm saying. You drop any and all suits you have the firm drawing up against me. You inform the insurance lawyers you've had a change of heart and want to go to a full trial if the summary judgment does not go Garland Lee's way. Don't for one minute get the idea that this is a negotiation. *It. Is. Not.* I'm going to hang up now, so you can have a discussion with Alvin and Robert. I'll get back to you later this afternoon. And while you're all in discussion mode, you might want to see if you can come up with a few more *star witnesses* for when we go to trial against Garland Lee. I know the firm does not like to lose. Neither do I, Henry. Neither do I." Forrester repeated what he'd just said a second time, to be sure that Henry Ballard was reading him loud and clear.

Sasha blinked, then blinked again, when

she realized the connection was broken. All she could hear were voices on Fox. She rubbed at her throbbing temples. The word *blackmail* swirled around and around inside her head. The boss was going to be absolutely ecstatic when he heard all of this.

Back in the conference room at the *Post,* Maggie continued to nibble on her nails as she waited for Annie to tell them what was happening. Her jaw dropped when Myra said, "I guess we should consider this Mr. Forrester's rabbit in the hat or the smoking gun, whatever you want to call it. He's going to blackmail the firm for something they did or allegedly did. I'm no lawyer, but that 'star witness' comment makes me think the star witness came out of the blue and perjured himself, and Mr. Forrester is privy to that information. Now, having said that, if it's true, we all know where this is going. Garland Lee will lose in court if it ever gets there because the firm will suddenly come up with some magical witnesses who will swear under oath whatever the firm wants them to swear to. Fraudulently so, but a loss is a loss. We promised Garland that would not happen," Myra said.

"Let's move our timetable up and plan for the snatch," Kathryn suggested.

"What about my epiphany and tomorrow's article on Garland?" Maggie asked.

"If you think it will help, dear, then go ahead, but I don't see it doing anything other than putting Mr. Forrester into a rage. I don't see it hurting us in any way whatsoever. So no harm, no foul. And it might also take a little wind out of his sails. Right now, I figure he's thinking he has the firm's senior partners right where he wants them, under his fist. So you might as well go ahead," Annie said. The others agreed.

"Forrester said he's going to be calling Henry Ballard back later this afternoon. I'm wondering if the three partners will go into the conference room to discuss this, or if they'll leave the premises," Nikki said. "Perhaps we should set up another conference call for late afternoon to see if it happens that way. In the meantime, Alexis, see if you can dig up the nitty-gritty on the case of *Tram* v *Oden.* If nothing goes down, we can at least discuss that during the call."

"Good thing we didn't make any plans to remove that listening device," Maggie said. "I'm starting not to have a good opinion of lawyers," she grumbled.

"There's good and bad in everything, Maggie, you know that. How many times have I heard or read about journalists who

196

made up stories to make themselves look good? Look at that TV guy, Brian Williams. That was a hot topic for a while, and now he's back on the air, doing breaking news reporting for one of the cable news channels. The public, as a general rule, is very forgiving. Not so much for lawyers, though," Alexis said. "And bar associations can be totally unforgiving."

The women talked for a few more minutes before the conference call ended, with Maggie's setting up the next one for five-thirty, after the end of the business day, and reminding someone to call Garland Lee to bring her up to date, as they had promised to do.

Maggie sat quietly at the conference table staring at her reflection coming off the highly polished wood. It was so quiet in here. She would be able to hear the proverbial pin drop — if she had a pin to drop.

Silence was not one of her favorite things. Silence offered up too much time to think and wonder. She much preferred noise and chaos, especially if she was the one creating the noise and the chaos.

Maggie let loose with a huge sigh as she heaved herself up from the table and headed back to the newsroom, which was rife with sound.

Intrepid investigative reporter that she was, she was in her element. She was exactly where she belonged.

CHAPTER 10

Henry Ballard felt like he had been kicked in the middle of his gut with a battering ram as he stared at the buzzing phone in his hand, a reminder that the call was over and he needed to hang up the phone. He did, marveling at how steady his hand was. He sat frozen in his custom-crafted ergonomic chair and chewed on his bottom lip. He wondered if he'd ever be able to move again. He also knew that with that one phone call, his life, as he'd known it, was never going to be the same again.

His mind moved then at warp speed. Fifty years he'd dedicated his life to the law, to this firm, fighting injustice every single day of those fifty years.

Fifty years! And now, with one phone call, it could all be washed down the drain. By one man! A cockroach of a man. All because of one mistake.

No, no, that's wrong. It wasn't a mistake.

He and the partners had deliberately done things they shouldn't have. *Guilty as charged by the cockroach.*

Henry Ballard was many things. The one thing he wasn't was a fool. "I did it, I own it," he muttered under his breath. It didn't help his thought processes when he recalled how Alvin and Robert had jumped on board immediately. But only because he had asked them. This was smack-dab on his doorstep, and he knew in his gut that both men would remind him of that fact.

What was the admonition he'd used back then to intimidate them into agreeing with his proposal? *Ah, yes . . . "Either you're a team player or not. If you're not, it's time to walk out the door."* Neither of them had walked out the door.

Henry let his gaze circle the opulent office until his eyes came to rest on his old-fashioned Rolodex. He spun the wheel until he came to the *S*'s, flipping the cards until he saw the name *Matthew Spicer,* along with his address and phone number. He removed the card and placed it carefully in the middle of his desk. He stared at it with loathing.

His star witness in the *Tram* v *Oden* lawsuit. Bought and paid for. A brand-new Jaguar and one hundred thousand in cash.

That was the day, Henry recalled, when he sold his soul to the Devil.

Henry almost jumped out of his skin when his phone shrilled. He really needed to get someone in here to make it buzz or chime. He pressed a button on the console to hear his secretary of thirty years telling him that he had a call from a Matthew Spicer. Did he want to take the call or return it later on?

"Put Mr. Spicer through," he said in a steady voice that surprised him. *Talk about timing. Unbelievable.* Forrester was clicking on all cylinders.

"Mr. Ballard, this is Matthew Spicer. I was wondering if you had time to speak to me. Outside the office. I just received a very . . . um . . . unsettling phone call from one of your firm's former partners. At least that's what he said over the phone when he identified himself. He asked to meet me and said he would make it worth my while. What's going on, Mr. Ballard? You assured me, swore to me . . . this would never, ever come up. I believed you and your partners. It looks to me from where I'm standing that rather than never coming up again, it is now front and center. So where would you like to meet?" Spicer asked, his tone belligerent.

Henry Ballard's mind raced as his stomach muscles tightened into a hard knot. Instead of responding to the question, he asked one of his own. "This caller, does he have a name?"

"Of course he has a name. I don't know if it's an alias or not, but he said his name was Arthur Forrester. He wants to meet tomorrow morning at a Starbucks in midtown D.C. He said he'd call me when he got into the city and give me the exact location. Listen, this guy knows everything there is to know about me. He knows where I goddamn live, Henry! He had my home phone number, and he has my cell phone number also."

Henry Ballard's mind continued to race. "Where are you now?"

"Here at my condo. In case you forgot, I give music lessons here six days a week."

"How long will it take you to cancel your students, say, for the next six months? How long will it take you to get in touch with your landlord, pay six months in advance, and take care of all your business as if you are going on a sabbatical for six months?"

"A few hours tops. Is this that serious?"

"I'm afraid so, Mr. Spicer. Can you have your bags packed and be ready to go by late this afternoon?"

"Depends on where you think I'm going.

I do not have a robust bank account. I used the money you paid me to buy my condo, but I still have a mortgage. I have to pay garage rental plus utilities. Are you prepared to take care of all that?" His tone lost none of its belligerence.

"Yes. How would you like to live in Maui, Hawaii, for the next six months? The firm has a house there that we use on occasion to entertain special clients. No one knows about it, but the name partners. It's right on the ocean, if you like water. There will be no cost to you, and it comes with a housekeeper and caretaker. There is also an Audi in the garage you can use. We can discuss this when we meet later this afternoon. When you do come to meet us, have your bags with you, as you will be leaving our meeting and heading for the airport. Disconnect your home phone. Contact your mobile carrier and get a new number. Can you do all of what I've just outlined?"

"It doesn't look like I have much of a choice, now, do I? The way I see it, either I agree, or I go to jail. Along with you and your partners. I also want it understood that I am not blackmailing you. Yes, it's all doable. I want it understood that when I get back, and if my students have found other teachers, that you will compensate me."

"Yes, of course. The word *blackmail* never entered my mind, Mr. Spicer. You helped us out when we needed you. We will take care of you now. In the meantime, if your caller should call again, do not answer the phone. Agreed?"

"Agreed. Where do you want to meet and when? Please give me a precise time?"

"Café Davino, five o'clock. I'll have your plane ticket with me. Thank you for calling me, Mr. Spicer."

"I wish I could say it was my pleasure, but it isn't a pleasure at all. I'll see you at five o'clock," Matthew Spicer said before he ended the call.

Henry Ballard dropped his head into his hands. At that moment in time, he knew that he was capable of killing. He wanted nothing more than to choke the life out of Arthur Forrester. He sat that way for ten solid minutes until he had his breathing under control and the knot in his stomach had dissipated. Then he sent off two in-house e-mails to Alvin and Robert, asking them to come to his office ASAP.

All it took was five minutes on the clock for Alvin Ballard and Robert Quinlan to appear in Henry Ballard's office. "Follow me," he said. "We're going to the conference room. What I have to tell you has to be said in a soundproof room." With that said, Henry led the way out of the office and down the hall to the conference room where he and the partners had met with Annie and Maggie and, later on, with Arthur and Nala Forrester.

Inside, he headed for his seat at the head of the table, then changed his mind. "Lock the door and sit down, please." The next thing Henry did was to press a button to tell his secretary he was not to be disturbed and to hold all his calls. He looked at his two senior partners, hating the look of alarm he was seeing on their faces, a look that he knew would turn to one of outright panic the moment he shared what was going on. He motioned for both men to head to the far corner of the room, to the seating area reserved for clients when discussions got too intense at the big table and a break was called for. He felt sick to his stomach when he sat down.

"For God's sake, Henry, what is it? You look like you've just seen a ghost, and it has you by the hand," Robert said.

"I have," Henry said before he brought both of the name partners up to date. When he was nearly finished talking, he ended with, "Let's not do the blame game here. That's over and done with. I think what I came up with will work, but I am not one hundred percent sure. I think Matthew Spicer will be as good as his word. If Arthur can't find him, there's nothing he can do. Everything he threatened hinges on Matthew Spicer's being available as a witness to what we did. Now, aside from us dropping all suits against Arthur, do we give him what he wants or do we fight him? He's going to be calling back. We need a solid plan here, boys."

Henry was not totally surprised when there were no recriminations from his senior partners. Still, he felt only relief. "I say we fight, but you have to agree. We can't let this bastard blackmail us like this. If we do, it will never end till he has bled us dry. Arthur Forrester is a son of a bitch whose greed knows no bounds. We all know how that works. Look at what he tried to pull off with Garland Lee."

"Are we absolutely sure we can count on Matthew Spicer?" Alvin asked.

"As sure as I can be at this point in time. If the monetary reward is sufficient, I think he will stay true. He hasn't gouged us and was content with his original payout. He has every right to look out for his own skin. We need to make it worth his while to stay loyal. We can pay him out of our own pockets. Six months in Hawaii is a dream come true for him. This thing, whatever happens, should be over in six months, one way or the other. He'll go back to his old life, pick up new students if his old ones leave. If that doesn't happen, we will continue to subsidize him. It's only fair." The two other partners stared at Henry hard and long before they nodded their approval.

"Robert, call Maui, alert Consuela that she is going to have a guest for the next six months and to treat him like royalty. I'll call Marta to arrange a first-class ticket to the big island for Mr. Spicer. He can take the puddle jumper from there to Maui. Alvin, arrange for certified checks so he doesn't have a problem once he's settled in. He's going to be taking care of his end today and will leave as though he's going on a sabbatical. Arthur will check, and that's what he will be told. I'm thinking a hundred thousand each."

"Does Arthur know about the house in Hawaii?" Robert asked.

"No one knows about that property but the three of us, our accountants, and the very few people we've had stay there over the years," Henry said.

"What if Arthur checks with the airlines?" Alvin asked.

"They do not give out that information, you know that," Henry said testily. "I grant you, he will almost certainly do a lot of blustering and blathering, but in the end, he'll be forced to give up on Mr. Spicer. That's not to say he still won't make waves and a lot of noise. So what we have to decide right now is, are we going to drop the suits we threatened him with?"

Alvin and Robert both said they were okay with that end of it, but they still wanted to pursue realistic settlement talks with Garland Lee and still go to trial if the talks fell through. "Perhaps that will show him we're being reasonable, but not the pushovers he was hoping for," Henry stated.

The three men stared at each other across the round table, which was littered with magazines. "I'm not going to let this firm go to hell because of Arthur Forrester," Henry said. "Our blood, sweat, and tears are tied up in this firm. We made one mistake. Just one, and, yes, we never should have gone down that road, but we did. We own it. We did our best to make it right during the following years, but we need to be honest — it was too late. We are guilty as hell, and no amount of money can change that."

"Then I guess we should get a move on it

and do what we have to do," Robert Quinlan said. "Wipe those sad-sack looks off
your faces. We'll get that bastard yet.

"I have an idea, so let's get the ball rolling
and order in some lunch. We'll eat right here
in the conference room. I have a bottle of
fifty-year-old scotch one of my clients gave
me for a job well done. I say we drink it up
with our lunch."

"Works for me," Henry said with no en-
thusiasm.

"Yes, that will work," Alvin said.

There was no backslapping, no handshak-
ing, because all three men knew it wasn't
all right, and that things would never again
be all right because they'd crossed the line
and had been found out. Now it was time
to pay the piper.

Twenty blocks away as the crow flies, Eileen
Mellencamp felt like her eardrums were going to explode at what she was hearing in
the conference room at Ballard, Ballard &
Quinlan. To think that one little gizmo no
bigger than a dime could give her all this
information was amazing. She quickly
uploaded everything and sent it flying
through cyberspace to Avery Snowden,
who, in turn, sent it flying to Charles Martin at Pinewood, who, in turn, summoned

Myra and Annie to listen to the firm's name partners' conversation.

It was Annie who clucked her tongue, and said, "In the words of Jack Emery, 'I did not see that coming.' " The others agreed.

"We have to tell everyone else. What time did Maggie say she wanted to have the conference call?" Myra asked.

"She said late this afternoon. But I think we should wait till after the partners meet with Mr. Spicer at Café Davino. We need to alert Avery so he can have his people at the café. We'll want pictures and, if possible, dialogue. He needs to have the café surveilled to see if it's even possible. I'm sure he can come up with something. The man has every listening device known to man, and some that aren't, at his fingertips."

"I'll do it," Fergus said as he tapped out a text to the superspy. "It's short notice, but he's been known to work magic for us before. Let's hope he can do it again."

"Find out who it is who will be following Mr. Forrester tomorrow, once he leaves his condo. Will it be Sasha or a male operative? Let's all remember that she has the key to Mr. Forrester's condo. If we take the last shuttle out tonight, we can stay overnight, and as soon as he leaves for the city, we can go in and wait for him to get back and do our snatch. When he gets back, he's going to be like a wet cat on a hot griddle," Myra said.

"I'm all for that," Annie said, smacking her hands together in anticipation. "We can talk to the girls when we have our conference call later on."

"I think you're forgetting something, Annie. The roads are flooded, and you will not be able to get to the airport," Charles said as he looked out the kitchen window. "The rain has stopped and is headed up that way. It's possible Forrester will get stuck in the city if Washington gets as much rain as we've gotten."

Annie grimaced. "Then we're right back to square one and a midnight entry at some point. What is Avery saying? What's taking so long, Fergus?"

"Patience, love. Avery is one man. He's doing the best he can on such short notice, especially since he is not in Washington now."

"If Avery were a woman, it would have been done five minutes ago," Annie snapped. Myra's head bobbed up and down to show she agreed with Annie. Fergus sighed heavily; he knew better than to argue because he could never win. Charles was suddenly busy banging pots and pans and getting nowhere fast.

"Tell him to speed it up," Myra said coldly. "We don't have all day." Charles dropped a heavy pot on the tile floor at his wife's tone. He absolutely hated it when his beloved got testy like this. He, too, sighed as he set about washing the pot.

"All right, Avery said he's got it covered. He will have a three-man detail set up at Café Davino by five o'clock. As well as a two-female backup. He said the feedback he's getting is that it is raining heavily, which indicates there probably won't be many diners. As a reminder to you, Avery is in Delaware with the boys."

"I'm bearing that in mind, Fergus. The man left us flat to scurry off to aid the boys. That little decision is going to cost him dearly on the next go-round. We are not chopped liver here. You might want to clue him in, or we can do it ourselves in case our message gets lost in your translation, *dear,*" Annie said, a bite in her tone. Fergus sighed again as he tapped out another text. Charles continued to scrub the pot in his hands, which didn't need scrubbing, for it already sparkled like a diamond.

Both men's shoulders sagged in relief when Myra motioned for Annie to follow her into the sunroom and out of earshot of their significant others.

"This is not good, Charles," Fergus whispered. "We gave Avery permission to go to Delaware to help the boys."

"No, mate, it is not," Charles said as he dried the gleaming pot in his hands.

In the sunroom, where there was not an iota of sun, Myra started to pace. "I hate this feeling of being marooned way out here on the farm. I hate feeling helpless."

Annie held up her iPhone. "We can still communicate with the outside world. We know what we know, so let's spread the word. Why wait for a conference call? I'll start with Maggie. I want to see what she's written for tomorrow's edition. That fact alone could change what goes down in the morning with Mr. SOP. Once he sees the morning edition, I think he's going to go flat-out berserk. What do you think, Myra?"

"I agree. The . . . um . . . men seem to have forgotten about that, which just goes to prove, yet once again, that women are the superior force. I'll call Yoko to see how she made out at the nursery with all the plants and this heavy rain."

Lady appeared in the doorway and woofed softly, a signal she needed to go out. Her offspring behind her, they formed a parade to the back door. Annie motioned for Myra to go ahead, that she would make the calls.

Myra opened the kitchen door, and admonished her charges, "Don't go in the mud, don't roll over in the water, and make it quick!" Lady looked up at her as much as to say, *Seriously, Mom?* In spite of herself, Myra laughed. "Go!"

Ten minutes later, Myra opened the door and stood aside for the stampede. "You know the drill. Go into the laundry room, and I'll dry you off. Then you get the treat." The dogs obediently did as they were told and suffered through the brisk rubdown. They waited for the words that would signal the treat was forthcoming. "Okay, guys, we are good to go. Five greenies coming up!"

Back in the sunroom, Myra was happy to see the smile on Annie's face as she read whatever she was seeing on her phone. When she ended the call, she looked at Myra and said, "Maggie did a good job. She said she had just finished when I called. Earlier, she sent Garland the rough draft, which she approved. I think it is safe to say Mr. SOP is going to pee green when he sees it tomorrow morning. Then, when he gets into the city and calls Mr. Spicer to find out he's flown the coop, he is going to pitch a fit. It's anyone's guess what he'll do at that point. Don'cha love it, Myra?" Annie exclaimed exuberantly.

"I do, I do. What do you think he'll do, Annie?"

"Well, for starters, after he sees the morning paper, he is going to be one angry man at all the money he could have had and lost. That's going to make him crazy. He'll be in a real state by the time he gets into the city, only to find out his secret weapon is nothing more than wishful thinking. So he'll head back home to plot and scheme some more. That would be my guess. I don't think he'll go to the firm. What would be the point? Without Mr. Spicer, all he has are empty threats that will get him nowhere. Is that how you see it, Myra?"

Myra nodded. "Too bad we aren't in the blackmail business. With everything we know, we could make a killing here." Myra laughed. "Weather permitting, I think we should plan on heading to Riverville later tomorrow afternoon. We either do the snatch tomorrow night or the following night. We really should put it to a vote. Are you okay with doing that, Annie?"

"Should we take the shuttle or should we take the *Post* van? Personally, I think we should take the van, since we're all going to be in attendance. We can switch up the license plates. Maggie knows how to do all that. We have a bunch of them in back of the van for . . . um . . . such things. We also have a box of magnetic decals. You just never know who is going to remember what. Some little old lady walking her dog might remember a white van with out-of-state plates, yada yada yada.

"Once we snatch him, we change the plates and the decals, and we're good to go. It's always worked before for us, so there is no reason to think it won't work again. Let's just think positive," Annie said, her eyes sparkling with the thought of the coming action.

"Avery's nose is going to be out of joint when he finds out we're doing this without his okay and his expertise," Myra said.

"He should have thought about that before he left us hanging to go to Delaware. He needs to know who is in charge here. I think he forgets sometimes," Annie snapped again. Suddenly she was feeling meaner than a junkyard dog.

"Reminders are good sometimes," Myra said, laughing.

"Of course, there is still that pesky problem of disposing of . . . what I mean is *relocating* . . . the package. Meaning Mr. SOP. That's spook speak, Myra. The package is another name for Mr. SOP."

"I get it, Annie. The plan is to snatch him, bring him here to the farm, and put him down in the dungeon. We don't need Avery for that. We can keep him forever in that cell we outfitted, if we want to. When we get tired of playing with him, we can tell Avery he's all his. By that time, Mr. Snowden will know better than to trifle with us."

"Myra, I just love and adore you when you think like that," Annie gushed. Myra beamed at Annie's effusive praise.

"Let's join the gentlemen in the kitchen. Charles should be done scrubbing that pot by now, and he and Fergus will both be looking to do something nice for us, like serving up that apple pie he baked earlier. Fergus made some ice cream in that fancy-dancy ice-cream maker you bought at Target last month. A good cup of coffee and pie à la mode might make me almost agreeable. What do you say, pal?"

Myra linked her arm with Annie's. "I think that's the second-best idea you've had all day, pal. And I'm really hungry."

Lady and her pups got up and followed the two women into the kitchen, because the kitchen was where the treats were.

CHAPTER 11

Café Davino wasn't exactly a landmark, but it was close to it if you counted all the years the Mongellos had operated their Italian eatery. Fifty long years of serving, with cheerful smiles, good Italian food, cooked by four different generations of Mongellos, constituted landmark status in the ever-changing restaurant scene in the nation's capital.

Natives to the area swore you could smell the garlic and cheese a block away. Tourists grumbled and complained because they couldn't get near the eatery to sample what was reputed to be the best Italian food in all of Washington, D.C.

There was nothing glamorous or upscale about Café Davino, which was little more than a hole-in-the-wall. It had all of twelve tables, which seated four to a table. A tiny counter with two stools for single diners completed the seating. On any given day, the Mongellos could turn the evening tables over at least four times starting at four o'clock, with the last diners being seated at nine o'clock. Lunch turned over three times.

The décor was simple, almost rustic, with red-checkered tablecloths, empty green Chianti bottles hanging from the rafters, the rattan chairs more duct tape than rattan, and sawdust on the floor. Napkins, along with containers of hot pepper flakes and grated cheese, graced every table. There were also the obligatory artificial flowers along the shelves that lined the walls and painted murals of long-ago Italy. In one corner stood an Italian flag, and next to it was the American flag.

The menu was simple and hadn't changed in the fifty years that the restaurant had been around. Diners were given exactly two daily choices, and that was it. Everyone knew what it was because it never changed. The eatery was known for its soft, yeasty, melt-in-your-mouth garlic twists, which were in the ovens by seven o'clock every morning. And that was the main reason the restaurant didn't open till 11:00 A.M. It took a long time to bake the delectable treats, which could also be bought by the dozen.

Today the dinner choices were lasagna,

with a side of meatballs, or shrimp scampi, with a side of spaghetti. Of course, there were also the garlic twists, which came six to a table. If you wanted more, you had to pay extra. No one complained, and everyone ordered more. Dessert was cannolis. And, of course, good, old, rich Italian coffee and espresso with which to wash it all down.

Seating time was ninety minutes. If you weren't finished by then, courteous waiters and waitresses, the Mongellos' offspring, appeared at your table with a take-home bag. It wasn't a subtle hint; it was a flat-out, time-to-go reminder. Again, no one ever complained.

The moment Matthew Spicer stepped out of the Town Car he'd engaged to take him to the airport, he swooned at the tantalizing aromas swirling around him. For years, he'd heard about the restaurant, but this was the first time he was going to eat there. At least he had assumed he was going to eat there when Henry Ballard had extended the invitation. He hoped he wasn't wrong.

With his bags in the trunk of the Town Car, Matthew instructed the driver to find a place to park and said he would text him when he was ready to be picked up.

Matthew made a mad dash to the front

door, but still managed to get soaked in the driving rain. The moment he opened the door, delicious aromas assailed his senses. He nearly swooned. A young girl, with rosy cheeks and sparkling dark eyes, handed him a pristine white towel to wipe his face and hair. She whisked it away the moment he handed it over. "I'm meeting some people here," he said as he stretched his neck to look into the small dining room.

He saw the law partners huddled around the table in the very back of the room. It wasn't crowded yet, with just three other tables filled with diners. Three young men dressed in jeans, sneakers, and ball caps, who looked like they had hearty appetites, and a table with two giggling girls, who looked like students and took turns eyeing the blackboard menu and the three studly-looking guys across from them. All the young people were drinking beer by the pitcher.

"Your hosts are waiting for you in the far corner," the rosy-cheeked girl said. "Just follow me." He did so, to the soft strains of Dean Martin singing some Italian ditty, which seemed to be coming from the kitchen.

Hands were shaken, and Matthew was told to sit. "We ordered for you, since you do not have all that much time to make it to the airport. We factored in the weather. You'll make it on time." Without further ado, Henry Ballard handed over a thin manila envelope. "First-class tickets to Hawaii. You'll change planes in San Francisco. You have only a one-hour layover. We took the liberty of writing out instructions. You'll land in Honolulu and take the puddle jumper to Maui. When you land in Maui, the caretaker will meet you. We've included three cashier checks in the amount of one hundred thousand dollars each. You will not have any expenses other than gas for the Audi. If you want to take ukulele instructions, you will pay for them yourself. We included the name of an excellent teacher, Tomas Aiola. Do you have any questions?"

"A dozen or so, but I can't think of one right this minute." All Matthew wanted to do was grab a handful of the garlic twists and shove them into his mouth, knowing full well he would reek of garlic for days. He didn't care.

"We want your assurances you will not be contacting anyone on the mainland, Mr. Spicer. I am, of course, referring to family, friends, and perhaps a lady friend. What backstory did you come up with?"

Matthew chewed the tiny garlic twist and

wiped at his lips. "The only family I have is a brother, who lives in Barcelona. We send Christmas cards, but that's pretty much our only contact. I only have two close friends, and both know about my brother. I told them I was going to stay with him for six months to help out because of some back surgery he just had. I was in a relationship, but it ended over the holidays. She wanted to get married, and I didn't. I told my neighbor, the only person on my floor I have contact with, the same story. My mail, such as it is, will be held for me at the post office. I do mostly everything online. I paid ahead for the garage fees, car insurance, utilities, and my mortgage. I literally cleaned out my bank account. My balance, in case you want to know, was a little under seven thousand dollars."

"When you get to Maui, you can open a bank account at the Royal Hawaiian Bank. You will be able to draw on your funds immediately, once you deposit the cashier checks. We allowed for a possible snafu and included five thousand in cash in small bills. I think we covered everything. To your mind's eye, did we forget anything?"

"No, I don't think so. I'd really like to know what's going on, Mr. Ballard."

Alvin Ballard cleared his throat, and said,

"We discussed this among ourselves, and we think it best if you don't know what's going on. Do not take that the wrong way, please. We want you to feel safe, and you will be safe if you play by the rules we laid out and follow our instructions. We have your back, and this will be put to rest very shortly. You need to believe us when we tell you that nothing at all will happen to you. Who knows? Perhaps you will fall in love with Hawaii and decide to relocate on a permanent basis. Are you comfortable with our assurances?"

Matthew Spicer looked at the three men across the table for a full minute before he nodded. "Who is this Arthur Forrester?"

"Not anyone you want to know, Mr. Spicer. Let's leave it at that," Robert Quinlan said. "Oh, here comes our food. Dig in, Mr. Spicer, and savor every mouthful so you can dream about it while you're eating pineapple in Hawaii and sipping on exotic drinks with little umbrellas."

Sixty minutes later, stuffed to the gills, Matthew Spicer stood up, shook his hosts' hands, and left the Café Davino with the manila folder clasped tightly in one hand. He didn't look back.

If he had taken a moment to do so, he would have seen the two tables of young people ignoring their dinners in favor of frantic texting. Nor did he pay any attention to the two giggling girls, who exited the restaurant right after he did. He did, however, notice them as he climbed into the Town Car, which had pulled to the curb. Just two girls out for an early dinner before they returned to their dorm to crack their books.

Back in the bustling dining room, where the three young men were still texting faster than lightning, with their dinners, now cold, sitting on their plates, Henry Ballard said, "I think that went well." He fished around in his wallet, looking for his black American Express card. He handed it over to the waiter, his gaze raking the customers. The place had filled up while they were eating, and he hadn't even noticed. Even the two single seats at the tiny bar counter were now occupied. Everyone was on their cell phones, tapping out messages. At least three of the people who were doing the tapping had already been seated when he and his partners had entered the café. Obviously, the two young women who had been there had left, for a waiter was busily clearing the table. He thought it odd that the dinner plates being cleared were still full, and the pitcher of beer looked like it had not been

225

touched. Strange, but not his concern. He wondered what would happen if, suddenly, cyberspace crashed. A massive meltdown for certain.

It was 6:20 P.M. when the three partners exited their favorite restaurant. Henry did notice at first that the three young men were right behind them. It was crowded under the long, narrow canopy that stretched almost to the street. And when he did notice them, he saw that none of the three carried a take-home box. He thought that was strange.

As the three partners waited for their driver to pull up, Henry reacted to the uneasy feeling he was experiencing. He turned to the three young men, and asked, "So, guys, how did you like your dinner? This was our first time here, and we all liked it," he added chattily.

Momentarily taken aback by the question, the tallest of the trio spoke up. "Best food in Washington by far. We come here at least twice a week. You get a lot of bang for your buck, and the owners are supernice. I'm stuffed, I can tell you that." His two friends bobbed their heads up and down to show that they were in agreement.

"Indeed," Henry said. He looked out into the street so as not to give away the fact

226

that he knew that the young man was lying through his teeth. His stomach tied itself in a knot. He knew in that instant that he and his partners, as well as Matthew Spicer, had been spied upon throughout their dinner together. He grappled with his thoughts as to the *how* and the *why* of it just as the company car slid to the curb. He was the last to climb into the backseat. "Take us back to the office, please, Stephen," he told the driver. His partners looked at him, but they said nothing. Company rule was never to discuss anything in the car that you didn't want to come back to bite you on the ass.

Since it was the senior partners' own rule, the men all settled back to discuss the rain, which was coming down in torrents. They were still talking monsoons and tsunamis as they took the elevator to their floor and strode to the conference room.

The second the door was closed and locked behind them, Henry let loose. "I would absolutely bet the rent on the fact that we were under surveillance this evening at the restaurant." He rattled on, hating the expressions he was seeing on his partners' faces. "I am as much a Neanderthal as the two of you are, but I'm betting one of the five young people who were there when we

227

arrived, the three guys and the two girls, had some kind of listening device, and that they overheard our conversation with Matthew Spicer."

Robert Quinlan loosened his tie and ran his fingers through his hair. "Henry, are you basing all you've said on the fact that they didn't eat their dinners and didn't have take-home bags with them when they left? Or did you see something else? The only thing I noticed was that the two giggling girls left right after Spicer did."

"The tall fellow lied to Henry when he said he was stuffed. How could he be stuffed if he didn't eat his dinner?" Alvin asked as he, too, jerked at his tie. He ripped it off and stuffed it in his pocket. "Should we alert Mr. Spicer? If all you say is true, whom do we blame? Arthur Forrester?"

"And give Spicer a coronary! I don't think so. For some reason, I don't think Arthur Forrester is behind this. That is if I'm even right. Let's think about this. How would Arthur know where we were going for dinner? Matthew had no other contact with Arthur, if he was telling us the truth, and he had no reason to lie. Especially to us. Of course, maybe I'm wrong."

Alvin Ballard, the most cautious and most methodical of the three partners, shook his head. "I don't think you're wrong, Henry. I tend to agree that Arthur doesn't have the chutzpah to pull off something like this. Besides, they were already seated when we arrived. So they couldn't have followed Matthew. Unless there is a sixth person hiding in the bushes somewhere. Which brings us back to the question of who knew where we were going. The answer is no one except the three of us and Matthew Spicer. Robert himself called to make the reservation. If my memory serves me right, we never discussed any of this outside of this room. Is that how you two see it?"

"Exactly," Henry said.

Robert threw his hands in the air. "This is the safest room in the building. Nothing can be overheard in here. I don't even know if this particular conference room has been used by anyone since Arthur was here with his wife. Except for the three of us."

"Unless it's bugged," Henry snarled.

"Did you just say what I think you said?" Alvin snarled in return. "Impossible! No one comes in here, just the staff and the clients. None of them have any skin in this game, so why would someone bug it?"

"Unless Arthur did it himself when he was in here with his wife. Maybe she did it? It did get a little testy there when she stood up to him. Our eyes were on her and what was going down between the two of them. Or he could have done it when she went into her *tirade,* for want of a better word," Robert suggested.

Henry scratched at the stubble on his cheeks. "Actually, there were some other people in this conference room, aside from staff and clients. Remember Countess de Silva's lawyer and the reporter from the *Post* were here. It was our idea to bring them to this particular conference room. Although why they would do something like that is beyond strange, to my way of thinking. They had no idea we would be speaking in here. I think we can rule them out and concentrate on Arthur and his wife. There is a real possibility it was all a plan on their part, create a diversion to distract us, and he plants a listening device."

Instantly the three partners moved as one. They pushed their chairs back from the table and dropped to their knees. "It's dark under here. We need a flashlight or something," Robert groused. "I don't even know what a listening device looks like."

"Just feel around. They're usually small, no bigger than a nickel. They have adhesive on the back. I saw that once on a television show," Henry said.

"I see something. Yeah, yeah, it's a little circle. Right where Arthur was sitting. He was across from us, remember? Okay, I got it. Stubborn little bugger. Good suction or good adhesive. Ah . . . I got it!" Alvin chortled.

The partners backed out from under the table and scrambled to their knees. They watched as Alvin dropped the little circle on the table like it was a white-hot coal. They all leaned forward to stare at the innocent-looking circle that had the power to ruin all three of their careers. No one spoke. All they could do was stare. Henry was the first to move over to the bar sink. He filled a glass with water, carried it back to the conference table, picked up the little circle, and dropped it into the glass.

The beautifully appointed conference room suddenly turned ugly and claustrophobic, thick with fear.

Henry sat down gingerly. He removed his glasses and massaged his temples. All he could think of was fifty years of trying to make things better in the legal world was all for naught, thanks to Arthur Forrester.

"What's our next move?" Robert asked nervously.

"I don't think we have a next move. That privilege goes to Arthur," Alvin replied.

"We're at his mercy right now. We wait for him to get in touch with us. It's all we can do," Henry said, putting his glasses back on. "I suggest we all go home and pick up tomorrow. Right now, I can't think clearly."

"What do we do with . . . *this*?" Robert asked, pointing to the glass holding the little black circle.

"Flush it," Henry said.

"Maybe we shouldn't do that. We might need it as proof or evidence if this gets away from us," Alvin said. "There might be a way for some forensic people to figure out who was listening on the other end. I say we keep it, just in case."

"I have a metal tin with some Altoids in it. I'll fetch it, and we can put the thing in there, close it, and forget about it for the time being," Alvin said.

"Sounds good, Alvin. Go get the tin," Henry said.

"Who has the pleasure of keeping this little gem?" Robert asked.

"Just stick it in an envelope, write our names on it, seal it, and put it in the safe," Henry said.

Ten minutes later, all three partners were in the parking garage and headed to their own cars for the drive home through the pouring rain. There were no good-byes, no handshakes, no claps on the back. The simple truth was that none of the three wanted to look at the other two.

They did, however, give airy backhand waves high in the air as they separated to go to their individual cars.

Their thoughts, however, were the same: *Tomorrow is another day.*

CHAPTER 12

Arthur Forrester paced the long, narrow kitchen, a glass of iced tea, which tasted like dishwater flavored with vanilla, in his hand. Tea he'd made himself. He whipped around the center island, the tea sloshing out of the glass onto the floor. He ignored the spill and let his gaze go to the clock on the stove — 4:49. Time to call Ballard, Ballard & Quinlan. He took another gulp of the tea, wishing that Nala had made it. He didn't miss her at all, but he did miss some of the things she did, like making tasty iced tea. She always made sure there was an extra pitcher, full to the rim, in the fridge. She even took the time to make ice cubes out of the tea so the tea wouldn't taste watered down.

Arthur set down the glass, which was sticky to the touch. He wiped his hand on the leg of his khaki pants before he picked up the receiver on the landline. He pressed in the digits of the firm and waited. When the receptionist announced the firm's name, Arthur identified himself and asked to be put through to Henry Ballard.

The cheerful voice on the other end of the line said, "I'm sorry, Mr. Forrester, but Mr. Ballard has left for the day. Would you like to leave a message on his voice mail?"

"No. Then put me through to Alvin or Robert, please."

"I'm sorry, Mr. Forrester, but they're also gone for the day. The senior partners left together fifteen minutes ago. Are you sure you don't want to leave a message?"

Arthur didn't bother to respond. Instead, he slammed down the phone and cursed under his breath. The bastards weren't taking him seriously. If they had, they'd be sitting in Henry's office, waiting for his promised call. Now what was he to do? Obviously, he needed to fall back and regroup. He headed for his office, the sticky glass of foul-tasting tea still in his hand.

Outside, in her car, Sasha Quantrell called Avery Snowden to report what she'd just heard. He, in turn, called Charles, who informed Annie and Myra, who immediately sent out texts to the sisters and Maggie, to keep them current.

Maggie sighed as she gathered up her

belongings into a neat pile. Her plan was to wait in the office until the next update on the law firm's partners and someone named Matthew Spicer. By then, the locally flooded streets should be safe enough to travel home. In the meantime, to pass away the time, she headed for the kitchen to see what she could scrounge up in the way of food. She carried a paperback novel with her, just in case she was unsuccessful in the food department.

Arthur Forrester looked at the bedside clock. He didn't think he'd slept more than twenty minutes after he climbed into bed. The digital clock said 5:30. He got up and headed for the shower. A shave was out of the question. His face was still red and raw, and his day-old stubble itched. He took a second to wonder what his blood pressure was. Well, after today, if his pressure was still high, it would come down when he settled things with his old firm.

Forrester stepped into the steaming shower, danced around as he lathered up, doing his best not to get his face wet. He made quick work of the shower, stepped out, and vigorously toweled himself off. He wiped the steam from the vanity mirror and winced at the condition of his face. He dabbed on two different prescription ointments. He dressed in his last pair of pressed khakis, along with a pristine white button-down shirt. As he peered at himself in the mirror, he made a mental note to take a trip to the dry cleaner, something Nala had always taken care of. As much as he hated the thought, he was going to have to apply the special blend of makeup his dermatologist had made up for him. He convinced himself that if he wore a ball cap, with the bill pulled low, and sunglasses, no one would stare at him. He didn't know why he cared, but he did. Vanity was the only thing he could come up with.

Unable to look at himself any longer, he quickly closed his eyes and brushed his teeth. His thoughts all over the map, Forrester left the bathroom and headed for the kitchen to make his morning coffee. In his opinion, there was nothing better than a good cup of coffee and the morning paper. Even if he read it online. No matter what else was going on. Today was a perfect example.

While he waited for the coffee to drip into the pot, Forrester leaned against the sink to stare out at the heavy rain battering the kitchen window. He absolutely, totally detested rainy days. Rainy days depressed him. A rainy day was for ducks. He wondered where that thought had come from. He felt a shiver course through his body. His second thought was that it was going to be one hell of a ride through the rain to the train station. Something else he had to deal with. The last plop of the coffee was like music to his ears.

Forrester filled his cup and carried it back to his office, where he turned on his computer. He waited patiently while it booted up. The time flashed on the bottom of the computer screen: 7:10. He clicked the keys, and his home page came up. He clicked again until he saw the large black headline on the front page of the *Sentinel.* He blinked, sucked air into his lungs, and held his breath until he grew light-headed. In a million years, he could never have anticipated what he was seeing. Especially today, of all days. His stomach roiled and his heart fluttered as bile rose in his throat. He fought to keep it down. He broke out into a cold sweat. *Shit on a shingle!* Now he was going to have to reapply the medical makeup. He swore then — every dirty, filthy word he'd ever heard in his seventy years of life. When he had exhausted all the words he knew, he made up more as he raced through the text on the *Sentinel*'s front page. Frenzied, he exited the article and clicked on the *New York Times.* Garland Lee smiled at him from his computer monitor.

Forrester bit down on his bottom lip. He fought with himself not to put his fist through his computer. He pushed his swivel chair backward with such force, the chair hit the wall. If he had not been gripping the armrests, he would have catapulted and bounced forward into the monitor, either cracking it or his head. As it was, whiplash was not out of the question. He struggled with his breathing. He dropped his head between his knees and took deep breaths. It seemed to take forever to get his breathing under control.

What he'd just seen was nothing more than a blip. A small bump in the road. Water under the proverbial bridge. Once Henry Ballard, the other name partners, and the firm got in line, it wasn't going to mean a damn thing. Once Henry fell into line, he'd own Garland Lee's tour. He took it one step further and told himself he would *own* Garland Lee. *Period. End of story.* He turned off his computer with a wild flourish.

Forrester looked into his coffee cup, surprised to see that it was empty. He made his way back to the kitchen. He was happy to see that his hands were steady as he poured coffee into his cup. *A blip.* He'd handled blips all his life. *What's one more?*

His cup full, Forrester sat down on the bar stool. He reached for his cell phone. Time to call Matthew Spicer. He scrolled through the numbers on his smartphone and placed his call. Spicer's cell phone rang five times before a metallic, robotic voice said, "The number you are dialing is no longer in service." Frowning, Forrester ended the call and pressed in the digits for the number again, only to get the same metallic, robotic message.

Forrester stomped his way back to the office and his file cabinet. He rummaged until he found the files for *Tram* v *Oden.* He searched through the loose notes in the folder until he found a background report on Matthew Spicer. He copied the phone number for his landline onto a sticky note. He closed the folder, returned it to the file cabinet, which he locked. He carried the sticky note back out to the kitchen, where he dialed the number for Spicer's landline. His eyes narrowed at the message he heard after the phone rang three times: "The number you are calling has been disconnected at the customer's request."

"At the customer's request." At the customer's request, my ass! More than likely, it was

at Henry Ballard's request!

Now it all made sense. The partners never left the office till seven o'clock so as not to sit in rush-hour traffic. Yet, the three partners had left before five o'clock yesterday. The fix was in, and Forrester knew it. Matthew Spicer was long gone, thanks to Henry Ballard and his cronies. Matthew Spicer could be anywhere in the world by now. The bastards had one-upped him. He gave himself a mental kick for not being one step ahead of the sons of bitches. *My bad. It will not happen again.* That was a given.

Forrester thought back to the headlines in the *Sentinel* and *Times.* If this wasn't a conspiracy, he didn't know what was.

Forrester drummed his fingers on the countertop as his mind raced. Obviously, a trip into the city was no longer necessary or even desirable. He was sure that if he went to where Spicer lived, he'd find a note on the door that said something to the effect that he was out of town to handle a family emergency. Thanks to his old law firm. He supposed he could go to the firm and confront the senior partners, but he didn't really have the stomach for that. If necessary, he could do the same thing over the phone.

All he had to do was think this through

and get his thoughts in order. He had the partners on the run, that was a given. Otherwise, they wouldn't have arranged a disappearing act for Matthew Spicer. What the partners didn't know was he had Spicer's Social Security number among the copious notes in his file. When it was time to lay hands on the man, he could hire an investigative firm to look for him. Sooner or later, Matthew Spicer would have to open a bank account somewhere. Also, somewhere there was a paper trail that would lead back to the damn partners, who thought they were so smart. No, he wasn't worried about Spicer. At least not now.

Forrester continued to drum his fingers on the countertop as his mind spun in circles. *So what is their game with the newspaper articles on Garland Lee? Do they think planting those stories will make me go off the deep end? Or . . . does it have something to do with the countess who's considering turning a four-hundred-million-dollar portfolio over to Ballard, Ballard & Quinlan to oversee? But according to Henry, the countess will only consider giving them her portfolio to manage if the case with Garland Lee is off the books. Yeah, yeah, that makes sense.*

And wasn't the other woman at that meeting from the Post? *Of course she was, and she also had the front page with Garland Lee.* Forrester was sure of it. He snorted, an ugly sound of displeasure. Then he started to mutter to himself. "You must think I'm really stupid, Henry, to fall for something so asinine."

Forrester reached for his smartphone and looked for the app that would give him the front page of the *Post.* He made another ugly sound in his throat when he saw the headline and Garland Lee's picture above the fold. He was right; it was all one big, gigantic conspiracy. He gave himself a mental pat on the back for his astuteness.

Now what was he to do? No knee-jerk reactions here. Knowing what he knew about Henry Ballard, Henry would think he had him on the ropes and that he'd buckle and drop the lawsuit against Garland Lee. Henry had always been a cocky bastard. It was about time someone cut him down to size, and he, Arthur Forrester, was just the man to do it.

There was not an iota of doubt in Arthur Forrester's mind that he was the man to do the job.

Pleased with himself, Forrester got up to pour himself the last of the coffee. Coffee he didn't need, but he was going to drink it, anyway. He did so hate waste.

With nothing pressing on his agenda, Forrester decided to while away the time by making himself some breakfast. By the time he did that, ate, and cleaned up, it would be time to place the call to the firm.

As he cooked, ate, and cleaned up, Forrester mentally rehearsed the conversation he would have with Henry Ballard. It would be a conversation where he did all the talking, and Henry Ballard did all the listening. Finally, at last, he was going to get the upper hand with the son of a bitch who had made his life so miserable for over thirty years.

He wished now, and not for the first time, that he had taken this route a long time ago. He never should have let the case drag on so long. No matter how many times he asked himself why, he had never been able to come up with an answer. Even now, with everything within his grasp, he still didn't know the answer. Maybe he would never know.

His arm snaked out to reach for his smartphone, when it buzzed. He looked at the caller ID, knowing he knew the number from somewhere, but couldn't quite place it. He clicked on and said, "Arthur Forrester."

"Arthur, this is Max Hubert. What's this I

see splashed across all the papers this morning? And you didn't call me to include my venue in Garland's tour. What? You want a bigger slice this time around? Negotiations are always good, Arthur. Why don't we get together and talk about this? What do you say?"

Forrester's heart started to pound. What to say? What not to say? He struggled to find the words. "It's . . . it's all still in the talking stages, Max. I do not know why the papers ran with it. You know I would never ace you out. I'll be in touch." The two men talked for a few minutes, the weather, the family, the entertainment business in general, before they ended the call.

Forrester's hands were shaking. He needed to calm down. Forget about the stupid call. Concentrate on what to say to Henry Ballard. He needed to decide if he should use his smartphone or the landline to make the call. Such a decision. He debated a full minute, finally settling on the landline. He pressed in the digits and waited for the phone to ring and for the receptionist to say the musical words, "Ballard, Ballard and Quinlan. How may I direct your call?"

"This is Arthur Forrester. Please put me through to Henry Ballard."

"One moment, please."

One moment turned into a full five minutes before Henry Ballard came on the phone. "Arthur, what can I do for you on this miserable rainy day?" Henry Ballard's flat-sounding voice suggested he would rather be talking to anyone other than Arthur Forrester.

"Actually, Henry, there's quite a lot you can do for me on this miserable rainy day, and you can do it all without moving from your desk. So let's get to it. I know that you arranged to plant that story about Garland Lee in all the papers, so do not think I am going to do something stupid in response to it. I am also aware that you spirited Matthew Spicer out of town. My guess would be you sent him out of the country last night. Or maybe you sent him to the Hawaii hideaway, which you think no one knows anything about, while, in reality, everyone in the firm knows about it and how you use it. But I'm not calling you to talk about real estate. I just wanted you to know that I know about Matthew Spicer. Just for the record, I have his Social Security number. If I need to find him, I will have no trouble being able to do so. You know the old saying 'You can run, but you can't hide'? Well, this is a perfect example of that little ditty.

"This is what I want you to do, and I want you to start on it the minute we disconnect from this call. Call the court and tell the judge we have all come to a settlement. That will put an end to the summary judgment motion that has still not been ruled on. You are to call Garland Lee's lead attorney to tell him two eyewitnesses have just come forward with damaging information concerning Garland Lee. So damaging that she will never be able to show her face in public again. Where you find these two eyewitnesses is up to you. Maybe wherever you found Matthew Spicer. Make them available to Garland's attorney at some point. I don't have to tell you what and how to do it, Henry. You're a pro. Just look at what you did for the Odens in *Tram* v *Oden*. They do say practice makes perfect.

"This business with Matthew Spicer is just a pimple on your ass, Henry, compared to what I am prepared to do to you and the firm if you don't come through. I do not want to hear any bullshit, any excuses. The only thing I want to hear from you is that you have two sterling witnesses ready to go on my behalf.

"If I don't hear from you in the affirmative, I will proceed with social media. Within forty-eight hours, your firm will be down the legal drain. The truth is more like twenty-four hours. Every client you have handled in the last fifty years will be screaming for your blood. You'll never be able to come back from that. *Never.* Every lawyer in the firm will be tainted. No one will hire them. You'll be defending yourself and the firm in the courts for the rest of your life.

"I think that about covers it. Do you understand everything I just said? Just say *yes* or *no.*"

"Yes" was the weary-sounding reply.

"Can you do this by the end of the day? *Yes* or *no*?"

"I'll do my best."

"Not good enough, Henry. Try again."

"Yes." The single word was a snarl sound.

"Good, good. We're on the same page. I'll expect your call soon."

Arthur Forrester replaced the receiver clenched in his hands into the cradle of the phone. *Well, that went rather well.* He frowned as he tried to imagine what Henry Ballard was doing right this very second.

What Henry Ballard was doing was crying. At that moment in time, he didn't know if he had the strength to call out to reception to call his brother and Robert Quinlan. *God Almighty, how did it come to this?* "Tell them to meet me in the garage immediately."

Henry Ballard felt every single one of his years as he tottered to the door that would take him to the service elevator and down to the garage, where he found both his brother and Robert Quinlan waiting for him, their expressions a mixture of panic and fear.

Henry took a deep breath and let it loose as he recounted the entire conversation he'd just had with Arthur Forrester. He steeled himself for the recriminations he feared were forthcoming. He was stunned when his brother just said, "So what's our game plan here?"

"What? Do you think I carry around a list of people who are willing to perjure themselves just because I ask them to? I don't know what to do. Arthur is right, we'll be ruined. Every case will be open for scrutiny. The lawsuits alone will be a tsunami. We could never, ever recover from something like that. Either we do as he instructed . . . or we shoot ourselves and leave the mess behind for someone else to clean up. To be honest about it, I don't know if I'm ready to give up the ship just yet."

"Where are we going to find two stupid people willing to perjure themselves? We didn't have to look for Matthew Spicer. He came to us because he couldn't decide if the information he had was valuable. All we did was steer him the way we wanted him to go, and he followed our lead. He never thought he was perjuring himself. What you're talking about now is out-and-out . . . evil. That's not who we are, Henry. And yet, I don't see any other recourse. We have to do it, but how?" Alvin said.

Robert Quinlan jerked at his tie. Then he took off his jacket and laid it on top of the hood of his car. "I might have an idea. How about we hire two actors. We set them up in the conference room and pretend we're doing a scene. We do the script. We tell them we're going to present it in court when the case comes to trial. Like in a few years down the road. We'll pay them well. Really well. Since we will be videoconferencing it, we can show it later to Garland Lee's lead attorney. Once he sees it, he'll know he has to convince his client to drop her case. In turn, the management company holding the escrow monies will release them to Arthur. That's all he wants, the escrow monies."

"Henry, did you record Arthur's call? By any chance, did you mention that we found the listening device he planted?" Alvin asked.

"Hell no. I didn't get the part about the

newspaper articles on Garland Lee. Arthur accused me of being responsible for them, but as he said, he wasn't buying into it. Whatever the hell that is supposed to mean."

"Then he will still have a hold on us, even after it's over," Alvin said.

"Not if Henry tapes the next call," Robert said. "We need to go back to the office. You two, Alvin and Henry, start to work on the script. Don't call the court just yet. Time enough to do that after I lock down my idea. I'll call the dean at Georgetown I did some work for him, and he owes me. I'll ask him to pick two of his best and brightest from the drama department and send them over ASAP. Once we lock that down, we should be good to go. When and after we pull this off, and we *will* succeed, only then will we deal with our consciences and Arthur Forrester. If it is humanly possible, we will make it right. If not, we will stand up and take whatever comes our way because we own it. This might be a good time for the three of us to think about stepping down permanently. We're too old to be dealing with bullshit like this."

Henry Ballard squared his shoulders, his face grim. He stomped his way to the elevator, his brother and partner behind him. "Once we hit the office, be careful what you say. We'll make our last call of the day to Arthur from here in the garage. My phone will record it all."

"Let's do it!" Alvin and Robert said in unison.

CHAPTER 13

The sound of the shrill landline's ringing in the quiet kitchen at Pinewood startled both Charles and Myra. It was rare that the house phone rang, and when it did, it was mostly the feed store or someone confirming an inspection for something or other. Husband and wife looked at each other. Myra threw her hands in the air as Charles swiveled around in his chair to reach for the phone. Myra did a double take when she heard Charles say, "Avery, why are you calling on this phone? Oh. No, it isn't a problem. You usually call on my cell phone, but, yes, I understand the weather is playing havoc with all things electrical, so I guess that is true of cyberspace as well. Myra and I are just trying to decide what to have for lunch. We're waiting for Annie and Fergus. The good news is that the rain finally stopped last night."

Myra threw her hands in the air again, her

expression clearly saying, *Get to the point of the call already, Charles.*

Charles listened to the old spy for ten solid minutes. Finally he said, "I must say that surprises me, but yet it doesn't. If that makes any kind of sense. The girls will go over the moon when I tell them. Keep up the good work, mate. I love solid intel like this."

"What! What!" Myra shouted. "What did he say that will put us 'over the moon'?"

Charles was about to expound on the phone call when Annie and Fergus whipped into the courtyard, sending Lady and her pups into a frenzy of barking.

"Why don't we wait for Annie and Fergus, so I don't have to repeat myself. Two minutes, Myra! Can you wait that long?"

Myra opened the door wide for the dogs to barrel through; then she stepped back as Annie and Fergus did the obligatory ear scratch and belly rub. Everyone hugged, even though they had seen each other less than twelve hours earlier. As Annie put it: "We're huggers." And that was the end of that.

"Hurry, hurry, you two! Charles has news. Avery just called, and Charles wouldn't tell me anything when he saw you drive through the gates, because he simply does not want to repeat whatever it is twice," Myra said as she handed out treats to the clamoring dogs.

"Well, we're here now, Charles, so spit it out. By the way, the water on the roads is gone, just so you know. That means we can go out and about. Well, Charles, what is it?" Annie demanded, her tone as impatient as Myra's.

Charles grinned. "I was just waiting for you to stop talking long enough so I could tell you." He then proceeded to repeat, virtually verbatim, everything Avery had told him about Arthur Forrester's phone calls to Henry Ballard at the firm.

"And Henry Ballard, pillar of the community that he is, agreed to find two people willing to perjure themselves," Fergus said, his voice full of shock. "What kind of lawyer would do something like that?"

"Why not? He did it once before, so why should this time be any different?" Annie snapped back.

"It's not the same thing, Annie. You read all the filings. Ballard, the firm, didn't hire Mr. Spicer to perjure himself. He came to them. They steered him, *guided,* if you prefer that word, to their way of thinking. In a way, it's really apples and oranges," Charles said. "What Arthur Forrester is telling them to do, mind you, *telling,* not asking, is to go out and find people who will outright perjure themselves for money. Standing in their shoes, they see their life's work going down the drain. They probably think Garland Lee has more money than God and won't miss those escrow monies. They get Forrester out of their lives, and the firm remains intact.

"If they do not agree to do what Forrester wants, too many people get hurt and have their lives ruined. They're between a rock and a hard place, and I would not like to be one of them. To see your life's work destroyed by one evil, angry, blackhearted man is, I'm sure, more than they can bear. I'm sure they weighed it all very carefully and decided to go along with him as the lesser of two evils.

"I find it very telling that Arthur is accusing the partners of being responsible for the newspapers' headlines this morning concerning Garland. And the partners are blaming Arthur for planting the listening device in the conference room. We need to thank the powers-that-be that Arthur did not discover the bugs in his own condo."

Annie looked at Myra.

Myra looked at Annie.

Myra reached for her handbag on the clothes tree by the back door as she followed

Annie out the door.

"Love, where are you going?" Charles called out.

"To take care of business," Annie shot back before Myra could respond.

"That was a really stupid question to ask, mate," Fergus said. "What's for lunch?"

"Whatever you make. I'm allowed a stupid question from time to time, Ferg," Charles said defensively.

"Yes, but that was a *really* stupid question. You should know the minute those two women hear something like what you just told them, they have to share it with the others. I hope you also realize that they did not invite us to go along with them — nor did they leave us with any instructions. Having explained all that just now, I ask you, what's for lunch?"

"Of course I realize that, Ferg. We're chopped liver. They're probably hatching a plan as we speak. By the time they get into the District, they'll have it down pat. Do not be surprised if we don't see them for a few days."

Fergus poked his head into the refrigerator and quickly withdrew it when he didn't see anything to his liking. "What do you think the plan will be?"

"They're going to move up their timetable

257

and go to Riverville and do the snatch right away."

A look of horror crossed Fergus's craggy features. "Without Avery in the background? Don't tell me that. That's . . . That's . . ."

"*Dangerous* is the word you're looking for," Charles muttered.

"Then we need to call Avery right now."

Charles looked at Fergus. "Think about what you just said. I wouldn't want to be you when Avery tells Annie you called him to step in."

"Ah, yes, I do see your point, Sir Charles. Some things I'm thinking are better left alone. Which brings me back to this. What's for lunch?"

"And my answer is the same as before — whatever you decide to make."

Fergus paced the vast kitchen, his face a mask of worry. He mumbled something that sounded like he did not, *he absolutely did not,* want peanut butter and jelly for lunch. Then he mumbled again about the best-laid plans of mice and men.

"Be serious here, Charles, what do you think they're going to do?"

"God only knows, Ferg, but whatever it is, it won't bode well for Arthur Forrester. That's a given. Stop fretting, those women can take on an army and come out winners."

"Uh-huh. Is that why you look so worried?"

"I was born to worry, Ferg. How about a ham-and-cheese omelet for lunch? Will that satisfy you?"

Fergus turned wily. "That depends on what you plan for dinner."

"I thought we'd go into town and have dinner. We haven't been anywhere in a few days, and I'm starting to get cabin fever. So an omelet or not?"

Fergus opened the refrigerator and reached for a bowl of brown eggs and handed it over to Charles. "I'll grate the cheese and chop the ham."

Charles nodded, his thoughts on his wife and Annie and what they were planning on their trip into the District. He told himself, over and over, till he was almost convinced, that perhaps it was better that he didn't know.

As Charles cracked eggs into a bowl, Myra and Annie were rattling on ten miles to the minute. Myra was so engrossed in their conversation, she didn't bother to chastise Annie for her hair-raising driving.

"I called Yoko, and she's calling the others

259

to meet up at the nursery. At first, I thought about calling the meeting at Nikki's law office or the *Post,* but negated that almost immediately. We don't want anyone to pay attention to us as a group. The nursery is the perfect place. Do you agree, Annie?"

"Absolutely. This is the part I like the best, Myra, when we all get together, forge the deal, and make our *move.*

"I keep thinking about the name partners at Forrester's old firm, and what he's forcing them to do so he can get all those escrow monies. I'm trying to put myself in their place and wonder what I'd do if I was up against it. It has to be a nightmare for them. I'm willing to cut them some slack with that case of *Tram* v *Oden.* Mr. Spicer went to them, and they, in turn, merely made it work to their advantage. I think it's even possible that no actual perjury was committed if Spicer believed what he testified to. So I'm not sure I wouldn't have done the same thing in that case.

"This, though, is a horse of a different color. This is deliberate subornation of perjury — I think that's the fancy lawyer's jargon I once heard Nikki use — on Forrester's part and the partners' as well. Plain and simple, he's blackmailing his former partners. What would you do, Annie, if you were them?"

Annie eased up on the gas pedal, turned on her signal light, and moved cautiously around a moving van that wasn't driving fast enough to suit her. Back in the right lane and cruising at a speed of seventy-five miles an hour, she said, "I'd like to believe I'd own it and step up to the plate. I'm not sure I would, though, if there was a threat to, say, you, the girls, and Fergus. I'd want to protect you at all costs. And myself as well. I don't know what I'd do, Myra, to be absolutely honest with you."

"I feel the same way. We can do something about that, Annie. We can do it right now, from this car, before we get to Yoko's nursery. We have the power to put the three partners out of their misery, and you know this thing is eating away at them. Their lives will be ruined, the firm will be in a shambles, and all sixty of the associates and partners of the firm will be tainted forever. The big question right this very minute is, do we do it on our own — without consulting the others — or do we wait and do it later? What do you think?"

"I think we should wait and put it to a vote. I know I'd get downright cranky if one or two of the girls did something without consulting us. I think you'd feel the same way. What we have going for us works because we work as a team."

"You're right, Annie. As usual. I guess I'm just anxious, and I so hate injustice. Not only is Arthur Forrester a sack of putrescence, but he's an evil little weasel in the bargain. I want to pull the skin right off his face and pour vinegar over him."

Annie laughed. "Why don't you tell me how you *really* feel about him. That's a joke, Myra. Do you think we'll be leaving for Riverville today or tomorrow?"

Myra nibbled on her thumbnail as she stared out the passenger-side window at the scenery that was passing in a blur. Today for some reason, Annie's heavy foot on the gas pedal wasn't bothering her in the least.

"Tomorrow makes more sense to me. But the girls might think traveling at night would be better. We'd have to find lodging if we leave tonight, or else we stay awake all night or take turns sleeping in the van. What's your preference?"

"As you well know, I prefer doing something as opposed to talking about doing something. I'm not sure traveling up to Riverville in the daylight is such a good idea. I know there are hundreds of white vans on the road, but why take the chance of someone's spotting us or remembering us?"

"Good point. Well, we'll put it to a vote when we get there. It's the next turnoff, Annie. You need to slow down, *like now*. Oh, my God! You took that curve on two wheels, and don't say you didn't! I have whiplash! Do you have some kind of death wish, Countess de Silva?"

"All you do is complain, Myra. Look, we're here! Safe and sound! Did you forget when I took those defensive driving courses you said were a waste of time? You are more of a danger on the road at the speed you drive than I could ever be. Plus, this vehicle is built *for speed*. I'm just trying to prove the engineers right! Otherwise, I'll take the car back for false advertising.

"You can get out now, Myra. The car is at a full stop, and the engine is already off. You also have to take your hands off those damn pearls, so you can open the door."

"I hate you!" Myra grated as she exited the low-slung sports car.

"Well, I love you, so get your ass in gear, the girls are waiting for us. Look alive, Myra!"

"I really do hate you!"

"Uh-huh," Annie said as she hugged Kathryn, who had run to her. The others followed until all the hugging and laughing was done.

Annie moved closer to Myra. "Do you still hate me?" She sounded like she cared.

"I should have pushed you off that cliff in Spain when I had the chance."

"But you didn't. And here we are."

Myra laughed. "Yes, here we are. And I wouldn't have it any other way," she said, linking arms with Annie.

"Me too." Annie grinned. "Okay, girls, let's get to it!"

"When you called earlier, I had the boys finish emptying out greenhouse three. We can conduct the meeting in there, and no one will bother us," Yoko said. "We can sit on the benches. The potting tables are cleaned off. Just follow me."

"It smells like gardenias in here," Isabelle said.

Yoko giggled. "That's because this is the gardenia greenhouse. We just moved them all out to put under the overhang. By the end of the day, they'll all be gone. So why are we meeting like this? What's up?"

Annie and Myra took turns explaining about Avery Snowden's earlier phone call to Charles. "What should we do, girls?" Myra concluded. "Do you want to leave tonight or tomorrow?"

"Night versus day," Annie said.

A long, detailed discussion followed as

each sister listed the pros and cons of day versus night travel, with Maggie having the last word. "I have to have the van checked out, and I'm going to have to find a Maryland magnetic decal for both sides, not to mention a Maryland license plate. The decals won't be too much of a problem, but the Maryland license plates will be. We might need to contact Avery Snowden for those."

Annie's eyes narrowed to slits. In a cold voice that could have thawed a rib roast, she said, "No, we will not be contacting Avery. He left us flat. You all need to remember that. We're on our own. Getting the Maryland license plates won't pose a problem. I'll just call Jackson Sparrow and have him deliver a set to the *Post*. He has contacts. I feel confident that he can have them to us by late this afternoon. If you can get the magnetic decals by then, we can go this evening."

"Which then raises the question, do we get a hotel room for the night? What will we do all day tomorrow while we wait?" Nikki asked.

"I need some time to gather stuff for my red bag. I have a client coming in at three, but I know him well enough to cancel without his being offended. That's if we're

265

still going with the plan we talked about out at the farm," Alexis said. "Are we going with that plan?"

The girls all nodded. "Okay, then, make the decision, tonight or tomorrow?"

The sisters kicked it around for a few more minutes, and the final decision was to leave around midnight. Nikki made reservations at the Riverville Inn for a one-night stay and booked four rooms. She went on to explain that a block away from the inn was a twenty-four-hour supermarket, where they could park the van and walk to the inn. "No sense giving anyone room to speculate why a bunch of women would arrive in the wee hours of the morning in a van. People notice things like that and remember them later."

"Good point," Maggie said.

"Who is going to get in touch with Avery's operative to secure the key to Forrester's condo? Maybe the question should be, will she give it up to us on our say-so? Or does she have to check with Avery Snowden?" Kathryn asked.

"I can send her a text, if you think it's okay," Isabelle said.

Annie bristled again at the mention of Snowden and his operative in the same sentence. "No, dear, I think I should be the one to contact Mr. Snowden's operative. I think her name is Sasha. Not to worry, she'll give it up."

"Avery is going to pitch a fit," Myra said. "He'll view this as going over his head."

"Really!" Annie drawled. "And who pays Mr. Snowden? I rest my case. And remember this, girls, he left us to run down to the boys in Delaware. That is so *not cool* in my book. You start a mission, you stick with it to the end. I think Mr. Avery Snowden, no matter how good he thinks he is, we're better. Agreed?"

No one disagreed. "Good. Myra, you call Jackson Sparrow while I send off a text to Sasha Quantrell. The rest of you finalize our plans, then there is one more item on our agenda before we part company."

Nikki looked across at Kathryn and winked. Annie was on a roll. This meant that life was about to get really, really interesting.

Business taken care of, the girls waited patiently for Myra and Annie to tell them the last bit of news. Myra took the lead and explained the situation with the partners at Arthur Forrester's old firm.

"It's my opinion that we can't let the partners go down that road when we plan to take out Mr. Forrester. We can't let them go ahead and ruin their lives and the lives of everyone who works at their firm. It's not right. They are not evil people. Forrester has them backed into a corner, and they don't see any way out. Myra and I talked about this on the way in this morning, and neither one of us could say for certain that we would not do the same thing if our feet were put to the fire. What we can do is call them and explain, or maybe even go to the firm and talk it out. I'm thinking they'll be so grateful they won't give us a bit of trouble.

"Don't let what you know about their case, *Tram* v *Oden,* color your thoughts. Yes, at first blush, we all went a little *schizzy,* but they did not recruit Mr. Spicer to commit perjury. He came to them. And if I am right, he probably believed what he said on the witness stand, so he did not even perjure himself, and they did not suborn perjury.

"They did what they did, but later made it right, or as right as they could. I say that's in the past, and this is now. We need to take a vote on what to do. But first, before you make your decision, ask yourselves, and be honest, how far would you be willing to go to protect all that you hold near and dear?"

"I think we should tell the firm," Maggie said. "I don't want it on my conscience that we could have stopped something this serious and didn't. I'm sure there is a serious cliché that I could trot out to support what I just said, but I can't think of one right now. There are just too many lives at stake here."

The others agreed. Annie and Myra both sighed in relief.

Another discussion followed to decide who the lucky person to make the call would be. In the end, the vote went to Kathryn. It was also agreed that the others would leave to do what they had to do, to make sure they got off by midnight. Yoko volunteered her office for the call to be made to Ballard, Ballard & Quinlan.

"You aren't nervous, are you, dear?" Myra asked.

"No. Don't jinx me, Myra. Make some quick notes so I get my facts straight. I think I have it, you all explained the situation very well, but you never know. I don't want to screw this up for us."

While Annie and Myra conferred and scribbled notes, Yoko made tea and offered her famous sticky rice cakes on a huge platter, which Kathryn immediately started to scarf down. Then she left the threesome to oversee what was going on with the greenhouse gardenias.

Kathryn scanned the scribbled notes carefully. She mumbled and muttered under her breath as she rehearsed what she planned on saying. Finally she looked over at Myra and Annie, and said, "I think I have it. Keep your pens and papers handy in case I make a goof and tell me what to say to correct it. Call the number!"

Annie punched in the numbers, but not before she blocked the call so the number would not show up on the firm's end.

Kathryn closed her eyes as she waited to be connected. She nodded to Myra and Annie to show the connection had gone through.

Kathryn's skin prickled at the cheerful-sounding voice. "Ballard, Ballard and Quinlan. How may I direct your call?"

Kathryn said, "I'd like to speak to Henry Ballard, please. Tell him it's urgent and it concerns Arthur Forrester."

"Who shall I say is calling?"

"My name isn't important. Mr. Ballard will understand that when you tell him this call concerns Arthur Forrester. I'll hold." Kathryn rolled her eyes at Myra and Annie, who just shrugged.

Kathryn sat up a little straighter when she heard the rich baritone that was Henry Ballard's voice. "How can I help you,

Miss . . ."

"Mr. Ballard, my name is of no importance, but what I have to tell you, and share with you, is. I know what Arthur Forrester has asked you to do. I know you agreed because you and your partners thought you had no other choice. I am calling you to tell you that you do have a choice, and that choice is for you to do nothing. My . . . um . . . colleagues and I will take care of Mr. Arthur Forrester.

"I know you found the listening device we planted in your conference room. What you do not know is that we also planted listening devices in Mr. Forrester's condo, so we could monitor the situation, which has now gotten out of control. We, my colleagues and I, have no desire to see you do something you will regret for the rest of your life. Now, having said that, I want you to call Mr. Forrester back and tell him that everything is under control. Tell him you have the two people who are willing to perjure themselves, but that it will take at least two days to get them comfortable with what you are asking them to do. If he says that's not good enough, hold your ground and say it is the best you can do and to take it or leave it. Trust me, he won't put up too much of an argument."

"Who . . . who are you? Why are you, whoever you are, involved in this? When the dust settles, are you going to blackmail me, too? This whole debacle is wildly insane," Henry Ballard blustered.

"I think you should consider me a very good friend right now, along with my colleagues. We mean you no harm. We simply want to help you so you do not make a mistake that will haunt you and many others for the rest of your lives. Let's leave it that my colleagues and I don't believe that the courts always get it right. When they screw up, we try to make things right."

"Oh, my God, are you . . . you are. . . . ?"

"The answer to your question is *yes*. Do you trust us?"

"If you are who I think you are, then *yes, with my life,* is my answer."

"All right, from here on in, the only thing you have to do is make the phone call and be sure to be convincing. You are 'off the hook,' as the saying goes. You'll know what to do legally to end this mess once . . . Mr. Forrester sees the light. Oh, one last thing, Mr. Ballard. This call never happened."

"What call?" Ballard said, but he was talking to dead air.

Ballard put his head down on his desk and prayed to everyone and anything he could think of. He prayed for thirty full minutes before he raised his head, with tears streaming down his cheeks.

"There is a God," he whispered to the empty room. "I always knew there was, but this proves it beyond a shadow of a doubt."

In the whole of his life, Henry Ballard never felt such peace as he felt at that precise moment in time.

Kathryn reached for the last sticky rice cake and popped it in her mouth. "We're good, ladies. He bought it. Poor thing, I felt sorry for him. Should we call Garland Lee?"

"I don't think so, not just yet," Myra said.

"Then if you don't mind my skipping out, I want to check on Murphy. Jackson Sparrow said he'd take care of him while I took care of business. He loves animals and watches out for Maggie's cat, Hero. Don't look at me like that!"

"Are you happy, Kathryn?" Myra and Annie asked at the same time.

Kathryn turned serious. "I never . . . I never thought I could ever be truly happy again after Alan died. I believed it for so long that I . . . Yes, yes, yes, I'm happier than I've ever been in my entire life."

The women hugged. All three had tears in their eyes. They continued to hug each other, crooning words only women knew to soothe the soul, the mind, the heart, and the body.

CHAPTER 14

One by one, the women arrived at the *Post*'s underground parking garage. The time was twenty minutes to midnight. With the exception of Alexis, who was pulling her red bag of tricks on a portable dolly, they all wore lightweight backpacks.

Even though the garage was empty of humans, the sisters still spoke softly.

"What do you think?" Maggie said, pointing to the Maryland license plates she'd just put on the white van. "Jackson Sparrow had them delivered to my office at seven o'clock this evening in a plain brown wrapper." She giggled at what she was saying. "There was a note inside saying that they were special plates with a magnetic backing, so they can be changed in and out in a hurry. He said they have a special set of plates for every state in the union at their agents' disposal. He also included a set of plates for a couple neighboring states, in case we have to do a switcheroo on short notice. We have to return them, of course."

"Did you have any trouble with the decals?" Isabelle asked.

"Yes and no. I had to wait awhile for the paint to dry on the phone number. This van now 'officially' belongs to the Rainbow Center for Senior Citizens. I picked this particular decal because the rainbow is so colorful. If you notice, the telephone number is painted yellow and very hard to see. I did that on purpose. The phone number is for the public library. I think it's all the cover we need, and if not, oh, well!"

"Then I vote to board this finely decorated vehicle and head on out of here," Annie said jubilantly.

The sisters piled into the van, with Maggie taking the wheel. She turned on the engine. It purred like a sleepy cat. She programmed their destination into the GPS and put the big van into gear. "Arthur Forrester, here we come!" The sisters hooted their pleasure as they started to discuss the operation that would take place the following night.

Gradually, all conversation petered out, with only Nikki keeping a running dialogue going so Maggie wouldn't get tired and fall asleep at the wheel.

"How far is it again to Riverville?" Nikki asked.

"About two hundred fifty miles, give or take a few. It's going to take us several hours. The weather isn't in our favor, either. This van is not built for speed, and I want to stay below the speed limit. Why, are you in a hurry?" Maggie joked.

"You know me. I like to be precise in my thinking. We're going to stop at least once, right? And this van has to be a gas guzzler, so maybe twice for gas, right?"

"Yes, ma'am. I was thinking I'd turn off at the next rest stop. I can use some fresh coffee and some donuts. You said you wanted to take a turn at the wheel, so you can take over when we start out. We're almost to the halfway mark. You okay with that?"

"Absolutely," Nikki said as she rolled her shoulders to loosen her tense muscles.

A couple of hours later, Nikki steered the van into the parking lot of the Big Super Saver supermarket and parked as far from the entrance as she could.

"Rise and shine, girls!" Maggie bellowed as loud as she could. "We're here, and the time is five-twenty in the A.M.!"

As Nikki Quinn parked the van, just blocks away from the Forresters' condo, Arthur

277

Forrester paced his kitchen like a caged lion. He felt like his pants were on fire. So far, he'd consumed two entire pots of coffee, eaten two bologna sandwiches, and swallowed twenty-two vitamin pills. In between, he lathered a cooling gel on his face four different times, cursing ripely at the burning sensation, and that was all before five o'clock. He cursed even more when he looked at his face in the mirror. He looked like a scary clown. He fumed and seethed. The rosacea was the one thing in his life over which he had no control. No matter what he did, no matter how many prescription medicines he took, no matter how much gel and ointment he applied, nothing helped. He refused to believe any of the doctors when they told him that stress aggravated the condition. He refused to believe his wife, Nala, who was a nurse practitioner and who knew a thing or two about medicine.

What do they know? I am not stressed. I never let stress get to me. Never! . . . "Liar, liar, pants on fire." *How apt that little ditty is.*

Forrester was stressed to his limits. No, the stress had gone beyond his limits. *Why lie to myself?* He didn't have the answer. *Well, now that things are coming to a head, my condition should improve, once and for all.*

278

He'd take all the escrow monies, thumb his nose at Garland Lee, the bitch, and the partners. He'd finalize the deal for the brewery and, from there, he would move directly to Easy Street, collect profits, and play golf.

Golf. His passion in life. Maybe what he should do was sell this condo and relocate to Hilton Head because of the superior golf courses. *Nala isn't coming back,* he knew that. *So why stick around?* He wouldn't miss this place one little bit. He didn't even miss his wife. He rarely saw his kids and grandchildren, so he wasn't going to miss them, either.

Being alone won't bother me, he knew that, too. He'd start a whole new life.

Everything was *almost* perfect.

Then what the hell is bothering me? What? That I crossed the line so many times I've lost count? That I turned into a blackmailer? The fact that, at least according to Nala, I'm a lousy husband and father? Again, according to Nala, that I have no conscience?

Forrester didn't like where his thoughts were taking him, so he switched mental gears and decided to make another pot of coffee, which he didn't want or need. He'd do it just to have something to do. He glanced at the clock on the range as he spooned coffee into the wire basket. It wasn't even six-thirty yet, and he'd already eaten two sandwiches. What the hell was he going to do to fill the hours till five o'clock this afternoon? It was raining the proverbial cats and dogs outside, so going for a walk or to the store was out of the question.

Forrester went back to his frantic pacing. He wished he had a friend to call to commiserate with, but he had no true friends, just acquaintances, people he said hello to, or acknowledged with a nod.

Maybe what he should do was swallow a sleeping pill and take a nap. The only problem with that thought was that the pills worked adversely on him; instead of putting him to sleep, they just wired him up more, something the damn doctors didn't understand. Even Nala said it was all in his head. Both the doctor and Nala told him he didn't know how to relax and was his own worst enemy. It was probably true, because he simply didn't know how to relax. He wondered if someday he would just keel over and sleep for a week. Maybe two weeks. What kind of bliss would that be? He didn't give it another thought because he knew it would never happen. If he did keel over, it would be because he was dead. And then he'd sleep forever. The thought depressed him.

With nothing else to do, he wandered back to his office. *Maybe I should tidy up? Why bother?* he asked himself. *I'll only mess it up again.* It was like making the bed. Why make it when he was just going to mess it up again when it was time to go to bed.

Forrester sat down at his desk and clicked the buttons on the computer's keyboard. His home page appeared. The scales of justice. Every lawyer at his old law firm had the same screen saver. He couldn't really remember now if it was mandatory at the time or not. Probably the computers at the firm came with that particular screen saver. He really needed to get a new home page. He'd long ago removed the word *justice* from his vocabulary. Maybe a cartoon or something funny to make him laugh. He couldn't remember the last time he'd laughed. Laughter was supposed to relieve tension and stress. "My ass," he muttered under his breath.

"Well, this is cozy," Annie said, looking around at the chintz-and-maple suite she and Myra were to share.

"I had to book four rooms. The good thing is there is a sitting room between each set of rooms. We can leave the doors open, and that way, none of us will get in each other's way. It's not like we're going to be sleeping here. When we leave this evening, we take all our belongings because we won't be coming back. I paid everything up front, so we don't even have to worry about checking out," Maggie said.

"I like it," Alexis said. "It's quaint and cozy. I might even bring Joseph and come back here someday. He'd really like this place."

"There's a minibar and a coffeemaker. Does anyone want coffee, or should we go down to the coffee shop and get some *real* coffee, not this instant stuff?" Nikki asked.

Myra shook her head. "I don't think it would be a wise move on our part to be seen as a group. We could order in. On the desk, there's a list of local eateries that deliver here to the inn. As Nikki correctly pointed out, the coffee they have here in the room would not meet with our approval, since we are such coffee aficionados. I think that ordering in might be our best bet, since it is still raining pretty hard."

The sisters talked it over and decided to follow Myra's advice.

While Isabelle took everyone's order and called it in to a restaurant called Wild

Ginger, Maggie explained to the others that there was a car-rental agency in the lobby. There were cars in the lot if they wanted to rent one for the day to cruise around, as opposed to going back out in the rain to the supermarket, where the van was parked. "We need to do something, or we'll go insane sitting here waiting for tonight."

"We'd need two cars," Annie said. "We have to get the key to Mr. Forrester's condo from Avery's operative, as well as the card that will allow us to park in the garage this evening. We need to find out where she is, so we don't waste time looking for her. What that means, Myra, is, you need to call Charles and set that up."

Myra squared her shoulders, took a deep breath, and hit the speed dial on her phone. Her gaze went to Annie as her hand snaked upward to clutch at her pearls. Whatever expression she saw on Annie's face made her shove her hand in the pocket of her jeans.

"Charles! I just wanted you to know we all got here safe and sound. We . . . I need you to get in touch with Mr. Snowden. Ask him how we can locate his operative to get the key to Mr. Forrester's condo. I also understand we're going to need a keycard to swipe the gate that leads to the condo garage. Call me back ASAP." She was about to end the call when she heard her husband say something. She listened, her lips narrowing into a thin, straight line. The sisters stopped their chattering to stare at Myra and listen.

"You need to tell that to someone who cares, Charles. I don't care, and neither do the girls. For former superspies, I would think that your tradecraft would be better than this. When operatives end their shifts, they pass on what happened during their shifts and turn over everything in their possession to their replacements, so do not tell me that Sasha or whoever is staked out at Forrester's condo might not have the key and the card. We want it *now*. No, I don't want to wait until tonight. We'll be leaving here soon, after we have lunch. What did you just say? Oh, I heard you, I just wanted to make sure you meant what you said. Don't get cute with me, Charles, Avery Snowden is *your* friend. He just works for us, and let me remind you he left us flat to go to Delaware to be with the boys. *We. Do. Not. Need. Him.*"

Kathryn looked around at the sisters, her eyebrows raised. "Whoa! I like her spirit." She grinned.

"Shhh," Nikki said. "She's not done yet."

"You *think* we should wait for Mr. Snowden, who you say is on his way here! And would that be because *you* told him what we're doing? Did you, Charles?" Myra listened a minute longer. "Oh, so now you're blaming Fergus for telling him! It doesn't matter who told him. It's none of his business what we do. I thought you understood that. Whose side are you on, Charles? Well?"

"Holy crap," Maggie hissed to Yoko, who was standing next to her.

Myra risked a glance at the girls as they slowly inched closer toward her, their sign that they were on her side. She winked at them.

"I want you to listen to me very carefully, and this time you have our permission, and by *our,* I mean all the girls, to tell Avery if he shows up at the site of our mission, Annie will shoot him right where the sun doesn't shine. Tell me you understand what I just said. And never mind the damn key and card. We'll manage on our own. Also, tell your great pal that the mission is over for them! We're not paying out another penny to him or his people. You're not saying anything, Charles. Say something." Myra listened. "That's not good enough. Good-bye, Charles."

Myra's phone rang immediately. She tossed it on the bed and looked at the closed circle surrounding her. "How'd I do?"

Kathryn laughed out loud. "You were smokin' hot, girl!" Myra grinned from ear to ear.

"Can I really shoot him if he shows up?" Annie asked.

"Yes!" the girls shouted in unison.

"So now we have a problem — how to get into the condo. I know Annie can pick a lock, but in the middle of the night, in a brightly lit hallway, that's not going to be easy," Nikki said. "What if there are security cameras?"

"Spray paint," Alexis said. "I have some in my bag."

Annie threw her hands in the air. "See! Problem solved."

"What about the gate? We need to be able to drive the van into the garage." Nikki said.

Kathryn raised her hand. "I'm a nuclear engineer, remember? I just drive an eighteen-wheeler for fun. I think I can figure it out. If necessary, I can even turn off the power and leave the gate open. With this weather, power shortages are going to be more common than you might think. No one will pay any special notice if I turn off the power. Trust me on that. Piece of cake."

The sisters clapped their approval.

"Do we know if Forrester has an alarm system? Worse yet, one of those silent alarms," Yoko said.

"He does. But I remember Avery's saying the cleaning lady told him they rarely activate it," Annie said. "Supposedly, it's a very secure building. We'll have to deal with it when we get there. That will go under Kathryn's purview."

"Now that we've got everyone's knickers in a knot, do we think Snowden will show up or not?" Maggie asked.

"Not if he wants to stay in Annie's good graces. And he knows, if he's half as smart as we think he is, not to try to cross Charles," Myra said gleefully.

"I'm not being a hardnose here," Annie said. "But we engaged his services, and we pay his astronomical fees, so we have every right to assume and demand that he stay on the mission until it's over. He just up and left us because he got a call from the boys. I've always secretly suspected that he resents working for a bunch of women. I could be wrong, but I don't think so."

"I think that Mr. Snowden thinks, or convinces himself, he is under contract to Charles. We're just a sideline," Myra said. "But he has always come through for us, we have to give him credit for that. Especially the extraction-and-disposal end of things. We need to think about that and make a plan."

"I might have an idea if it comes down to that," Kathryn said. "Jackson Sparrow and I were talking, and I asked him what his most memorable case was, the one that had the most meaning. The one that got under his skin that he still thinks about. You all want to hear it?" Everyone said they did, so they sat down in the sitting room and formed a virtual circle.

"We have quite a bit of time until our meal gets here, so expound away, my dear," Annie said.

"It all started when Jackson was a rookie agent, fresh out of Quantico. It was his third assigned case. 'Routine' was the way he put it. The night before, his whole team sat down together for dinner. Some kind of fish. The whole damn team got food poisoning. He didn't, because he avoided the fish. As he put it, it was drowning in some kind of white sauce. That left a one-man team, so they assigned him to a seasoned team. He said the guys were in their forties, and they'd been around a long time and seen it all. He was young, twenty-three, and in awe of those guys. As you all know, the FBI is strictly domestic. The CIA is not domestic. They operate on foreign soil. This particular case had the CIA *and* the FBI working together. Jackson loved the danger the CIA spooks confronted on their assignments, not that working in the field for the FBI wasn't dangerous, because it was, but nothing like working in the field for the CIA. And by the end of that case, he'd made friends with some of the CIA guys. Who, by the way, are still his friends to this day.

"Jackson excelled, and he moved up the ladder really quickly. Flash forward five years. He was so good at what he did that this one guy from the CIA asked the powers-that-be if they would lend Jackson to their group for a special case. It was a case that lasted three full years. It was a case that involved this man named Nigel Bly. Jackson called him a chameleon. He had his mani-cured hands into everything — he was an arms dealer, a money launderer, a drug ped-dler, and anything else he could be to turn a dollar. He worked both sides of the law. The CIA paid him off the books. The other side paid him off their books. The one thing Bly would never agree to was prostitution and slave trafficking, although he was privy to it. He'd even inform the CIA of times and dates so they could raid the places. I guess he was worth his weight in gold to the CIA. The CIA would set him up with false intel, and he'd pass it on. Nothing important, just to keep the guy in the other side's good graces and in the game. Flash forward again, to when something bad went down, and there was a lot of gunfire. Jackson said it was the first time he'd ever fired his gun in the whole of his career.

"When the shooting stopped, Jackson was wounded, and so was Bly. Bly more so, but Jackson carried him to safety, and eventually the CIA got them both to safety. It took a long time for Bly to recover. The CIA set him up in Barbados, where he rules like a king. The place is like a fortress. He has his own network of agents. He still plays both sides and collects monies from both sides. To this day, he has never left the island. 'It works for everyone,' Jackson said.

"During his tenure at the FBI, Jackson said he called on Bly many times for help, and it was always given. Once a year, he goes to see him."

"And this means what?" Annie asked.

"What it means, at least to me, is, if we need to replace Avery Snowden, we have Mr. Nigel Bly standing in the wings. It's an option, nothing more, nothing less. If we decide to forgive Mr. Snowden for his . . .

rash decision to abandon us, then we don't have to ever revisit this. Like I said, it's an option. Oh, I almost forgot something. Jackson told me that Mr. Bly knows Mr. Snowden very well and considers him a thorn in his side, as Snowden believes Bly to be to him. That's it, the end of the story."

"And just in time," Maggie said, running to the door to take delivery of their food.

"I think we should tuck all of that away for the time being. What I especially like is that now we have a name we can bandy about where Charles and his superspy are concerned," Annie said.

"Maybe I'll try it out on him later when I call." Myra giggled. "I'll put him on speakerphone so you can all hear his reaction. If Mr. Snowden is familiar with Mr. Bly, then I am sure that Charles is, too." Myra giggled again as she reached for a napkin and plastic fork.

"I think we're on a roll, girls," Nikki said as she eyed a carton of Chinese food.

"Hear! Hear!"

CHAPTER 15

"You have already washed that omelet pan three times, Charles. Do you want me to dry it, or are you going to wash it again?" Fergus asked, his voice sounding jittery.

"This is not good, Ferg."

Fergus sighed. There was no use pretending he didn't know what Charles was talking about. "You're right, this is not good. We have to decide whose side we're on. And we need to decide right now."

"Is that how you see it, Ferg? As Maggie would say, 'It's a no-brainer.' I don't fancy seeing myself sleeping in the barn, and I wager you aren't looking forward to sleeping in Annie's toolshed."

Fergus twisted the dishcloth he was holding into a knot. "This is how I see it. Myra and Annie are right to be upset that Avery left them high and dry on this mission. He has never done that before, so they have a right to be upset. Yes, he left capable people in place. We got the information within minutes of his people's relaying what they found out to him. He might not have been on the mission physically, but nothing went down or awry while he's been gone. In all fairness, Charles, we need to cut the man some slack here."

"And you're right. The boys needed him. Physically needed him. How can we argue with that? We're one of them. Or we're supposed to be. The thing is, and you know it as well as I do, you never leave the mission once it gets under way. We were trained that way, and Avery took it upon himself to step outside the box. And even though I did not try to argue him out of it, even gave him permission, he knew full well that he had stepped over a line by not bothering to clear his decision with Annie or Myra. And that, in itself, was a clear indication to the girls that he doesn't take them seriously. It's women's thinking, Ferg. I learned a long time ago never to argue with their brand of logic because I knew I would never win."

"Will you please rinse the pan, so I can dry it, Charles? This kitchen is not tidy, and I know how much you like, no, insist upon, a tidy kitchen."

Charles rinsed the omelet pan and handed it over to Fergus, who undid the knot on

293

the towel and dried the pan. "There! How hard was that? Now we can sit down with a cup of coffee and ponder our dilemma."

Charles listened to the gurgle of the water rushing down the drain and wished that he could go right along with it. He hated times like this, times when he had to make decisions he didn't want to make. He looked around to see if Fergus was right about the kitchen. It sparkled. With his jaw clenched, he sat down at the old oak table and reached for the cup of coffee Fergus poured for him.

"Have you noticed, Ferg, that this past year, maybe the last year and a half, that the girls seem — I say *seem* — to be trying to outdo the boys? They no longer call on them for help. They seem bent on proving something. To whom, I don't know. Themselves would be my guess. That whatever the boys can do, they can do better. It goes without saying, the girls are beyond competitive. This situation we find ourselves in right now just goes to prove it. Do you agree or not?"

"Sadly, yes, I have to agree. But, Charles, let me take that one step further. I believe they are better. We've seen what they can do. They have no limits. When they did call in the boys for help, it was always more a matter of expediency than anything else. All they have to do now if they fire Avery is plan a little more carefully. We both know they can do it. The boys just don't have the fire burning in their bellies that the girls have."

"Avery is not going to take this well, I can tell you that," Charles said.

"He's a big boy, Charles. He had a choice to make, and he made it. On his own, without any consultation with his clients, the ones who were paying the freight. Now he has to live with the decision and the manner in which he implemented it. I have to wonder how the boys will react to the news when they hear it. Oh, and one other thing. I think the two of us need to decide if we're on shaky ground here or not. By that, I mean with the guys and the sisters."

"There is that," Charles said morosely as a vision of him sleeping in the barn on a pile of straw flashed through his mind. He'd be eating wilted apples and carrots and munching on hay. He shivered. "How big is that toolshed where you might be sleeping, Ferg?"

Fergus turned white. "Annie has so much junk in there, I'd have to sleep standing up or on top of the John Deere." He thought of his and Annie's pretty bedroom, which was neither feminine nor masculine, and in which he'd been sleeping lo these many years. He loved the thousand-thread-count sheets, the special pillows that didn't give him a stiff neck, the downy blankets, and the soothing scent of lavender dispersed throughout the room. The toolshed, on the other hand, smelled like manure and motor oil. His stomach rumbled.

"I'm no fool, Charles, and neither are you. Let's get this over with. Call Avery and tell him just the way it is. We'll deal with the fallout when it happens."

"Before I make the call, we need to talk about something else. How are the girls going to get Arthur Forrester out of the condo? I don't know this for sure, but I think their game plan is to bring him back here to the farm and stash him in the dungeon. Which then brings up the question of when they're . . . um . . . done playing with him, what are they going to do with him? Until now, they've always relied on Avery for the final relocation. How are they going to make him . . . um . . . disappear? Avery has the resources to make that happen. If you're thinking you and I can do it, think again."

"Maybe they'll just leave him in the dungeon to rot?"

"Then he'd smell, Fergus."

"What do you want from me, Charles?

Between the eight of them, and I'm including Maggie, I have to believe they have a plan in mind. We just don't know what it is, and I, for one, have no intention of asking. You can do whatever you want. Make the damn call, already, Charles. All this chitchat is nothing more than delaying the inevitable."

Charles reached for his specially encrypted cell phone, compliments of Avery Snowden, which came with a price tag. He punched in the number three on the speed dial and sat back to wait.

"Snowden. Talk to me, Charles, and talk loud because I can't hear a blasted thing with the way the rain is pounding down here."

Charles didn't bother to mince words. He did, however, raise his voice. "The girls called me to call you and tell you you're fired. You are to immediately recall all of your operatives. And before you can ask the reason, it is because you left the mission. Without *their* authorizing you to do so. Where are you?"

"Ninety minutes outside Riverville. Are you yanking my chain, mate, or is this for real?"

"It's for real. So turn around and go back to Delaware. The girls no longer need your services."

"I understand everything you just said. This is a stupid decision, Charles. All I was doing was babysitting and not adding anything to the operation. The fellas *needed me* — and that is an understatement. I actually saved the ladies money by leaving. I'm not going to beg here, if that's what you're thinking. My people and I have given the ladies a hundred percent on each mission over the years. I'll stand by that until the sheep wander home. I'll recall my people and put an end to the mission. No hard feelings, Charles. I know what it took for you to call to deliver the news. I do have a question, though. Do you all have any objection to my telling the boys I've been terminated? I like to be as transparent as I can be. As you know, that's paramount in this business."

"I don't think that will be a problem, Avery. I'm sorry I was the one to have to call you."

"Me too, mate, but someone had to do it, right? I guess I'll . . . I'll see you when I see you. It's been nice working with you, Sir Charles."

Charles bit down on his lower lip. He threw his hands in the air. "It went better than I thought it would. Still, I feel lower than a snake's belly, Ferg."

"I know, but Avery broke his own rule. There have to be consequences when that happens. You, me, Avery, back when we were in service, we had to follow the rules and orders given us, even when we felt they were wrong. That's how we were trained. Avery himself drummed that into the girls. While I wasn't here at the time, you yourself told me about his many pep talks and how essential it was for them to learn how things in this . . . field they entered into operated. It will be interesting to see what the boys do, once Avery tells them. I can't even guess what their reaction will be. What do you think, Charles? If they need a defense for their decision, it will be that sometimes there are extenuating circumstances that have to be dealt with, and this was one of those times. That's just my opinion. Ferg, you got one you want to share?"

"I think they'll keep him on. After all, they're the reason the girls sacked him. They won't cast him to the wolves. There is a lot to be said for loyalty. Actually, it's paramount. I'm with you on that. It might or might not cause a problem with the girls, but knowing how they operate, they'll put it all behind them and refuse to discuss it. In other words, they'll get over it."

Charles nodded sagely. "We still have a lot of files to clean up where Mr. Forrester is concerned. I suggest we go down to the war room and do something constructive. With any luck, we can have things all neat and tidy for the girls when they get back here tomorrow. We're still dining out, right?"

"That's my vote," Fergus said agreeably.

"You go ahead, I'll take Lady and the pups out for a spell. You know what you have to do. Bind everything in the yellow folders. Be sure to make duplicate copies of everything. By the way, did we ever get any solid information on the brewery Forrester invested in?"

"No."

"We need to work on that. Although with tonight's invasion, I imagine the girls will get that information out of him a lot more easily than you and I can do on endless computer searches."

As the hours crawled by, Arthur Forrester realized that his anxiety level was reaching a new high. He was starting to feel light-headed, out of sorts. Without stopping to think about it, he went to the closet and pulled out a rain jacket and hat. He looked for an umbrella, but didn't see one. He made sure he had his wallet and house key in his pocket. A walk in the spring rain might be just what he needed. Yes, he would get soaked to the skin, but when he got back, he could take a hot shower and put on clean clothes. It was one way of eating up the time until five o'clock. He looked at the clock over the doorway in the kitchen. One o'clock. Four more hours to go. He didn't bother to set the alarm. The alarm was Nala's thing, not his. He hated the damn thing. For no reason at all, it would go off and he'd have to spend an hour on the phone with the alarm company to reset it. And for that privilege, he paid ninety-nine dollars a month. He made a mental note to terminate the contract now that Nala was gone and wouldn't be on his case about setting the alarm even when he went downstairs to collect the mail. Nala was a pain in his ass. Always had been, come to think of it. Canceling the alarm service would probably eat up an hour of his time when he returned.

Five minutes into his walk, and Forrester already knew that he had made a big mistake. He was soaked to the skin; his rain jacket, which had seen better days, was simply not fit for the deluge under which he was walking. He squished and sloshed as his sneakers filled with water. The baseball

301

cap did little to shield the raw skin on his face. And this rain wasn't the warm spring rain he'd expected. This rain was hard-driving and almost cold. He walked on, then turned the corner and started back the way he'd come.

As miserable as he felt, he was relieved to find that the overwhelming anxiety he had been feeling had dissipated. So, as uncomfortable as he was, the decision to walk in the rain had been correct. He shivered and tried to quicken his steps, but his sodden shoes only allowed for a slow pace.

Back at the condo, he started to strip down the minute he walked through the door. He left a trail of water and sodden clothes behind, along with his sneakers, which felt like they weighed ten pounds each. Maybe he'd just dump the whole lot in the trash so he didn't have to do a whole load of laundry. He had plenty of clothes, and at least six pairs of sneakers.

The clock on the nightstand said he'd used up an hour. Fifteen minutes to shower and get warm again, ten minutes more to dress, another ten minutes to anoint his face, then a half hour with the alarm company, possibly more if they put him on hold to search for his records or try to convince him not to cancel his service.

At least two hours accounted for. Then he could make coffee and a sandwich and whittle the time down even more. Worst-case scenario, he would pace the kitchen and dining room for an hour and a half until the phone rang at five o'clock. He had no idea what he would do after the phone call. It bothered him now that he hadn't thought about that part of the equation. Maybe that would be the perfect time to think on the matter while he paced for the last hour and a half.

Forrester followed his own instructions to the letter. When the phone rang, he congratulated himself on how steady his hand was when he picked up the receiver on the landline. He let it ring three times to show Henry Ballard that he wasn't sitting on top of it, waiting for it to ring.

"Arthur, this is Henry Ballard. The partners and I have agreed to your terms. We've placed all the wheels in motion. Tomorrow morning, at nine o'clock, our two surprise witnesses will be here. We're going to need the better part of the day to . . . ah . . . rehearse with them. We've written out a script, but they have to memorize it and be comfortable with it. I was assured they would do a good job. For the money we're paying them, I certainly hope so. We should wrap this up the day after tomorrow. When do you want us to call the court?"

"The minute you have it on film and are satisfied no lawyer can trick them. I'm holding you responsible. I also want to see the video."

"Of course, Arthur. Do you have any other instructions for us?"

Arthur suddenly didn't like Henry Ballard's accommodating tone. "You're suddenly pretty damn agreeable, Henry. Why is that? Earlier you were full of piss and vinegar. You had better not be trying to pull a fast one on me. Because if you are, you will come to regret it more than you can even imagine."

Henry Ballard sighed so loud, Forrester could hear it. "I'm trying to make the best out of an intolerable situation. We all realize it is useless to fight you, Arthur, the senior partners and I realize that. We did everything you said. What more do you want?"

"What else I want is for the escrow monies to be released to me within an hour of your speaking with the judge and Garland Lee's lawyers. That's when it's over."

"I'll certainly do my best, but I do not know if it can be done that quickly. You know as well as I do that I can't force the judge to do anything. If I'm too demanding, he'll dig in, and it could be weeks before he approves the terms of the settlement. Is that what you want?"

Forrester knew that what Henry Ballard said was true. Judges did not like to be told what to do. Not ever. "You damn well better make the best case you can then, Henry."

"Is there anything else, Arthur? If not, I want to go home and forget about all of this for a little while."

Forrester didn't bother to respond; he simply hung up the phone.

Not sure what he was feeling, Forrester picked up the phone again and ordered his dinner, a pizza with pepperoni, sausage, peppers, onions, and garlic, with a side order of Tony's famous garlic twists. *Nala would have a fit if she heard this order,* he thought. *Well, Nala isn't here.* Pizza had all the food groups, as far as he was concerned. Next week, when things were finally settled and all his decisions made, he would go back to healthy eating and living. *In crisis mode, you do what you have to do to survive. That's why they call it a crisis,* he told himself.

When his pizza arrived at six-thirty, Forrester carried it out to the kitchen, aware that he had forgotten to lock the door. But he could do that later. Right now, he wanted to eat the pizza while it was still reasonably hot. Sitting at the kitchen table, he downed it with two bottles of Budweiser. He couldn't remember anything ever tasting so good.

Not only that, he felt good. *Really good.* He thought he would finally be able to sleep. Optimistically looking forward to a good night's sleep, he left the mess in the kitchen and made his way to the bedroom, where the messy-looking bed he hadn't bothered to make when he woke waited for him. He stripped down to his boxers and, at the last second, decided to take a sleeping pill to ensure he really would sleep the night through. He gulped at it with half a glass of water before he tottered back to his room, where he fell into bed.

For some crazy reason, he started to think about his neighbors and whom he would call if there was an emergency he couldn't handle, now that he was living alone. He didn't really know any of them. *NalaNala-Nala* . . . Forrester's eyelids started to droop as the sleeping pill began to take effect. *Nala-Nala* . . . He was on his own. Maybe he should think about getting one of those medical alert bracelets.

Forrester's eyes finally closed. His last conscious thought before he fell asleep was

that he had forgotten to lock the door to
the condo.

CHAPTER 16

The sisters were tense as they tried to while away the hours until midnight, at which time they planned to make their move. They alternated between their suites, muttering and mumbling among themselves, as they stared out at the early-evening rainy day. All four televisions in the suites were tuned to various channels: Fox, QVC, the shopping channel, and a station carrying reruns of *Castle.* No one was paying attention to anything on the screens, even though they were staring at what was playing out in front of them. Only Maggie was off by herself, busily tapping away on her laptop.

The time was two minutes to eight and it was almost dark outside. On cue, as if some unheard bell had rung, the sisters all moved as one. They met up in the middle of Annie and Myra's sitting room, where Alexis was pawing through her red magic bag of tricks for what she called the evening's upcoming festivities. Only Maggie remained outside the circle, still tapping furiously on her laptop.

"I wish I had a magic wand so I could move time forward," Isabelle complained. The others agreed.

"We could tidy up here and get rid of all our trash from the two meals we ordered in. We can't leave anything behind because we are not coming back. If you like, we can do another rehearsal, girls," Myra said.

"What's to rehearse, Myra? We're going in blind and will be winging it. How do you rehearse something like that? We're going to take the stairs while Kathryn scouts out the utility room, where the main electrical breakers, or whatever you call them, are. At least that's the plan for now. It could change. Annie is going to pick the Forresters' lock with the aid of a penlight. How do you want to rehearse that?" Nikki asked, irritation ringing in her voice.

"Well, dear, when you put it like that, I guess there is nothing to rehearse," Myra said. "We're all on edge, so let's just try to calm down since we still have hours to go."

A whoop of sound ricocheted through the room as Maggie literally catapulted into the room. "Wait till you hear what I have! I should get a medal for this!" she continued to shout.

"Well, damn, girl, share," Kathryn said.

"Okay! Okay! Do you all remember my telling you about Carlie Mason, my colleague at the *Sentinel*? She got us coverage for the Garland article. I e-mailed her and asked her if she could dig out some information on the building where Arthur Forrester lives. She came through in spades. I just uploaded the schematics to your phone, Kathryn. You'll know exactly where to go when we get there to do whatever you have to do on the power grid."

"That's great, Maggie. Going in blind does have its disadvantages."

"What else did your friend tell you, dear?" Myra asked.

"Plenty. I have the skinny on the whole building. It has sixteen floors. Five of the sixteen have seven condos. Those are floors three, six, nine, twelve, and fifteen. The other eleven floors just have six condos, because the seventh space is used for a laundry room, a room with a huge ice machine, and a third room for a utility room. Arthur Forrester lives on the ninth floor, one of those that houses seven condos. Carlie managed to dig out the ownership records, and I have them right here. In addition to that, she Googled all the owners and was lucky enough to Facebook all of them. It's all right here!" Maggie said, pointing dramatically to her laptop. "She was good enough to compile a summary of each tenant from what she got off their Facebook pages. Believe it or not, the Forresters are the only ones who do *not* have a Facebook page. Guess they are not into social media."

"Are we going to like what you tell us?" Annie twinkled.

"Oh, yeah," Maggie drawled. "You ready for the good news?"

"We are *soooo* ready, you cannot believe," Yoko all but screamed. "Just tell us!"

"Okay, here goes. First I'll tell you who the condo owners are. And then I'll give you their Facebook histories. Inga Kitchel is an airline hostess for British Airways. Mimi Davis is one of the owners, and she's retired. Jacob Little is also retired. Martha and Clement Carlton are a married couple. They're also retired. Angela Evers is also retired, and the last owner is a guy named Kurt Meyers. And, of course, Arthur and Nala Forrester. Jacob Little, Mimi Davis, the Carltons, and Angela Evers all paid cash for their condos. The others have mortgages, including the Forresters.

"Their Facebook pages are interesting. Ac-

311

cording to Carlie, the retirees spend a lot of time Facebooking kids, grandchildren, friends in other parts of the country. Inga Kitchel spends, if she's lucky, two nights a month in her condo. She bought it for tax purposes, according to what she told friends. She has several boyfriends in different parts of the world. She's young, thirty-three. Pays her mortgage on time. She has a snappy little BMW sports car she keeps in the garage.

"Mimi Davis is a grandmother. She spends a lot of time on Facebook with her kids and grandkids. She appears to have something going on with Jacob Little. She just alludes to it. She wears two hearing aids. Her grandkids tease her about not calling because she can't hear on the phone. It seems Mr. Little also has two hearing aids, so maybe that's what drew them together. Both are in their late seventies. Mimi tells her kids that she goes to bed at eight o'clock at night, except the nights she and Jacob Little play bingo at their church. Little likes to play poker on the Internet and spends a lot of time at it. He goes to sleep early, too. I do not know if the two of them are sleeping together. It doesn't say anything about that on Facebook." Maggie giggled.

"The Carltons are world travelers. That

appears to be their job in life. They return for the Christmas holidays to spend time with their kids. They leave again right after the New Year and don't come back till the next Christmas. Their Facebook page is full of pictures of their travels. As of two days ago, they were in Russia.

"Then there is Angela Evers, who spends most of the year in Florida. From her Facebook page, she's single, but has tons of friends. She is a retired schoolteacher. She comes back around Easter and stays through Christmas, then leaves to go to Florida to spend the winter in a warmer climate.

"The last owner is a thirty-eight-year-old bachelor with 'bookoo' girlfriends. He is rarely at the condo he owns. He's a pharmaceutical rep and on the road five days a week. He bragged on Facebook that last month he did not spend a single night in his own bed.

"What all this tells us is tonight should be a piece of cake. Talk about lucking out here. It looks and sounds to me like the only people who will be on the floor are Mr. Little, Ms. Davis, and Arthur Forrester. Maybe Kathryn won't have to turn off the power. Think about it, the two seniors go to bed early. No one else is there unless the bachelor happens to be spending one of those rare nights at home, which sounds most unlikely. His last post was last evening, and he said he was in Rhode Island for the next few days. It's not Easter yet, so Evers is still in Florida. The Carltons are wherever they are, someplace in Russia, according to their last Facebook posting, and won't be back till Christmas. That leaves Kitchel, and she's in Denmark, or at least she was as of yesterday morning. That's it!"

"What a wonderful treasure trove of information, dear. Thank your colleague for us. It would appear we will have no interference this evening. But bear in mind, one never knows, the young yuppie man might suddenly decide he wants to sleep in his own bed for a change. Ms. Kitchel might be landing at the airport right now and looking forward to an evening in her own home. Any number of things could still go wrong. I don't think we should assume anything at this point," Annie admonished the others. The sisters all agreed.

"Did your colleague share anything else about the building?" Alexis asked.

Maggie looked down at her computer. "It was built in the fifties. Very well maintained. It was originally apartments that were converted to condos. Maintenance fees are on the high side. Security is so-so. Nothing elaborate. You need a Medeco key to get in the front door. There is a reception area with someone at the desk twenty-four/seven. The mailroom is on the first floor. Small seating area, that's about it. It's not top of the line, but nor, by any stretch of the imagination, is it shabby. I guess the Forresters felt they fit in there."

"So, do I turn off the power or not?" Kathryn asked.

"Off the top of my head, I vote no," Nikki said. "What about security cameras on the different floors? If they have them, who monitors them? Who owns the building?"

"According to Carlie, there has never been any kind of reported incident at the building. There was/is a security camera on each floor, located by the Exit sign. But most of them do not work, and that is supposed to be the main topic of conversation at the next condo association meeting, a meeting that virtually no one goes to. No one ever shows up, because the meetings are always about being assessed for some improvement or other. I guess it's something they don't consider too important. Carlie got that information from Mimi's Facebook page. Of all the people on the ninth floor, she seems to be the most vocal. Guess it doesn't matter that she can't hear, as long as she can talk.

"Carlie was unable to dig up information about who owns the building on such short notice. I don't see that it matters one way or the other, do you?"

"No," Yoko said. And the others nodded in agreement.

Alexis patted her red bag, which was sitting in front of her on the floor. "Just to be on the safe side, we can still spray-paint the lens of the camera. Sounds to me like we're good to go." The others concurred.

"Good work, Maggie. At least now we won't be going in blind. We will have to be quick, though. And stealthy," Nikki said.

"And how are we going to get him out and down to the garage? What did we decide to do about the garage opener?" Kathryn asked.

"We didn't decide. If it's like most underground garages, like the one we have at the *Post,* you can walk around it, and it's a tight fit, so Yoko, who is the smallest of us all, will have to do it. There's a button on the bottom you can press that will keep the bar open in case a truck making a delivery has to pull through. I don't foresee a problem, especially that late at night," Maggie indicated. "Oh, one other thing. I remember seeing something in one of Avery Snowden's reports that the Forrester condo would go silent, meaning the television would go off after the eleven o'clock news. That has to mean Forrester goes to bed at that time. I think our timing is spot-on, all the way around."

"I am seriously starting to get excited," Annie whispered to Myra, who was staring down at the vibrating cell phone in her hand. It was Charles.

Myra held up her hand for the sisters to go quiet. She pressed the SPEAKER button so the girls could hear both ends of the conversation.

"Hello, dear."

Charles cut to the chase. "What' going on, *dear*?"

"Not much, *dear*. We're all just sitting here listening to the rain. We still have some time till zero hour. Did you call to tell me you miss me?" Myra asked, tongue in cheek.

"I'm calling to tell you I'm worried about you girls. Fergus is worried, too. We are both upset that you . . . terminated Avery. That was not a wise move on your part, Myra. And just so you know, Avery handled the termination better than I thought he would. You girls need to give some consideration to how invaluable he's been to all of us over the years."

"Really. He should have thought about that before he left us to fend for ourselves. Well, I am happy to report we have it all under control, and we even found someone to replace him. His fees are on par, and he comes highly recommended. You might even know him, *dear.*"

Charles chuckled. "Myra, you know as well as I do that there is no one out there who can replace Avery and his team. He's the best of the best. The queen still calls on him from time to time. So who is this mysterious person you *think* can take Avery's place?"

"His name is Nigel Bly. I have to go now, dear. It's time to leave. Do not call me, because I'm turning off the phone the way we always do as each mission gets under way. The way you taught us to do it."

Kathryn's fist shot high in the air. "Way to go, Myra!" The sisters clapped their hands in glee. Myra beamed.

"We still have a few more hours to while away," Annie said. "Whatever shall we do?" she asked dramatically to ease the tension in the room, which was so thick you could slice through it with a butter knife.

"Back to the boob tube," Nikki said.

Finally, three hours later, blessedly, as Annie put it, it was time to leave.

"Last check, everyone!" Maggie called out.

"We're good," Yoko responded.

"Okay, everyone, you know the plan," Nikki called out. "We leave in pairs. Maggie is going ahead to get the van and will pick us up down at the end of the driveway. Alexis can handle the red bag, since she had wheels put on it. Go!"

Maggie shifted her backpack more comfortably over her shoulders and sprinted from the room. She slid the van to the curb at the end of the driveway within fifteen minutes, the windshield wipers swishing furiously back and forth. She brought the van to a smooth stop and opened the door for the sisters, who were drenched to the skin, even though they were huddled under a leafy, umbrella-like tree.

The decibel level inside the large van increased to a dull roar as the van started rocking back and forth as the sisters started to shed their clothing to put on the outfits Alexis was handing out.

"Three minutes and counting," Maggie bellowed to be heard over the clamoring sisters. "I'm going to need time to change," she continued to bellow.

"Not a problem, dear. We have all your things ready for you!" Myra shouted.

Annie let loose with a shrill whistle, calling for silence. "We're almost to the gate. Quiet, everyone! You're up, Yoko. We're beneath the overhang, so you won't get wet. Please do not hurt yourself when you squeeze through."

"Who said anything about squeezing through? I'm going to vault over the gate. It's the first thing you learn in ninja training," she quipped. A second later, she was out the door and cartwheeling over the sturdy black-and-yellow bar. A minute after that, Maggie barreled through the wide-open space. Yoko hopped in, and Maggie tore off down the center aisle to the ramp that would lead to the fifth-floor parking area that the Forresters' vehicles were assigned to.

Annie nudged Myra, and whispered, "Even on our best day, back when we were young, do you think we could do what Yoko just did?" Her voice was so fretful, Myra almost laughed out loud.

"And show our bloomers! I don't think so!"

"I so love your witty repartee, Myra." Annie giggled.

Maggie cruised up the winding ramps that would take them to the fifth-floor parking level. "We shouldn't have a problem finding a parking space, since each owner is assigned two spaces. Forrester's wife took her car, so we'll just park right next to that luxurious Mercedes, whose lease is paid for with Garland Lee's money. Yep, there it is!" Maggie said gleefully.

"And I see a big security camera over there to your left. What should we do about that?" Nikki asked.

Alexis was out of the van before Nikki stopped speaking. She held a container no bigger than a prescription bottle in her hand. She ran, dodging between cars, until she came up right alongside the mounted camera. She reached up, and then the lens was covered with black paint in an instant. She ran back to the van as the others climbed out.

"How do we look?" Isabelle asked.

"In a word, *awesome*!" Alexis said, laughing. "If I woke up out of a sound sleep and saw us, I think I'd die on the spot."

"We're taking the steps, right?" Yoko asked.

"It's just four flights," Kathryn said. "Short flights," she clarified. She held the door. Yoko was the first one through; the others followed, with Annie and Myra bringing up the rear.

"I can't wait to get my hands on that

weasel," Annie hissed.

"Forget that for the moment. Do you have your picklock in hand?"

"Right here!" Annie said, holding up her right hand. "I hope it's not one of those complicated locks."

"What I hope for is that there is no alarm system," Myra said. There was an edge to her voice.

"As a rule, men do not turn on alarms. It's women who usually require that safety feature. At least that's what I've read. With Mrs. Forrester gone now, I'm thinking he wouldn't bother," Annie said. "Still, we should have given more thought to Kathryn's turning off the power to the ninth floor. We're winging this, as it is."

"Too late now," Myra said, heaving a deep breath as the sisters huddled in a group outside the door that would lead them onto the ninth floor and Arthur Forrester's condo.

Kathryn held up her hand for everyone to go quiet. "No talking, once we go through the doors. Hand signals only. Annie, you're up as soon as Alexis sprays the camera that is right outside this door. Are you ready?"

Annie inched forward, Myra right behind her.

"Wait! Wait!" Nikki hissed. "We need to

turn off the overhead light in the hall. It's right outside the Forresters' door. Open the door, Kathryn, and take a peek. I remember seeing it on the plans. The ceilings are relatively low. You're the tallest of us all, so let Yoko get on your shoulders and just twist it off. The Exit sign at the end of the hallway will give you more than enough light. Go! Go!"

Both sisters returned breathless from their exertion. "You're up, Annie." Kathryn opened the door for Annie to step through.

Annie immediately backed up. "It's too dark. I'm going to need more light than what my penlight provides. Does anyone have a flashlight?"

"I have a mini Maglite," Alexis said as she fished around in her pocket. She handed it to Myra. "Good, good. Let's go, Myra. Make sure someone is watching both ends of the hallway. Dressed like we are, we certainly don't want to scare the life out of any of the owners if they suddenly show up."

"We have your back," Kathryn said. "Pretend there is a rattlesnake on your trail. Move already!"

Both women moved faster than greased lightning. Annie dropped to her knees. "Hold the light steady, Myra." Annie let out her breath in a long swoosh of sound.

"Thank God, Myra, this is just a standard lock. A piece of cake."

"Make it snappy, then, Miz Wizard, and do your thing," Myra said, looking over her shoulder to where the sisters were huddled in the dim doorway.

Annie reached for the doorknob to steady herself, for she was on one knee. She turned slightly to get into a better position, now that she had a good grip on the door. When it moved of its own volition, she almost toppled over.

"That was quick! Damn, Annie, you really are a wizard!"

"Shut up, Myra! I didn't do anything. The door opened by itself."

"Oh, dear God! He knew we were coming and set a trap for us! Run!"

"You run! It's not a trap. The sack of pus probably forgot to lock the door. There is no way he could know we were coming here tonight. Fetch the girls, Myra. Like *now* would be good!" When Myra didn't move, Annie hissed, "You waiting for a bus, Myra?"

Myra turned and ran down the hall. "The door was open! Do you believe that? I think it might be a trap, but Annie says no."

"It's not a trap. There's no way that weasel could know our plans. No way. Ready, girls!

Slow and stealthy. Hug the walls," Kathryn said, leading the way.

Annie held the door open wide so all the sisters could slip through. Kathryn immediately homed in on the keypad next to the door. She twirled her finger in the air, the sign that *all was okay.* The alarm was off. Annie closed the door. Alexis pointed her mini Maglite at the floor and turned it on.

Kathryn made a wide circle with her hand, which meant *take stock, get your bearings.* She led the way down the short hall to a long, narrow living room. She stopped again. She pointed left. Alexis pointed the Maglite in the direction Kathryn was pointing. The kitchen. Kathryn pointed to a short hallway. The light cast enough light so they could see what looked like an office, which was now totally dark, and what also looked like a bedroom, also dark.

The sisters crept forward silently, with Alexis pointing the mini Maglite at the floor for light.

Kathryn held her arm straight in the air. *Stop.* The door to the master bedroom was halfway open. Her arm still upraised, she moved forward. Alexis waved the mini Maglite around till the light it shed came to rest on the sleeping form in the king-size bed. Kathryn's arm came down, to be replaced with a circling motion. The sisters circled the bed. *No escape.* Kathryn pointed to the wall switch. She held up three fingers. On the count of three, Nikki would turn on the overhead light.

Kathryn's index finger went up. *One.*

Kathryn's middle finger went up. *Two.*

Kathryn's ring finger went up. *Three.*

The overhead light came on in Arthur Forrester's master bedroom.

"Rise and shine, you sack of pus!" Kathryn roared.

CHAPTER 17

Arthur Forrester came out of a deep sleep and bolted upright, his corkscrew hair standing on end, his eyes glazed as he struggled to make sense of what he was seeing in his bedroom. It was a bad dream gone *really bad.* He felt like he'd swallowed a mouthful of cotton. *Damn the sleeping pill!* He never should have taken it, especially after drinking two beers. It took a while for him to get his tongue unglued. He uttered a string of expletives that would make a grown man blush.

"What in the goddamn hell . . . ," he blustered as he stared at eight black figures, dressed in ninja attire and circling his bed, staring at him. *Ninjas!* Forget a dream gone bad. This was the kind of nightmare Hollywood made into movies.

"Cursing is not allowed, Mr. Forrester. Do not make me tell you that again," Myra said in a conversational tone that belied the circumstances in which it was said.

"Who are you? Is this a home invasion? I don't have anything. I'm retired. My wallet is on the dresser. Take it. There's no jewelry here. My wife left me and took all her jewelry. Get out of here. You must have me mixed up with someone else." He hoped his voice sounded reasonably optimistic.

Forrester tried to burrow deeper into the bed. He grabbed for Nala's pillow and clutched it to his chest. He smelled her shampoo. He wished now that she were here.

Kathryn yanked at the comforter and threw it on the floor. "Get up! Now!"

Annie stepped closer and looked down at the man on the bed. "You are a scrawny little man, aren't you?"

"We don't want your money. Well, that's not quite true, we do, but we want the bank accounts, not what's in your wallet. And we do not have you mixed up with anyone else. You are our quarry. We can do this the hard way, or we can do it the easy way. My colleague told you to get up," Nikki said. "Oh, one other thing, you are not dreaming. This is as real as it gets, Mr. Arthur Forrester, attorney at law and a disgrace to the legal profession."

Son of a bitch. They even know my name!

Forrester shoved himself violently back against the headboard. The glaze in his eyes was fast disappearing as he finally began to come to terms with what was happening in his very own bedroom. This was no dream. Nor was it a nightmare. This was reality.

I have to do something. But what?

They want me to get up. Like that's going to happen.

His cheeks started to itch. *Scratch or not to scratch?* His face felt like it was on fire. *What the hell is going on?* He jerked his head upright, wishing he had his glasses on. "Who are you?" he managed to croak.

"We're whoever you want us to be," Nikki said in a singsong.

"What do you want?" Forrester asked, his voice sounding so strange that he could hardly believe it was his own. *"They're women,"* an inner voice warned him. He wondered why that would matter to him.

"We want you! And we want your house in Hilton Head, your car, your bank accounts, and your brokerage account. Oh, and your interest in that craft brewery you are so hot to acquire full ownership of. Plus, we want you to drop your lawsuit against Garland Lee. We also want you to sign off with your old law firm. It's against the law to blackmail one's former employer. It's against the law to blackmail *anyone,* as a matter of fact. Since you're a lawyer, you should know that," Nikki said. "Then again, it is a violation of professional ethics to cheat one's client by double-dipping. But that did not stop you, did it?"

"You're working for Ballard and Garland Lee?" Forrester barked. "I should have known. Well, screw you and the horse you rode in on. I'm not giving up anything!"

The sisters took a step closer to the bed. Annie held up her hand. On cue, the scabbards attached to each sister's waist belt came alive as they pressed a button that released long, vicious-looking blades, which hit Forrester's body like a well-practiced choreographic move. Eight pinpricks of blood glistened on his chest under the overhead lighting.

Arthur Forrester fainted.

"Crap!" Maggie said. "Now we have to wait for him to wake up."

"No, we don't," Kathryn said as she reached down, grasped Forrester's corkscrew hair in her fist, and dragged him from the bed. He landed with a loud thump. She kicked him to get up. He rolled over, gripping his stomach. Then he almost retched.

"You puke, and you're cleaning it up!"

Alexis barked as she pressed the button for the blade to retract into the scabbard. The other sisters did the same thing.

"This guy is a hot mess," Isabelle said.

"No problem. We'll cool him down so quick, he won't know what happened to him," Myra said.

Kathryn yanked him upright and slammed him against the wall.

"Get dressed! *Now.* If you don't, we'll take you as you are, in your boxers and bare feet. Doesn't matter to us one way or the other," Annie said.

"I'm not going anywhere with you! You can't kidnap me! That's against the law!" Forrester squealed as Yoko kicked the clothes he'd been wearing closer to where Kathryn was still holding him pressed up against the wall. The sisters burst out laughing.

"You wanna bet?" Nikki asked. "Like I said, you are not dreaming, Mr. Forrester. You are not having a nightmare. You are not going to wake up later thanking God this was all just a bad dream. Nightmarish as it is, this is as real as it gets. Get dressed *now.* You have five minutes."

Arthur Forrester's shoulders sagged. *The damn ninja is right, this is no dream. I'm being kidnapped.* He eyed the black-clad figures through narrowed eyes. There was suddenly no doubt in his mind that these women, and they were all women, would cut him down in a nanosecond. But maybe if he stayed alert, he could find a way to get out of this predicament with his skin intact. Once again, for some inexplicable reason, he wished his wife were here with him.

Resigned, he pulled on his messy, wrinkled clothes and stepped into his boat shoes. Whatever was coming next, he was ready. A thought suddenly struck him. His shoulders straightened imperceptibly. *The cameras in the hallways. Someone will see these crazy people kidnapping me.* By the time they got him to the garage, he figured, the police would be there.

"Okay, everyone, listen up. We need to find the listening devices. We need to pack up his gear, at least some of it, so it looks like he walked away of his own free will. We need his files, his computer, his cell phone, his iPad. And the kitchen needs to be tidied up. Are we taking the car or not?" Nikki asked.

Though she knew the answer already, Kathryn asked, "Is that fancy Mercedes in the garage leased or do you own it?"

Forrester knew better than not to respond. "It's leased."

"We knew that. Just checking to make sure you were not going to lie to us," Nikki said. "Who has the eye?"

"I do," Isabelle said. "Fifteen minutes, people."

The sisters scattered, leaving Kathryn in charge of Arthur Forrester.

"What listening devices?" Forrester asked with a catch in his voice.

"We had them planted a week or so ago. We know everything you've been doing, everything you said. We also planted one at Ballard, Ballard and Quinlan, in the conference room where you had your meeting. By now, you should realize this is not a Mickey Mouse operation. We know exactly what we are doing."

"How . . . how did you get in here?"

"We were ready to pick the lock and walk in, when, to our extreme delight, we found that you had left the door open. Shame on you, Mr. Forrester. No more questions."

"Ask him what medicine he needs!" Nikki called from the bathroom.

Forrester's shoulders sagged. This was too real. "Everything on the counter." His voice came out as little more than a whisper.

"Everything on the counter," Kathryn yelled, relaying Forrester's response.

"There are twenty-two bottles of vitamins

in the kitchen," Myra called out. "Ask him, where do they deposit the trash?"

Forrester rubbed his temples. "Leave the vitamins. The trash chute is two doors down from this apartment." He wasn't going to get away. He just knew it, and the thought devastated him. He was so close. *So close!* He'd been stupid enough to celebrate last night. Still, he had to try. "Who's paying you to do this? I'll double it, whatever it is, if you walk away now."

Kathryn laughed. The effect was so eerie, so evil-sounding, coming through the black ninja mask, Arthur Forrester felt his insides crumble. "You can't afford us. But I'm going to answer your question, anyway. No one is paying us. This is pro bono. You being a lawyer, you should know what that means, even if you have never done anything pro bono in your entire life, you greedy money-grubber. We're all about justice. Something you obviously know nothing about or choose to ignore. You are one bad-apple lawyer, Mr. Forrester."

Forrester absorbed Kathryn's words. He wanted to lie down and die. *No, there has to be a way to get out of this.* He wasn't going down without a fight. *They are women. Dressed up in costumes. How stupid.*

Kathryn tilted her head to hear Alexis say

334

she had left something in her red bag. "Ask him where he keeps his."

"What?" Kathryn bellowed.

"Duct tape!" Alexis bellowed in return.

Before Kathryn could get the words out of her mouth, Forrester said, "Bottom drawer, next to the sink." *They must need it to tape up boxes,* he thought. Little did he know, it was to tape his mouth shut for the journey down to the garage.

"Five minutes and counting!" Isabelle shouted.

The sisters responded and were side by side, black rucksacks on their backs loaded with Forrester's belongings. Yoko tossed a bag of trash toward Kathryn, who caught it deftly with one hand.

"Who wants the honor?" Maggie asked, holding up the roll of duct tape.

"What are . . . What . . . No, no!" Forrester yelped, finally realizing the women's intent. *And I damn well told them where the frigging tape was. How stupid was that?*

"You need to shut up. You talk too much for someone who has nothing meaningful to say," Kathryn observed as she cuffed him upside the head.

"Give me the tape," Annie said.

Annie ripped at the bright purple duct tape. A *long* strip. The sound was like thunder in the quiet room.

"That's a pretty big piece of tape. His mouth isn't *that* big," Maggie said.

"I know. I'm going to wrap it around his whole head so when we pull it off, his hair will come with it. Roots and all," Annie said gleefully. "If I tore off a big-enough piece, I might be able to run it down his nose. Then he'll have a cross on his head and face."

The sisters stomped their feet and hooted their approval.

Arthur Forrester sagged in Kathryn's grasp. He'd always been proud of his full head of curly hair, which he wore to below his ears. His brothers were bald. Even his two sons were partially bald.

Annie went to work. Within minutes, Arthur Forrester looked like he was ready to star in a horror movie.

"Good show! I like your technique. Do you practice much?" Myra giggled.

Annie bowed low. "No. This was my first time. If I have to do it again, I'm certain I can shave four seconds off my time. Are we really going to leave his arms free? I have lots of tape left."

"Then, by all means, shore him up," Maggie said as she shifted her rucksack more firmly on her shoulders. Annie obliged.

Arthur Forrester was so light-headed, he

would have toppled over if Kathryn hadn't yanked him upright by the collar of his IZOD shirt.

"Time to go, ladies. Did we get everything?" Isabelle asked as she looked around.

"We're good," Myra said.

"Look around, Mr. Forrester. Take a last look. You're never coming back here. Just so you know."

Tears of anger and frustration burned in Arthur Forrester's eyes. He stared straight ahead.

Yoko opened the door. "Clear!" she said.

The sisters sprinted in pairs of two down the hall to the EXIT door.

Kathryn and Nikki were the last to leave, with Forrester between them. He didn't make it easy, digging in his heels and forcing them to drag him between them.

Both sisters were winded with their effort as they finally pushed the lawyer through the EXIT door. At this point, Nikki shoved him up against the concrete wall and hissed in his ear, "Try that again, buster, and my foot will be so far up your ass, you'll be able to pitch a tent. Nod if you heard and understand what I just said."

Arthur Forrester knew when he was beaten. His head bobbed up and down. She jerked him forward. This time, he cooperated.

By the time they reached the door leading into the garage on the fifth-floor level, Maggie had the *Post* van idling at the door. Nikki looked around to make sure there was no activity to be seen. The garage was quiet. She looked out over the half wall to see that it was still raining. She stepped to the side as Kathryn shoved Forrester into the van. Isabelle and Yoko hauled him inward, then dragged him to the back of the van and tossed him in a seat.

"Do we buckle him in, or don't we care?" Yoko asked.

"We don't care," Alexis said. Yoko shrugged as she sat down across from him.

The van moved; then they were out of the garage.

Yoko chirped up again: "Do we care if the gate remains up?"

"I don't think we care about that, either," Annie replied.

The moment the van hit the street and headed out to the boulevard, the sisters' fists shot high in the air.

"Avery Snowden who?" Annie shouted. The women's fists hit the air a second time.

"Take us home, dear," Myra ordered.

"With pleasure," Maggie replied.

■ ■ ■ ■

A few hours later, with only one pit stop for bathroom use and a gallon of coffee to go, the *Post* van blasted through the open gates at Pinewood. Even inside the van, the sisters could hear Lady and her pups barking a welcome-home greeting.

The kitchen door opened. The dogs rushed out. Not so Charles and Fergus, who waited inside, not knowing what to expect by way of a greeting, which didn't happen. Both men watched as the sisters exited the van, then held what looked to be an intense discussion. No one even bothered to look in their direction.

"This doesn't look good from where I'm standing, Charlie."

"You're right, mate, it does not look good at all. I'm not seeing the prize they went after."

"Trust me, he's in there," Fergus said, his voice sounding sour. "Stands to reason he'll be the last one out."

Both men continued to watch as the sisters stepped aside to allow Kathryn and Yoko to drag Arthur Forrester from the van. He crumpled to the ground and had to be jerked upright.

Fergus glued himself to Charles's side. "They did it. I'm actually seeing him. Are you seeing him, Charles?"

"Of course I am. Step aside, mate, this is one of those times the ladies will not want our help, so do not even bother to offer. Don't even ask them any questions. We've been scorned, so act humble. Not that it will work, but it's worth a shot."

Myra was the first one through the kitchen door. She looked around, not knowing quite what she expected to see, but whatever she did see seemed to satisfy her. "Good morning, Charles. Give us an hour, then we'd all like some breakfast. The works. Maggie wants some of everything, so please outdo yourself," she said sweetly.

Annie stepped forward and pecked Fergus on the cheek. "Did you miss me?"

Fergus was all over himself as he said how bereft he had been with her gone. Then he made a mistake and asked Annie if she missed him.

"Not one little bit, dear. I was too busy." Fergus hung his head in shame as Lady pawed at his leg for a treat. Charles would take him to task the minute the girls were out of sight for asking such a stupid question.

And then both men did a double take

when they saw Kathryn and Yoko dragging their prize through the kitchen door.

"This . . . um . . . person will be our guest for a short while. His name is Arthur Forrester. We're going to take him . . . um . . . down to the lower level to his new accommodations," Myra said.

Charles knew he shouldn't ask, but he bit his tongue and asked, anyway. Maybe it was the steely glint in his beloved's eyes that made him go for the gold. "May Fergus and I help?"

"I think we have it covered. Annie?"

"Oh, we do have it covered." She ran into the laundry room and returned with the ironing board. "Slap him on there, girls, and we're good to go. Use his belt, so he doesn't slide off. Alexis, dear, quick, open the secret panel."

With their eyes wide, jaws drooping, the two men watched as Kathryn and Nikki secured Arthur Forrester to the ironing board. Forrester, his eyes frantic and full of tears, stared up at Fergus and Charles, imploring them for help.

"Let's go, so we can get this over with!" Maggie yelled. "I am so hungry!"

"Careful on the steps with all that moss!" Alexis shouted as Nikki and Kathryn hefted the ironing board to follow the sisters. Lady and her pups barked and howled at these strange goings-on.

Arthur Forrester prayed that he would die on the spot as he felt himself going down a steep incline that smelled wet and moldy.

Back in the kitchen, Fergus and Charles looked at one another. "I don't know about you, Charles, but I don't think I would ever have come up with that ironing-board solution. Ah . . . I'll make the pancake batter while you do . . . whatever you want to do. We are *soooo* in the doghouse here."

"Do not say another word, Fergus Duffy, or I will clobber you with this frying pan."

Down below, in the dungeon, Annie ripped the purple duct tape from Arthur Forrester's hands. He flapped them back and forth to get his circulation moving. His eyes begged them to take the tape off his head and mouth.

Kathryn gave him such a shove he literally fell into the hard bunk inside the spacious cell. The sisters gathered around him, still in their ninja gear. One by one, they removed their head masks. "Doesn't matter now if you see us or not, since you aren't going anywhere," Yoko said.

Forrester struggled to sit upright on the hard bunk. He waited for whatever was to come next. Kathryn didn't make him wait long. She ripped at the tape. Skin from his lips stuck to the purple tape. Hair came out, roots and all. His scream was so primal, the sisters had to cover their ears. Small drops of blood trickled down his neck. Myra held out a bottle of water. Forrester's hands were shaking so badly, he couldn't hold the bottle.

"Open your mouth, and I'll pour it in," Myra said, not unkindly. Forrester obeyed as his eyes rolled back in his head. He toppled over onto the bunk. "He'll come around in a minute or so," Myra said. "He sort of looks like a skinny monk, the way the hair came out, don't you think?" The sisters leaned over to better observe Forrester's head.

A long discussion followed as to whether they should or shouldn't put ointment on his head. The vote was eight to one for *No*.

"Can we hurry this up? I'm starving," Maggie said.

"Now that you mention it, I'm hungry myself," Annie said. "Maggie, turn on the music. Nikki, turn on the overhead lights."

"Done, and done," both sisters said.

"He'll be listening to Garland Lee at full decibel level twenty-four/seven, with five hundred watts of light shining on him for the same amount of time. I'm thinking by tonight, he might, I say *might,* be willing to give us what we want. We need nourishment and a few hours' sleep right now. Forrester is safe and sound. Who has his medicine?"

"I have it," Alexis said. "I'll just leave it here on the stool."

Out of sight of the dungeon cell, the sisters high-fived one another before they scampered up the moss-covered stone steps like sure-footed billy goats.

"We did good, girls! Real good. We can be proud of ourselves today," Nikki said.

"Truer words were never spoken, my dear," Annie said.

"Amen," the others chorused.

CHAPTER 18

Fergus Duffy eyed the platter of brownies, loaded with nuts and raisins, which were cooling on the kitchen counter. He looked over at Charles, who was putting the finishing touches to a standing rib roast, which would go in the oven shortly. Charles's guilty offering to the girls. But it wasn't going to work. He knew it, and Charles knew it, too. He shrugged.

"I hear water gurgling in the pipes. That means the girls are finally up." Charles looked around. The coffeemaker was ready, the brownies just waiting to be eaten. "It looks like it's going to rain pretty soon, Ferg. Let's take the dogs out now. I could use some fresh air. And perhaps a new perspective will come to me."

Both men stood aside as the dogs raced through the open door and ran toward the barn. Charles and Fergus followed. "We should have owned up last week, Charles, to our part in the Avery Snowden fiasco. When he asked permission to leave the area to go to Delaware to help the boys, we should have said no. Or we should have told him, at least, to make his case with the girls. It was up to *them,* not *us,* to decide. I still can't believe he didn't rat us out."

"That's not who he is, Ferg. You know that. I'm sure he doesn't have a very high opinion of us right now, and justifiably so. I'm supposed to be the leader, and as such, I call the shots. He was simply babysitting, when his special talents were needed elsewhere. It was a good decision, though not as good as making him ask the girls. Still, if it was up to me to decide, I'd make the same decision again if I had to."

Fergus looked up at the dark clouds weaving their way across the sky. Charles was right that it was going to rain shortly. He could feel the dampness settling into his knees and hips.

"I shouldn't have to explain every decision I make. This is not your fault, Ferg. It's mine and mine alone.

"I don't know about you, but I think once I finish the preparations for dinner, I am going to head into the District. Camping out in the BOLO Building sounds like it might be a good idea. I feel very unwelcome here. And I don't like that feeling. You can either come along or go home, your call."

"We're in this together, Charles, so I am with you all the way. If I have a say in the matter, I think we should explain to the girls about Avery. If you don't want to do it, I will. We owe it to Avery."

"You're right. I'll do it. It's time to go back, anyway. I just felt a drop of rain, and Lady is already on her way. We'll just grab our stuff and head out."

"Is that before or after you explain about Avery?"

"After, of course," Charles snapped irritably.

"Just asking, mate, just asking."

The minute the kitchen door closed behind him, Charles eyed the sisters sitting around the table and eating the brownies he'd made and drinking the coffee he'd made for them. He checked the oven temperature and slid the prime rib inside.

He turned to the women, who were staring at him, puzzled expressions on their faces. They knew something was off, something different about the two men standing in front of them. They waited. Then, as one, they sat up straighter in their chairs when they saw Fergus return with the two traveling bags in his hands.

Charles didn't waste any time or mince his words. "I have a question for you all, then I have a statement to make. Am I, or am I not, the leader of our . . . organization?"

The sisters looked at one another, and they all nodded.

"In that case, I have two statements to make. Being the leader, I am therefore the person who makes decisions — some of which you might like and some of which you might not like. Up until now, we've never had a problem, and I've never steered you wrong. First and foremost, your safety has always been my main concern.

"I am the one who authorized Avery Snowden to leave the mission. He was, as he put it, doing 'babysitting' duty when his expertise was required elsewhere. He asked my permission to leave, and I granted it. Perhaps I should have had him ask you, but that did not occur to me at the time. I would do it again, too, if I had to. Manpower is something you never want to waste. Fergus and I do not require an apology, but you do owe one to Avery. He is loyal, and he has served us all well over the years. It is to his credit that he did not defend himself out of respect for me and the years we served Her Majesty together.

"That's my statement. Your dinner is in the oven. Fergus and I are going into the District and will remain there until such time as you all feel that you want all three of us back in the fold. If not, we will make other arrangements. One last thing, so I guess that means three statements.

"Earlier you mentioned the name Nigel Bly. There should be no bad blood between him and Avery, but there is. Avery saved Bly's life — not once, but twice — and the life of his wife. No one has ever figured out what turned Bly against Avery, unless it was his own wounded pride that he'd failed on a mission, and Avery and his people saved the day. See ya around, old girl," Charles said, offering up a snappy salute.

"You have my number, Annie," Fergus said, following Charles out the door. Lady reared up, threw her head back, and let loose with an earsplitting howl of displeasure, her offspring doing the same thing.

The sisters looked at one another, but no one said a word. Seconds and minutes crawled by, and still no one said a word. Lady and the pups stopped howling and had progressed to whining as they frantically paced the kitchen.

"I think someone should say something,"

Maggie said as she reached for the last brownie on the platter.

Annie cleared her throat. "I hate to have to admit it, but it appears we might have made a mistake in regard to Mr. Snowden. Everything Charles said is true. I'm willing to take the full blame for the decision we made in anger and haste."

"It doesn't work that way, Annie. I agreed with you, and so did the girls. We did what Charles has always told us to do — 'Stay on the mission, no matter what.' He never explained to us that extenuating circumstances could change things. We know better now," Myra said unhappily as she swiped at a tear in the corner of her eye. "We're not infallible, even though at times we think we are."

"Right now, we're all feeling pretty proud of ourselves. We do not deserve to feel proud. Possibly humble. Which is hard for us to do, but sometimes you have to suck up some things you don't like. Avery was the one who planted the listening devices. He is the one, along with his people, who tailed the Forresters and listened in to what was going on both at their condo and at the law firm. Yes, Annie and Maggie planted the bug at the law firm, but that bug came from Avery. And it was Avery and his people who listened to what was said, not us. Without Avery's contribution, there would have been nothing we could do to help Garland. We need to fall back and regroup right now," Kathryn said.

"I'm all for that, but I think we need to check on our . . . um . . . guest. He is probably hungry by now. We only left him with a bottle of water. I say we take care of him first, then come back up here to the kitchen and talk out our problem. And make no mistake, it is our problem," Nikki said. "Raise your hand if you agree." All eight hands shot in the air.

Alexis headed for the refrigerator. "Cheese and bread should do it, along with another bottle of water." She looked around for a bag of some sort, found one, and tossed the food and drink in. "We're good here."

Garland Lee's voice thundered at the sisters as they made their way down the moss-covered steps to the war room, where Lady Justice stared down at them. From there, they made their way to the dungeon and its cell, which Isabelle had redesigned from the days of slavery, when Myra's family aided those in need and got them to a safe harbor as a part of the Underground Railroad's route to freedom.

Kathryn turned down the volume on the

stereo and lowered the overhead lighting.

"Good afternoon, Mr. Forrester. We brought you a little nourishment," Alexis said.

"Keep your nourishment," Forrester croaked from his position on the hard bunk. "I don't want anything from you, not now, not ever."

"Nicely said, Mr. Forrester, but that is not going to change your current circumstances. As we said earlier, we want something from you. You will not leave here until you give us what we want. Right now, you are reasonably comfortable. That can — and will — change, the longer you fight us," Nikki said.

Forrester snorted. He looked awful — the bald strips on his head were bloody and scabbing over. His lips, where the skin had peeled off, looked even worse. His ruddy cheeks were like circles of fire. "What the hell else can you do to me, except kill me? Go for it, put me out of my misery, but I am not doing what you want."

"See, now you aren't thinking clearly. Eventually you will do what we want. How long you can hold out until that happens, only you can answer. It's a given that you will do what we want. Even the best of them, and I'm referring to soldiers and agents of our government, who over time found themselves in the same position you are in now, gave it up when they were tortured. No one can hold out forever. Sleep deprivation, ruptured eardrums, infections, and starvation. That's what you have to look forward to under our care. You don't look like a man of steel to me, you sack of pus," Kathryn said.

"Just for the record, Mr. Forrester. We do not kill people. What we do, do, however, is make certain people wish for, indeed long for, death. Keep going as you indicate you will, and I suspect you are going to turn out to be one of those people," Myra added with a smile.

"Last chance, Mr. Forrester. Are you going to sign off on the escrow monies being held until the lawsuits involving their rightful ownership are settled? And are you willing to drop your lawsuit against her? Think carefully before you respond," Annie said.

"I don't have to think. I will say to you what I said to the senior partners at my former law firm. Go to hell, and kiss my ass on the way down. Just leave me to my misery."

"I guess we have our answer," Yoko said.

Annie advanced closer to the bars on the cell. "We're going upstairs now to prepare our dinner, which will consist of prime rib, baked potatoes, salad, and fresh garden peas, along with homemade bread. We'll come back later this evening to start the festivities in your honor. We're going to have an early Halloween party just for you. We're going to have you dunk for apples. Only in this case, there won't be any apples. That's just another way of saying we're going to be waterboarding you. The president may have forbidden the CIA to use so-called *enhanced interrogation,* another way of saying *torture,* but we never got the message. Even if you manage to avoid drowning, think about what it will do to your head and those luscious, ugly lips of yours."

Nikki joined Annie at the bars. "Mr. Forrester, you really need to understand something. You do not — and I repeat, *you do not* — get to press the reset button. The reason for that is that there is no reset button."

Arthur Forrester swore as his fists pummeled the paper-thin mattress he was lying on. A strangled sound coming from his ravaged mouth permeated the room.

The sisters laughed as they left the dungeon area to make their way out to the war room, where Kathryn turned up the volume on the stereo and turned up the overhead lights.

■ ■ ■

Once again in the kitchen, Myra made fresh coffee, while the girls took over the dinner preparations. As always, when they worked as a team, things progressed perfectly. All that remained to do was to set the table when dinner was ready.

Annie poured coffee. "We need to talk, girls."

Always the most vocal of the group, Kathryn let it fly. "Just say it, Annie, we screwed up. Now we have to make it right with Avery. I wouldn't blame him a bit if he told us to go pound salt. Speaking strictly for myself, I am ashamed of what we did."

"Avery and I have had our differences over time, but I agree with Kathryn. We treated him shabbily. I won't have a problem apologizing. The kicker here is, will he accept our apology?" Maggie asked.

The others weighed in, and, in the end, they all agreed that each of them would go the distance and apologize to the old super-spy.

"He's a professional," Annie said curtly. "I might be wrong, but I think he will chalk it up to a bunch of women PMS-ing all at the same time, and he'll let it go. I will say this, though. I think we should finish up this mission *on our own* and start fresh the next time around. We've gotten this far mostly on our own, and, yes, I am giving credit where credit is due to Avery, so let's just finish it up and go on from there. We learned a hard lesson, and life is all about learning."

"Very well put, Annie," Myra said. "We need to take a vote, so we are all on the same page." All hands shot high in the air, even Annie's.

Nikki swiped at imaginary sweat on her brow. "Whew! I'm glad we settled that to our satisfaction. We still have time before dinner is ready. I suggest we call Mr. Snowden now and get it over with. Then we need to call Garland and give her a progress report. Who wants to do it?" All eyes turned to Annie, who nodded in response.

The kitchen turned silent as Annie hit the speed dial on her phone. The sisters listened carefully as Annie extended hers and their apologies. What she received for her efforts was a brisk reply: "Not a problem, Countess. Call me if you need me."

Myra had both hands on the pearls at her neck. "I think that went better than we had any right to expect." Everyone at the table looked relieved, Annie more so than the others.

"Coffee anyone?" Alexis asked. All the sisters nodded.

While Alexis poured coffee, Nikki checked on the prime rib. Yoko placed the potatoes on a baking sheet and slid it on the top shelf of the double oven, while Isabelle chopped a purple onion and some tomatoes into a salad bowl full of fresh lettuce from Charles's greenhouse. It was all done, just as Alexis poured the remainder of the coffee into her own cup.

"I guess I'm the one to call Garland," Myra said, reaching for her phone. "Do any of you think we should ask her out here so she can —"

The sisters all spoke at once with an overwhelming *no* as their response. Myra shrugged as she hit the number 9 on her speed dial. Garland picked up on the third ring, sounding as cheerful as ever. Myra quickly brought her up to speed and was rewarded with a laugh of pure joy. The two women made small talk for a few minutes, and Myra signed off.

"I wonder what she would think if she knew every song she ever recorded is blasting in Forrester's ears twenty-four/seven?" Maggie asked.

"I guess the next question is, should we call the firm and . . . at least give them a heads-up?" Isabelle asked.

Another vote was called for. *Not yet* was the decision.

"Then, girls, I think we're all good here. All we have to do is eat this fine dinner awaiting us," Myra said.

"I think we forgot something. Actually someone," Nikki said.

"I guess you mean Charles and Fergus," Myra said.

"Exactly." Nikki grinned.

"Not just yet." Myra grinned in return. Annie agreed.

"Whose turn is it to set the table?"

"Mine," Isabelle said as she got up to get the dishes from the overhead cabinet. "I have the peas, too."

"I'll do the rolls," Maggie said.

"I'll do the dressing for the salad," Alexis said.

"I've got the potatoes," Yoko said.

"I do the gravy," Kathryn said. "I know, I know, no lumps."

"I have the roast," Nikki said, pulling the platter from the cabinet.

"And Annie and I will just sit here and wait for it all to come to the table."

As was their custom when the sisters dined together, Annie said grace.

■ ■ ■ ■

While all their heads were bowed, Arthur Forrester was pacing his new living quarters like a raging, caged lion. He cursed at the top of his lungs, but he couldn't even hear himself, what with Garland Lee's singing coming close to rupturing his eardrums. The blinding white light overhead made his head pound like a drum. He felt disoriented as he paced, his legs wobbly, his equilibrium off. He had wet toilet tissue stuffed in his ears, but it was nowhere near to lowering the horrific sound that shook the old stone walls. He wondered how long it would be before he went out of his mind.

He wished Nala were here with him, the way she had been when they were first married. She would pat him on the back. She had gentle, caring hands. Nala to his rescue. It wasn't going to happen, and he knew it. He was on his own and batting zip. His loss.

Forrester's legs finally gave out. He flopped down on the hard bunk and dropped his head into his hands. His head ached, inside and out. His scalp felt like a million bumblebees were eating at his exposed flesh. His lips, where the skin had peeled off, were wet and slimy, and he saw in the mirror over the sink that pockets of pus were forming at the corners of his mouth. It hurt just to open his mouth.

Maybe it was time to give it all up and hope these evil people would just let him go. Their paraphrased message — *"We don't kill people, we just make them wish they were dead"* — ricocheted inside his pounding head. The tall one, the mouthy one, had vocalized that. And he believed her implicitly.

If he gave it all up, where would he go? What would he do? They were going to take all his money. Could he live on his Social Security and what little was left in his pension fund? He would have to, since there were no other options.

Maybe he could plead with Nala to take him back. Nala had money. What a stupid thought that was. That bus had already pulled away from the curb.

All he had to do was sign his name, and, hopefully, those ugly, hateful people would turn him loose. God, how he hated them.

Forrester wondered what time it was. He looked down at his wrist, only to see that it was bare. The damn thieves had even stolen his Rolex watch. He looked around, but there was no way to tell if it was night or day or how many hours he'd been here. It seemed like an eternity. Maybe their plan was to keep him here till he went insane and was a drooling idiot. Freedom never looked so good. He would never take it for granted ever again. Providing he got the chance to savor it after this.

There had to be a way out of here, some way to trick them into letting him go. There just had to be. He felt a sob catch in his throat as he realized it was all wishful thinking on his part. They would never let him go until he did what they wanted. His gut told him that even then they were not going to let him go. He wondered what plans they had for him, since they didn't kill people. He'd probably end up in some third-world country in some gulag. Who would mourn his disappearance? No one, that's who. Not Nala, not his kids. Not his grandchildren, whom he hardly knew. It was a bitter pill to swallow.

Forrester lay down on the hard bunk. He brought his arm up to cover his eyes, to shield them from the blinding light, as Garland Lee kept singing about her man and unrequited love. If she were within arm's reach, he'd stick his hand down her stringy throat and yank her tonsils out. That would shut her up, once and for all.

He cried then, the way he'd cried when

he was five years old and one of his brothers had called him a *pissant.* His brother had mocked his curly hair, which his mother loved. He had mocked his crooked teeth, which his mother promised would be beautiful when they all came through as he got older. He'd mocked his big ears, which he called *elephant ears.* His mother hadn't promised anything in regard to his ears. It was the ugly nickname of pissant that bothered him the most. Even to this day, that brother still called him pissant. He hated him almost as much as he hated Garland Lee and the name partners at the Ballard law firm. He realized in that moment of time that there wasn't one single person he loved unconditionally, not even his children or grandchildren. The only person he loved was himself. And look where that had landed him.

Forrester cried then because there was nothing else for him to do. Except wait, and he could cry while he waited. When the first tear rolled down his cheeks, he knew he'd made a mistake, as the salt in his tears was eating at the rosy patches on his cheeks. He howled in pain as he beat the brick walls with his bare fists. Another mistake, he realized when he looked at his bloody knuckles.

"Just let me die already," he moaned. "Just let me die."

CHAPTER 19

Annie looked at Myra's kitchen clock. In fifteen minutes, it would be the witching hour. "I think it's time to head downstairs and get the promised festivities under way. It's almost midnight. The perfect time to get a party in motion."

"Where's the galvanized tub?" Yoko asked.

"Nikki fetched it from the barn earlier. It's in the laundry room. We are forgoing the apples, aren't we? Or are we going with the charade of bobbing for apples?" Alexis asked.

"Bring some if it will make you feel better. Personally, I don't see the point, since we already alerted Forrester to the waterboarding," Isabelle said as she rooted around inside the vegetable bin for some apples. Finding some, she tossed them into a grocery sack. She wiggled her eyebrows and rolled her eyes, just for the fun of it.

"If luck is with us, we might not even need

any of this," Myra said, motioning to the galvanized tub and the sack of apples Isabelle was holding. "By that, I mean he's had almost seven more hours of bright lights and blasting sound. If we're lucky, he might be ready to give up the ghost by now. I'm pretty sure I would be if I were in his shoes."

Maggie scoffed. "That guy is going to hold out until the bitter end. Part of it is *us*. He got skinned by a bunch of women. Right now, in my opinion, his greed is secondary."

"He's got to be one huge mass of pain. It must be true what they say, that greed is the most powerful motivator in the world. I know I couldn't handle what he's going through, and I'm no wimp," Nikki said.

"What choice does the man have? Really, think about it. He signs off and he's got nothing left, except a few dollars and his Social Security, and I do believe he has a pension. That's it. He assumes he's going to be set free, so he's looking at living in a one-bedroom garden apartment and driving a pickup truck. How would he explain that to his very wealthy brothers? That's his thinking. I could be wrong, but I don't think so," Myra said.

"Then let's put it to the test," Annie said. She picked up the tub and headed for the secret stairway.

The time on the digital kitchen clock read: 11:55.

Arthur Forrester heard them coming. His stomach muscles started to spasm. Garland Lee turned silent just as the lights were lowered. Hardly daring to breathe, he waited for the women to approach. The moment he saw the huge, galvanized tub, he grew light-headed. He noticed the handsome legal briefcase one of the women was carrying. *Ostrich skin. Ostrich cost a fortune.* He should know, since he'd actually priced them last year. Plus, his brother's medical bag was made out of ostrich skin. *She must be a lawyer* was his second thought. They were talking, but he couldn't hear what they were saying. One of the women pointed to her ears. He felt stupid when he reached up to remove the toilet-tissue plugs he'd jammed into his own.

Kathryn unlocked the cell door, told him to step aside, then attached a hose to the faucet. She threaded it through the bars. Maggie turned on the nozzle, and the tub started to fill with water.

Forrester's mind raced. He'd read somewhere that a person could die in just a few inches of water. He wondered if it was true. It looked to him like they were filling the tub to the brim. He blinked when he saw one of the women drop four apples into the water. He'd always liked apples. Nala said apples were good for you, something about the pectin in them. When it came to health and vitamins, his wife was usually spot-on. *I'd give anything right now, Nala, if you were here right next to me.* What totally stunned him was that he realized he meant it.

He waited; then he flinched as he watched the tall, mouthy female turn off the faucet. This was his moment of reckoning. He sucked in a deep breath.

"When was the last time you dunked for apples, Mr. Forrester?" Nikki asked.

Forrester didn't respond because he simply couldn't remember if he'd ever dunked for apples or not. What he did say, and he said it with no authority, was "It's against the law to waterboard a person."

As one, all eight women pointed to the apples bobbing up and down in the tub of water.

"Flexicuff his hands behind his back," Isabelle said. "Otherwise, he'll try to fight it."

In the blink of an eye, Alexis had Forrester's hands secured behind his back. She jerked him forward.

"Wait!" Nikki said. She unzipped the ostrich briefcase and withdrew a sheaf of

367

papers. She advanced and waved them under Forrester's nose. "All you have to do is sign your name. And this will all be over."

"And you're going to let me walk out of here, wherever *here is,* right?"

"Absolutely," Annie lied with a straight face.

"Bullshit."

"So that's a *no*?" Nikki asked.

"Goddamn right that's a *no.* And all you will get out of me from now until doomsday is a *no.* Go ahead, do your waterboarding. But you better know this, I am *not* going to hold my breath, so I'm going to drown. You crazy people said you don't kill people. I guess I'll be your first kill. Let's just get this over with."

The sisters looked at one another.

Kathryn moved faster than a streak of lightning. "It's instinctive to hold your breath," she said as she shoved Forrester's head into the water. "Count, Yoko!"

Kathryn yanked him out of the water on the count of ten. She waited until he stopped sputtering and gulped in a huge mouthful of air. His head hit the water immediately. Yoko counted again. Kathryn let her get to eleven before she pulled him out. He was shaking as he sputtered and spit out water. He struggled to take deep breaths.

"Give up?" Kathryn asked.

Forrester cursed. Down went his head. Yoko did the number count in a singsong.

This time, Kathryn yanked him out on the count of twelve. The lawyer slipped out of her grip and fell to the floor, where he coughed and sputtered, spitting out water he had inadvertently swallowed.

"Okay, I give up," he gasped. Alexis removed the flexicuffs. He rolled over, vomiting water.

There was no moment of joy among the women.

Isabelle tossed Forrester a towel. "Dry your head. Be careful because you are bleeding."

"We brought ointment for you to put on your head where the tape was. It's not looking good, Mr. Forrester. Your face appears to be raw. We're going to allow you to use your medicine. The moment you sign the papers we have for you, the stereo will be turned off. Garland Lee will just be a memory. The lights will be dimmed. We're going to give you a decent meal, and then you are going to be permitted to sleep. When you wake up, we'll tell you all about what will happen next. You did the right thing, Mr. Forrester," Myra said quietly.

"Sit him upright, Kathryn," Nikki said as

she held out a clipboard and pen. "Sign your name where you see an *X*. Make sure your signature is legible. We don't want any signatures that look like a doctor's signature when he writes out a prescription. Don't screw up now. We can wait a few minutes if you feel your hands are too shaky. Alexis is a notary public. She will witness Annie's and Myra's signatures as witnesses, and then affix her stamp to all the documents."

Ten minutes crawled by before Arthur Forrester reached for the pen Nikki was holding out to him. He signed his name six times, making sure his signature was legible and met with the women's approval. Annie and Myra signed their names just as carefully and handed each document to Alexis, so she could fill out her information and affix her notary stamp.

"We'll bring your dinner down in a few minutes. And then you can sleep, Mr. Forrester," Annie said.

Forrester sighed. "Don't bother. I'm not hungry."

Kathryn's touch was gentle when she led the lawyer to his bunk. She eased him down gently. "Sleep well, Mr. Forrester. We'll see you in the morning." She exited the cell, locked it, then checked it by rattling it to see that it was indeed securely locked.

"We're done, girls."

There was no hand clapping, no high-fiving. No smiles, no laughter. Instead, the women simply turned and made their way to the war room, then out to the stone steps that would take them to the main floor of the house.

The time was one-thirty, and it was a new day.

The girls sat around the table while they waited for Myra to get glasses and a full bottle of her favorite Kentucky bourbon out of the overhead cabinet. Annie dropped ice cubes into the glasses as Myra poured generously.

"Here's to the completion of another successful mission. Well done, girls!" Nikki said.

Eight glasses clinked against each other. It was a pleasant, successful sound.

The sisters straggled into the kitchen, one by one, to find Maggie making breakfast. "Pancakes and bacon. I'm not Charles, guys. I can only do two things at a time. Coffee is ready, and so is the juice. There is blueberry pancakes with blueberry syrup."

"That sounds lovely, dear," Myra said.

"Anything sounds lovely to you, Myra, as long as you don't have to cook it," Annie said, tongue in cheek.

"You should talk. If it were your turn to make breakfast, you'd call IHOP and have them deliver it," Myra snapped in return.

"Are we serving breakfast to Mr. Forrester? I still have some batter left," Maggie asked.

"Yes, we'll take it down with us. He passed on dinner last evening. I'm sure he's hungry, unless he plans on going on a hunger strike," Nikki said as she dived into her stack of pancakes.

Kathryn waved her fork in the air as she posed the second question of the morning. "We need to make a decision here. Do we call Mr. Snowden for the relocation, or do we go with our original plan?"

"I, for one, have given it a lot of thought, since I didn't sleep well. I think we should finish up on our own. That's a personal thought, however. My reasoning is that I think our original intention was to prove we didn't need Mr. Snowden to complete our mission. We can still do that, even though we had to pivot and apologize. We should take a vote, and, as always, majority rules."

The sisters stopped eating. Even Maggie. "Raise your hand if you want Mr. Snowden to . . . um . . . relocate our guest." No hands were raised.

"Raise your hand if you vote to finish up

on our own." Eight hands shot high in the air.

"Well, all right, then. Who wants to make the call?"

Kathryn grinned. "I will!" The sisters groaned good-naturedly. "As soon as I finish these delicious pancakes."

The sisters started to giggle as they watched Kathryn psych herself for the upcoming call.

Five minutes later, Kathryn got up and carried her plate to the sink and rummaged in her rucksack for her cell phone. She scrolled down until she found what she wanted and punched in the numbers. She had the sisters' undivided attention.

The phone rang five times before there was a response. The response was guarded, cautious. "Pearl! This is Kathryn Lucas. I'm out at Pinewood with the girls. We need your help. Like right now."

As if on cue, the sisters took a deep breath. They all knew about Kathryn and Pearl's contentious relationship. They all leaned forward to hear Pearl's response.

"Define what you mean by 'like right now,' Kathryn?"

"*Right now* means *right now.* That means you get into that SUV of yours and head on out here to Pinewood. There are no excuses that will be accepted. Are you locking up and getting under way?"

Pearl Barnes knew better than to argue with Kathryn Lucas. "I am. I have to stop for gas. I should get there in ninety minutes, give or take a few." Kathryn looked down at the phone and laughed out loud as she clicked END.

Years ago, Pearl Barnes had retired from the Supreme Court to organize an underground railroad network that, instead of transporting freed slaves, protected abused women and children. Pearl had left the Court after her only daughter had been threatened by her vindictive and abusive husband. Working on her own, Pearl had secretly transported her daughter and her granddaughter to a safe haven. Since her son-in-law had legal rights to his daughter — Pearl's granddaughter — she knew that what she was doing was illegal, so she'd resigned from the Court. Within a year, she had established a workable network, which was now in its twelfth year. To date, over that period of time, she had managed to arrange a safe haven for over seven thousand bruised and battered women and children.

The only problem with Pearl and her very successful network surfaced when she approached Myra and Annie for help when things got too dicey for her to handle on her own. When they asked for records and background, Pearl refused to divulge any details and said it was all in her head, saying the reason her underground worked was because she couldn't trust anyone but herself. To Pearl's dismay, the sisters refused to help her, saying they didn't work blind. Kathryn took it one step further and threatened to turn her in to the authorities unless she gave up the records, so she could be helped. Pearl took one look at Kathryn and buckled. The records had been produced and were at that very moment locked in Charles's safe.

"She's going to have a bird when she sees what she is transporting," Alexis said.

"I don't think any of us cares about that. Right now, she's working on credit with us. We bailed her butt out on three separate occasions. To put it in plain and simple language, she *owes* us," Kathryn said. The sisters all agreed.

Maggie finished the last of the pancake batter and fixed a plate for Arthur Forrester. The sisters got up and, with their usual efficiency, had the kitchen looking in record time as good as if Charles had left it.

"Time to check on our guest," Annie said

gleefully as she led the parade to the secret staircase.

"It's so quiet," Yoko said as she turned on the lights.

They approached the spacious cell to see Arthur Forrester sitting on the edge, staring at his feet. "We brought you some breakfast. You need to eat something before your trip."

Forrester was about to say he didn't want any breakfast, when it dawned on him what the woman had said. "Did you say *a trip*?" His voice sounded like he had a frog in his throat. "Are you releasing me?"

"In a manner of speaking. It won't be till tonight, however. We work best in the dark. I'm sure you understand that."

Kathryn opened the cell. Maggie set the tray down on top of the lone metal chair, which was bolted to the floor. Kathryn re-locked the cell door. She followed the sisters to the war room, where they all saluted Lady Justice, before they headed back upstairs to the main part of the old farmhouse to wait for Pearl Barnes. Pearl was as good as her word and arrived in eighty-seven minutes.

Pearl Barnes was a slim woman, wiry, actually, with a crop of curly gray hair. One look at her, and you knew she was a capable person, up to any task she undertook. Annie said it was in her DNA. There were no hugs, no special greetings, because, as Pearl said, she did not cotton to displays of affection. The only thing she did was make certain she was nowhere near Kathryn Lucas.

Annie poured coffee as Nikki explained the situation. "We'll bring him to you tonight. Just tell us where to meet you. He's never to return here — that has to be understood. We don't care if you ship him out of the country or not, and we know you have contacts who can handle that end of things. Are we clear on this, Pearl? If he ever surfaces, we will come after you and show you no mercy. So, are we clear?"

"We're clear. I'm going to need some time. You know how it works. All the relays. Are you going to drug him? What time are you shooting for?"

"If you want him drugged, you'll get him drugged. Whatever time works for you will work for us," Annie said agreeably.

"I just want him sluggish, not out cold."

"Understood," Myra said.

Pearl finished her coffee. "Let's shoot for midnight, to be on the safe side. Meet me at the deserted depot, where we met the last time. If things change, I'll be in touch."

Myra escorted Pearl to the door. Pearl merely nodded a good-bye.

"She is one tough cookie," Yoko said.

Kathryn laughed. "When are we going to tell Garland and the law firm?"

"Not till he is out of our care. Too many things can go wrong," Nikki said. "Tomorrow is soon enough."

"It's a long time till midnight. How do you all feel if Nikki and I check in at the office? We'll come back late this afternoon," Alexis said.

"You can all leave if you have things to do. Annie and I can hold down the fort," Myra stated.

After the younger sisters all left, including Maggie, it was just Annie and Myra in the kitchen. Annie poured fresh coffee. "You okay with the way it all turned out, Myra?"

"I am, Annie. You?"

"I don't see how we could have done anything differently. The only blight is that snafu with Avery Snowden. And I can forget that very easily. What exactly did we ever decide in regard to Mrs. Forrester?" Annie asked.

"Actually, we didn't. I'm thinking we should let the law firm handle all that. We'll make her financial situation part of our deal with the law firm. They can handle her divorce if she wants to go that route. She's going to need some good representation with respect to Arthur's share in the brewery. In the end, she'll be okay — probably, all in all, better off, her own kids and the kids she helps out as well. We'll be okay, too.

"You look exhausted, Annie. You said you were up all night. Go upstairs and take a nap. I'm going to take the dogs out for a long run. We can have ham sandwiches, if you wake up before lunch. We also have to think about dinner, if the girls are coming back out."

"You think about it," Annie said, stifling a yawn.

"Like I'm going to think about anything else," Myra muttered under her breath as she opened the door for the anxious dogs.

It was nine-thirty when the sisters descended to the dungeon. Once again, Kathryn unlocked the cell door. "Time to go." Forrester didn't move. He looked terrible. "Someone put his meds in a bag for him." She nodded to Yoko, who pulled a syringe out of her pocket. Kathryn hauled him upright. He didn't fight her, but his eyes narrowed with hate. Before he knew what was happening, Yoko jammed the syringe into his arm.

"What the hell . . . What did you do to me?" Forrester bellowed.

"Oh, pipe down. It's just something to make you relax. We're going for a ride, and we really do not want to have to tie you up. Behave yourself, and this will be over before you know it," Kathryn said.

Forrester wanted to fight, but his body just wouldn't cooperate. He had no choice but to let the crazy women push and shove him up a set of steps, which smelled moldy and were slippery under his feet. Then he heard dogs barking and saw a herd of them heading in his direction. They circled him, sniffing him and growling. Then he was outside and walking across stones. Strong arms held tight to his upper arms. Finally he was being pushed into some kind of vehicle. It smelled familiar. Probably it was the same vehicle in which he had been brought here, wherever *here* was.

"Where is this place?" he asked, his mouth dry. His tongue felt too big for his mouth. He'd never been more miserable in his life, and he didn't even care. All he wanted was to go to sleep.

Forrester sat down in the van, aware that someone was on each side of him. The van started to move. He closed his eyes.

An hour later, the *Post* van came to a stop in the parking lot of the deserted depot. Maggie turned off the engine and the lights as well. Ten minutes later, headlights lit up the parking area. Annie got out of the van to greet two men, who looked like sumo wrestlers. Pearl brought up the rear. "Is he ready?"

"He's ready. What that means is he's sound asleep. I don't know for how long he'll be sluggish when you wake him up. He didn't put up a fight. He's resigned to whatever is going to happen from here on out. Do not tell him anything."

"Understood."

"Okay, here he is," Annie said as Nikki and Kathryn stood alongside Arthur Forrester in the open doorway. "He's all yours!"

One of the wrestler types picked Forrester up like he was a rag doll. He put him in a fireman's carry and stomped his way to what looked like a Hummer.

The sisters stood in the spill of light from the Hummer's headlights and watched until the boxy vehicle was out of sight.

The sisters high-fived one another, then grinned.

"We did it!" Annie chortled.

"Did you doubt this would be the outcome?" Yoko asked.

"Not for a minute. Let's go home and celebrate. All in favor, say *aye*!"

The empty lot rang with the happy sound of laughter.

EPILOGUE

The sisters were seated around the dining-room table at Pinewood. It was a little past noon. They were about to make a toast to the mission they had just brought to a successful conclusion.

"I still can't believe that the Ballard, Ballard and Quinlan law firm wanted to pay us for all our help. I have here in my briefcase all the documents everyone signed off on. Do you believe they didn't want to know where Arthur Forrester is? Not that I would have told them. All they wanted was my assurance that he would never rear his ugly head in their direction. They fell all over themselves, and though I had to decline their offer of payment, I did want their promise, in writing, that they would take care of Nala Forrester pro bono. They were happy to sign off on that. Arthur's share in the brewery, along with her own money, will take care of Mrs. Forrester and her family for the rest of their lives. I left it up to them to get in touch with her. I trust them to follow through. Henry Ballard and the others were ecstatic," Nikki said.

"How much did they want to pay us?" Isabelle asked.

"It doesn't matter, I turned it down. It was the right thing to do," Nikki responded.

"I have something to share with all of you," Myra said as she reached behind her for two envelopes on the sideboard. She made a big production of opening them, until Kathryn, who had zero patience, snatched one of them right out of her hand, opened it, then let out a loud whoop. "This is a check for five million dollars and made out to cash! It's from Garland Lee. There is a note that says if we send it back, she'll just send it again. I say we keep it, as that's what she wants. Raise your hand if you agree!" Every hand in the room shot high in the air.

"And this beautiful square envelope is an invitation to a private concert at Garland's personal recording studio. One month from today. It's for one hundred of her closest friends. It's her private retirement concert. It's for all of us, plus we can each bring a guest. And the dogs, too, if we want."

The girls were ecstatic, saying that nothing and no one could keep them from attending.

"I hate to be the first one to leave, but leave I must. I have a date," Kathryn said as the girls stood up to leave the table.

"It's okay, girls, Annie and I will clean up here. Go. Go. We'll catch up when Annie and I get back from our trip."

"Have fun on your trip," Nikki called over her shoulder. The sisters all burst out laughing.

"Oh, we will," Annie said.

And then pandemonium broke loose as Lady and her pups pushed past the girls as they raced to the kitchen door.

Yoko turned, and hissed, "It's Charles and Fergus."

"Ah, yes, I thought they would be back around this time," Myra said as she started to gather up the cake plates and champagne glasses. She carried them into the kitchen. "Hello, dear. You're just in time to clean this up. Annie and I are pressed for time right now." She turned and bolted for the door, Annie behind her, as she blew kisses to Fergus.

Nonplussed, Charles looked at Fergus and shrugged. He rolled up his shirtsleeves as he prepared to clean up the sisters' dishes.

"They're up to something, Charlie. I can

actually smell their excitement."

Fifteen minutes later, Charles looked around at his kitchen. Spick-and-span. Just the way he liked it. "Coffee, Fergus?"

"Sounds good. We haven't had a good cup of coffee since we left."

Lady bounded to her feet the moment she heard her mistress's footsteps on the stairs. She waited, panting, to see if maybe she was going on a car trip. When Lady saw the small travel bag Myra was wheeling behind her, she knew she was being left behind at Pinewood.

Charles pushed the coffeemaker's ON button just as Myra and Annie came into his line of vision. He saw the travel bags at the same moment that Fergus saw them. He looked at his beloved. Not for the world was he going to ask her where she was going. He would never lower himself to question her. *Absolutely not.*

"Where are you going, dear?" he asked cheerfully.

Myra looked at Annie.

Annie, whose hand was on the doorknob, looked back at Myra.

Myra smiled from ear to ear. "Why do you ask, dear?"

"Because I want to know. We always tell each other when we go on a trip."

"That's not quite true, Charles. I can recall three different times when you didn't follow your own rule." Myra was still smiling.

"Myra, where are you going?" Charles asked a second time.

"Barbados."

Charles absorbed that one-word response, just as Fergus did.

"Did Myra just . . . ?"

"Yes, Ferg. They're going to Barbados."

"Isn't that where . . . ?"

Charles nodded; then he laughed out loud. "Looks to me like we're going to be bachelors again for a few days. I know my wife. They're going to Las Vegas. Trust me on that. Annie loves going to Vegas to stir up trouble, once a mission is finished."

Fergus looked doubtful, but he had to admit that Charles was usually right.

An hour later, Annie and Myra stepped off the portable stairway of her private Gulfstream and entered the plane. Her pilot greeted them, and said, "They're having perfect weather in Barbados, ma'am."

"That's nice to know. I'm tired of all the rain we've had," Annie said as she headed toward the luxurious seating area and buckled up.

"I'm excited. Are you excited, Annie?"

"I am. I've never been to Barbados. Have you?"

"I have not."

"You do realize that Charles and Fergus think we're going to Las Vegas, even though you told them the truth, right? It all comes down to *need to know* in the end." Annie laughed so hard, Myra had to slap her on the back, so she could catch her breath.

When Annie's breathing was back under control, the two women high-fived each other.

"You did call ahead for an appointment?"

"I did."

"I think life is going to get interesting real quick." Myra giggled.

"That it is, my friend, that it is."

ABOUT THE AUTHOR

Fern Michaels is the *USA Today* and *New York Times* bestselling author of over 150 novels and novellas, including *Holly and Ivy, High Stakes, Crash and Burn, Fast and Loose, No Safe Secret, Double Down, In Plain Sight, Perfect Match, Eyes Only,* and *Kiss and Tell.* There are over 160 million copies of her books in print.

Fern Michaels has built and funded several large daycare centers in her hometown, and is a passionate animal lover who has outfitted police dogs across the country with special bulletproof vests. She shares her home in South Carolina with her five dogs and a resident ghost named Mary Margaret. Visit her website at www.fernmichaels.com.